BUNKER MENTALITY

BUNKER MENTALITY

A NOVEL

COPERNICUS PAUL

MOUNT
WILSON
PUBLISHING

This is a work of fiction. Names, characters, organizations, places, events, and incidents are either products of the author's imagination or are used fictitiously.

Published by Mount Wilson Publishing, San Diego, CA
www.mountwilsonpublishing.com
www.copernicuspaul.com

Cover design: Emily Weigel
Project management: Sara Addicott
Image credits: cover © Shutterstock/ MARGRIT HIRSCH

ISBN (hardcover): 979-8-9899347-1-3
ISBN (paperback): 979-8-9899347-0-6
ISBN (ebook): 979-8-9899347-2-0

Library of Congress Control Number: 2024913199

First edition

For those hungry to understand why this world sometimes feels like a colossal clusterfuck, I offer you this warm blanket.

AUTHOR'S NOTE

History, alas, occurs only once, yet is often interpreted thereafter in a thousand different ways. My depiction is but one of those ways.

This is an artifact of a moment in time, cast as an adult story.

If words might offend you, please read at your own risk.

1

Shuffling and whispers cloaked those deplaning after me. A handful of children livened up as they carried with them presents from a Christmas spent far away. At 5:50 a.m., Philadelphia International had yet to come to life. Except for a janitor working a mirrored finish onto the tile, I found myself alone and with nine hours until my connecting flight. I'd been here before. Not this place specifically, but this moment—wishing to join the distraction of hurried people. I wanted to follow them home, but I made a promise.

Confidence permeated the unyielding world I was leaving in Strategic Air Command, or SAC as we called it. One might find it hard to associate peace with the constant threat of imminent annihilation, but better this tenuous position than a life of totalitarian Soviet thought or control. At SAC, survival and freedom were the result of childhood "good versus evil" allegories taken to a real-world logical extreme. Those entrusted with America's thermonuclear arsenal existed in this extreme.

As the last deplaned passengers faded from view, I found a quiet seat in the arrival gate. I tucked my feet under the chair, crossed my arms, then bowed my head. While adrenaline had kept me from napping on my red-eye, it took a jarring terminal announcement to wake me from the hardest hour of sleep I'd had in a week.

"You're snoring, mister," said a young boy in a full-body parka, analyzing me.

I squinted at him. "OK."

"Momma, he woke up!" the boy shouted, running away in struggled half steps.

Several dozen passengers now filled the gate area. I picked up my briefcase and Class A uniform carrier, then headed for baggage claim.

"Excuse me, ma'am. Can you tell me where I can find bags for Eastern flight 224?"

My flight was no longer listed on any of the baggage-claim belts.

"What you ask me?" the rotund, uniformed lady replied.

"Eastern flight 224, ma'am," I said. "Do you know where I can find the unclaimed baggage?"

I studied the impatience on her face at my politeness.

"I'm just looking for my bag."

"You late," she said, pointing toward a mash-up of luggage at the far end of the hall. "Unclaimed is over there."

After locating my duffel bag, I took an escalator to the departure level. A flight status board directed all active-duty travelers to a location in another terminal. My connecting flight would be on a World Airways / Military Airlift Command charter. While civilian clothes would be fine for a commercial flight, one could fly MAC only in uniform. I stopped in a restroom, changed into my Class A's, then caught a shuttle to my departure point.

At noon, famished and overtired, I ate a sandwich I'd packed from home, positioning myself on a bench where I could spy on the check-in counter. Interspersed with transiting civilians, soldiers and airmen joined the rush of travelers.

When the World Airways clerks approached their counter, I queued second, with several other active duty behind me. I checked my duffel bag. When I left the counter, at least twenty more had lined up. I proceeded to the gate.

In the gate area, the faded green paint had chipped and peeled along one wall. Windows high on the opposite side allowed sunlight to blister a daily path. Some untold number of travelers before me had fidgeted holes into the vinyl of my beam-seat chair. They'd meticulously removed the foam padding along the front edge of most of the seats.

Chain smokers arrived and began pacing as if awaiting a jury verdict. Their predecessors had long since worked shiny paths into the carpet. As the afternoon deepened, rays of sunlight found their way to my knees. I put my hands out to warm them. The number of smokers increased, pacing more quickly now. Their last gasps of nicotine would need to suffice until we were airborne.

A thud barked out of the PA system as a clerk struck the microphone on the counter. The gathering jumped in unison.

"Ladies and gentlemen," the clerk began, "World Airways MAC flight 29 will begin boarding in thirty minutes." I received position 327, one of the last to board.

2

December 27th, 1986

Dad,

By the time you read this, I'll have arrived at my new duty station.

For the moment, I'm in hurry-up-and-wait mode between connecting flights.

Hope all is well with you.

I'll write again soon.

Roy

3

As the jets spun up, months of anticipation ended. I contemplated my worth. When I was growing up, Dad's earning power meant that clothes were passed down brother to brother, while our bicycles would be no newer than secondhand. Family vacations, if taken, were spent within a day's drive of home. Back then, I had a rich kid in my grade school. He often bragged about summer vacations in Europe. Damned if he wasn't a complete dick for it, since my only recourse to "visit" Europe rested with Funk & Wagnalls.

All I now owned fit into one duffel bag, uniforms mostly. Inside the plane, no room remained for even a walk up the aisle. Carry-on luggage that should have been stowed created an obstacle course. To replenish the troops overseas, the Department of Defense chartered aircraft to herd the replacements and their dependents over the Atlantic. Every seat was taken, with those single and junior in rank like me used to fill the holes that remained after all senior ranking and families boarded. Some laps had babies on them. Many people had bags under their eyes.

The plane rolled the entire runway to get off the ground. I

gripped my armrests as the concrete ran out beneath us. We veered upward, then northeasterly, and the United States became a fainter and fainter image. Sitting as I was on the port side, I could see the coastal areas for a while. However, as the craft flew into the shortened eastbound night, all visuals of America were lost.

Though I'd never crossed any ocean, I had flown before. Flights nowhere near as full as this one had shuddered and creaked during air turbulence. This plane didn't flinch. We barreled through with the weight keeping us on an even keel. The chiseling-cold outside air radiated through the skin of the aircraft, and there wasn't anything I could do. Every other seat was taken, and the guys next to me had jumped claim on the two blankets for the three seats in my row.

From my window position behind the wing, I could see the Atlantic cloud cover lit up neon white by the moon's reflection. I sought out the lights of cities, ships, anything. Most of the others had found a way to contort themselves to sleep in their narrow seats. The moment we hit altitude, the No Smoking light went out and the aircraft lit up like a chimney. As I was in the last nonsmoking row, I would be mainlining a pack of cigarettes every hour courtesy of the addicts behind me.

Fortunately, the flight was tranquil early on. The whooshing of the cabin air calmed me. Except for the occasional whining kid, I had solitude in my mind.

I recollected the thread of my life to the soundtrack of classic rock and Motown, falling into distant childhood memories of Los Angeles life. Over one of those summers, I rode several times with my cousin and his girlfriend in his Chevelle as "Someday We'll Be Together" played on eight-track. One time we drove the winding road up to Mount Wilson, music blasting. I thought that summer would never end.

I spent the remainder of the flight recalling my prejudices about how life should be lived "over there." That, interspersed with the occasional fear and doubt about the miles that lay between me and the East Coast. Without America, without the Marshall Plan, Europe would be nowhere. Enough film motifs had ingrained in me the image of narrow cobblestone streets, cars I couldn't name, and people grateful for what we, *America*, had done for them.

My early beliefs about war had been forged from the snippets of Vietnam newsreels presented to the country during evening news hours in the late sixties and early seventies. There, in my family living room, my brothers and I were asked to look away from the graphic footage. What did I care? The reality of my life was shaped by the sun of Southern California days. Besides, I had firsthand experience with combat two houses down from mine, at the residence of a returned Vietnam veteran.

Day in and day out, Sergeant Clegg unearthed a fortification around his backyard. He would pop his head up once in a blue moon to see if he could spot Charlie's eyes. The patrol in his bunker occurred most often by day, but sometimes at night. My friends and I used my backyard fence as an observation deck, climbing up on the top two-by-four and stationing ourselves at our command post on lookout duty. Silence is all we got in return. No words, no noise, only various maneuvers conducted to hide down deep.

One summer Saturday morning, I woke at daybreak. I filled my camping canteen with ice cubes and water, left quietly to hop my back fence, then ran across the backyards of the two neighbors behind me. I looked in at Sergeant Clegg's fortification. He was not on duty. Jumping his perimeter fence, I hustled in low to drop my canteen at the edge of his encampment, then scrambled back to my command post. For ten minutes I pulled sentry duty, observing for any movement. None came.

I checked a few more times that day and spotted him at one point looking directly at me. I saw only his eyes under a helmet. From his nose down, he was under the cover of his embankment. I jumped off the fence. After waiting a minute, I inched up again, but only enough for my eyes to crest the top of my command post. His stare remained locked. I held up my right hand, palm open to him as a brother in arms. He retreated at that moment.

Two days later, on a recon mission, I spotted a tiny American flag stuck in the ground under a pomegranate tree located at my fence line. I retrieved the flag and found my empty canteen on the back side of the tree trunk. I scampered to the top of the fence, scanning the horizon for Sergeant Clegg. He popped up with his eyes focused directly on me. He was helmeted, and otherwise under the cover of his bunker, so that's all I saw. I held up the flag.

"Got it!" I yelled.

Sergeant Clegg quickly raised his right hand and gestured for silence, his index finger over his lips. He then retreated. I observed for any further movement but lost him after that. For the next few months that summer, I completed my reinforcement runs. I'd place the flag next to the canteen adjacent to his bunker. When he needed a resupply, he planted the flag and placed the canteen under my pomegranate tree.

It had to be done covertly, to not be seen or noticed and subsequently questioned by enemy intelligence. I'd wait and look right before reinforcement runs, to determine if he was up or out at that early hour. He never was but I never presumed. I had no intention of startling him. I would not let myself be confused for Charlie. At some point during the week, the flag and empty canteen always ended up back in my yard. I remained committed. No war would be lost on my account.

4

Midflight over the Atlantic, I traced this moment to four months earlier when Senior Master Sergeant Crowley broke the news.

"You've got orders," he said, handing me the documents.

Sergeant Crowley would never be consumed by opinion or supposition. His daily life centered on squared corners and zero tolerance for ambiguity. Strategic Air Command required it.

"To *where*?" I asked.

"Good question," he said. "You're going to the front line of this game—West Germany."

"I still have a lot to do here."

"It's a done deal."

As this revelation dug in deeper, I realized the obvious but less apparent extent of this "game." I was a game piece.

"It's one of those places that exist, but no one discusses *that* it exists—at least not in any official capacity."

"I understand," I said.

"Keep in mind," said Sergeant Crowley, "when you're on the front line, you're also at the end of the line."

At such moments, I did not interrupt. Instead I read in

Sergeant Crowley's eyes the patience and discipline of a career spent entirely assigned to SAC. I knew his stories—his tales as part of missile combat crews. These were positions that required the utmost in mental stability, predictability, and unwavering commitment to kill scores of millions on the other side at the earliest confirmation of enemy attack.

America's No First Use policy meant that we would never strike first with nuclear weapons. The solemn oaths taken to protect our way of life meant that our weapons were purely defensive. It would be preposterous for anyone to think that we had them for any other reason, let alone wanted to use them. Unless the Russians did first, in which case we would annihilate them.

For Sergeant Crowley and SAC, this was a clean war. If you received the order to execute your duties, at least it would be from the comfort of a chair, be that in a cockpit, a missile silo, or a command center. In fact, after a launch, you'd probably have time to file your nails. For Sergeant Clegg, war was a mess—a mess of trenches and bush and filth and death within feet and inches of the enemy. If Sergeant Clegg had a fingernail file, he'd have probably had to use it to stab someone.

"Just do what you need to do."

"Do you know anything about this place?" I asked.

"I do not, but you'll find out soon enough."

At that moment, Sergeant Crowley went hard-core SAC. He trained his eyes on me. "You're taking with you the one thing you need to know."

"Set the course, maintain the bearing?"

"That's how you survive."

"Yes sir."

"The colonel wants to have a word with you before he presents your medal. Be at the auditorium fifteen minutes prior."

"Understood."

Sergeant Crowley connected his hands as if in prayer, then

pointed them toward me. "By the way, do you know how you ended up here?"

"A benevolent kick in the ass from Air Force assignments?"

"That would be easy. No. We handpicked you from tech school and now you proved yourself."

I tilted my head and squinted.

"You're in the pipeline."

"How's that?"

"It's like the Mafia," Sergeant Crowley continued. "You know too much for them to let you go."

I nodded.

"That's how this works," said Sergeant Crowley.

"Yes sir."

"Since you're now officially a SAC graduate, join me tonight at the club for a drink to celebrate."

"That sounds great," I said.

"You are legal?"

"Twenty-one this past October."

"Perfect. I'll see you at the ceremony."

The aircraft arcing down woke me from that memory. I needed a splash of water on my face and a leg stretch, so I used a restroom toward the front of the plane. As I returned to my seat, I had to reenter the molasses-brown cigarette smog, which by now had pushed three rows into "nonsmoking."

Slow. Shallow. Breathe. Slow. Shallow. Breathe.

As we began our descent, *course and bearing* echoed in my mind.

5

"Good morning, ladies and gentlemen," the pilot radioed back. "Local time is 7:15 a.m. with Frankfurt reporting twenty-eight degrees Fahrenheit. We should be at the gate in about twenty minutes."

We finally broke through the cloud cover. I could make out the traffic below. This didn't appear to be so foreign—forests, direction of traffic on roadway lanes—it all conformed. For the time being my homesickness faded.

We landed at Rhein-Main Air Base, situated opposite the Frankfurt civilian airport. This had been the US military's gateway to Europe ever since the American occupation of West Germany at the end of World War II. As the plane taxied to the terminal, I got my mind in order and collected my excitement. I planned to round up my bag, meet my sponsor, then head to my new duty station.

The last time I'd had a sponsor was during my confirmation. The ceremony requires an adult Catholic to vouch for a young person's worthiness. A response I gave that day must have made mine seem questionable.

At our Catholic school, my classmates and I had been

drilled the week prior on everything the cardinal loved to quiz the confirmands on during the ceremony.

"What is the Seventh Commandment?" asked the cardinal.

All the kids raised their hands. He picked me.

"Thou shalt not kill," I said in front of God and everyone. I knew I was wrong as I said it, but I had been running through all ten of them in my head during the service. I was on number five when he picked me, so I said what was on my mind at that instant.

The whole church broke out into hysterics. My sponsor must have been mortified. I didn't turn around to look. I knew the answer, but simply running through answers from rote memorization can lead to unintended consequences.

I pressed my way to the conveyor belt to get my duffel bag.

"Airman Chisolm, proceed to the information desk," said a voice over the intercom.

I wove through the throng of people toward the designated point, where five people stood, all staring at me.

"Staff Sergeant Hlavacka?" I asked.

"'At's me." Hlavacka was a dead ringer for a young Jack Klugman, right down to the big, pimply nose and starched-in-place hair.

"Welcome to Germany," Hlavacka said, shaking my hand. "Got your stuff?"

We immediately headed toward the exit.

"Yes sir."

Hlavacka cocked back his head, scowling at me. "Please don't call me *sir*."

"Alright, Sergeant Hlavacka."

"Cut it out," he said over his shoulder and kept walking.

"How long is the drive to the base?"

"About two hours, give or take."

"OK, I couldn't find Borlingau on any map to know how far we were going."

Hlavacka cleared his throat, laughed, then piped up. "Borlingau, the *Bunker*, isn't where we're going. Immelbrücken, the Brook, is where we're going. The Bunker is where we do the work, and it ain't on any map. The Brook is our support base."

Hlavacka nodded toward a car with occupants. "Family's along for the ride. They needed a chance to get the hell out of there."

"Understood."

Hlavacka looked at his watch. "Let's get going."

I threw my duffel bag in the trunk and climbed into the front passenger seat. Hlavacka's wife and children were in the back seat.

"Nice to meet you," I said.

"Welcome to West Germany, Roy."

"Hello," I said to Hlavacka's shivering children, as they stared at my intrusion into their morning.

"Hello, Roy-O," said the older looking of the two. The other boy giggled.

We left Rhein-Main heading south, covered the next thirty miles in just over fifteen minutes, then turned west on Autobahn 6.

"That's Mannheim in the distance," Hlavacka said. "This shit was leveled during the war."

"Jack, the boys," Hlavacka's wife chided. "Please."

"Yeah, alright," Hlavacka said, eyeballing his sons as they giggled.

"How fast are we going?" I asked. Hlavacka's wife was worried about his language. I was worried about my life at our speed.

"Hundred and twenty now. It's an autobahn. No speed limit."

Farther on, we crossed the Rhine River, conjuring images of the surrounding landscape being blown to hell. Forty-odd years later, Americans still maintained a presence.

Along the way, we passed many smallish farms. Villages were set back from the autobahn, preventing me from discerning their age. They showed gray and dreary brown, as portrayed in movies filmed in these locales. Absent entirely were the ubiquitous gas stations, fast food outlets, and roadside motels of home.

These were not the manicured lawns and lives of my Catholic school friends. God and Country dominated, with the Pledge of Allegiance as our compass. Derivatives of our ancestors, we lived according to the belief that hard work and commitment would take you anywhere you wanted to go. That is, unless you were an outsider.

Clive Portnoy was a kid in my Catholic grade school. He was big—big like he'd gone through a box of Wheaties every morning for breakfast. We sometimes biked to school together since Clive's route took him past my house. His shirt was always sweat-soaked by the time we met up. I knew that Clive lived at some distance. My inquiries as to where exactly were always met with "Way the fuck out there."

He lived with his mom. Never did I understand his dad's absence, nor did I ask. Not having Mom and Dad at home seemed incomprehensible back then. Clive was also the only black kid in my school. These two facts seemed very odd to me.

Sometimes one can be struck speechless by the discovery of something that will never fit into your worldview, and the experience permanently changes you. That happened to me one fall day. I recall the autumn leaves had begun to change. On this day, four big high school kids were riding on the sidewalk in the opposite direction as Clive and me. They didn't yield so much as an inch of sidewalk space.

"What's wrong with you, asshole?" asked the kid whose handlebars struck mine.

"Sorry," I said.

"Fucking *asshole*," another chimed in.

They didn't try to jump me, though the one I hit pushed me and yanked his bike back.

"He *said* he was sorry," said Clive. He'd been riding behind me and veered off into the grass.

"You're on the wrong side of town, asshole," said one of the other high school kids to Clive.

"Kick his ass," added one of the boys in the back.

"I just might," said the one I collided with. "You idiots need to get out of the way."

"*You're* the idiot," I said.

After taking a punch to my mouth, I attempted a swing. It was blocked and I was thrown to the ground by one of the other kids.

Clive rushed in behind me and landed a punch, nailing the guy who hit my bike. Then he took one to the gut and doubled over.

"Goddamn idiots," said the boy who hit Clive.

Clive and I pulled ourselves up; the other boys gave my bike a kick as they walked away. I wiped my mouth and got blood on my hand from a busted lip.

"How bad is it?" I asked Clive.

"Doesn't look bad, but you're dripping blood."

"You OK?"

"Yeah, I'm OK."

We pressed on to a gas station a few blocks up. I used paper towels from an outside dispenser to cover my lip and stop the bleeding.

Then, silence.

Where we had always bantered while riding, we spoke not a word the rest of the way.

I hadn't seen prejudice before except maybe in an old movie, or while joking around among my white buddies, who were essentially my only buddies. White, middle-class, Catholic, manicured-lawn buddies. We joked about anyone and everyone who wasn't like us. We even joked about us, but this was different. There was nothing much to think except that I was white, and some other white kid just pointed out the obvious—and not in a joking way.

Clive and I never spoke about that morning. Something changed, though. America changed for me. There were insiders and there were outsiders. It all depended upon what one saw.

6

We entered the last leg of our journey, heading north on Autobahn 26. The final half hour went over like two full hours. Maybe I should have been more excited. The New Year was only days away. I wasn't homesick. I just wanted to sleep.

"When do I sign in?" I asked.

Signing in meant formal recognition that one had arrived at their new duty station. You're never "in" until signed in.

"We'll do it tomorrow morning."

"OK."

"Ain't no rush. I'll drop you in your room today. Sleep and I'll come by tomorrow and show you around."

We crested the final hill of our drive, then descended below a low fog cover. A cluster of buildings appeared in a valley. Hlavacka turned to me, paying unnervingly little attention to the road.

"That's it. *That's* the Brook."

I clenched my teeth in despair. The Brook stood in a tight valley of solitude overlooking itself.

"You serious?"

Hlavacka laughed, his eyes darting toward me to register

my reaction. His wife and sons stared out their windows in silence.

My heart took a dive to the floor. There was no city, not even a village in sight for miles. On this last stretch of the autobahn, I tallied no more than a dozen vehicles heading the opposite direction. No golden arches. No civilization. Just low and thick cloud cover.

"There's not much to see," said Hlavacka. "It's a freeway to nowhere."

The highway terminated in this valley. We pulled off at the end of the line and made our approach. Hlavacka showed his ID to a gate sentry, who glanced at our faces. The sentry was in a uniform, but something wasn't quite "uniform." No words were exchanged. The sentry put a cigarette back in his mouth and waved us in.

"Locals," said Hlavacka in a huff of sarcasm. "They keep us safe."

My self-interrogations began again. This time, as to what measure does what I want out of life coincide with what America—land of the free and of those who held that tenet— would make of me?

We proceeded to park in front of the dorm.

"Back in a minute," Hlavacka told his family, exiting the car.

"Nice meeting you all," I said to Hlavacka's family.

"Bye, Roy-O," said the older boy.

The younger boy turned to his mother. "I'm hungry, Mom."

"Say goodbye to Roy," Hlavacka told his younger son.

"Goodbye, Roy-O-O."

Hlavacka's wife moved to the front seat once I got out.

"Don't let this place get to you, Roy," she said.

I turned away from the haunted look in her eyes, retrieved my belongings from the car, then took a deep breath. I followed Hlavacka up the steps. Ours were the second and third sets of footprints to crunch the fresh-minted ice crystals. Frost covered the dead grass and the barren branches of two nearby trees. I glanced around. The frost gripped everything in sight.

I followed Hlavacka to my room. He'd already retrieved my room key. I dropped off my things, then walked him back out of the building.

"Thank you," I said. "I appreciate you getting me this far."

"She's right," said Hlavacka, as he returned to his car. "Don't let it get ahold of you."

"Right," I said.

"I'll see you in the morning."

"Oh-seven-thirty?"

The typical Air Force duty day always began at 7:30 a.m. "If you're early, you're on time. If you're on time, you're late," Sergeant Crowley used to say.

"Thereabouts," said Hlavacka.

At 07:20 the next morning, I stood on broken glass just inside the front door of the dorm. Dressed in my Class A's, gloves, a scarf, and an overcoat, I would have preferred to sit but there was no chair. I peered out the one-foot-square window in the door, waiting for Hlavacka to show up. He arrived at 08:14 and parked his car in front of the dorm. I descended the steps toward him.

"How can you show up to the orderly room in civilian clothes?" I asked.

"It's the holidays, Chisolm. Lighten up. Besides, you're the one checking in, not me."

We walked about a hundred yards along the edge of the perimeter road. A stand of trees followed along the outside perimeter. Beyond the trees, a barbed wire fence encircled the Brook.

"This is it," said Hlavacka.

We came upon several steps leading up to an aged building with a white facade. Hlavacka and I entered.

The office space was filled with 1950s-issue steel government desks. The steel chairs from the same era were ergonomic only to the extent that they allowed you to sit. No heat had been running this morning. Only half the fluorescent lights were turned on.

"Timmons, this is Chisolm. Chisolm, meet Timmons."

"Welcome, Mr. Chisolm."

Timmons was the only person in the office. He was also in civilian clothes, so I couldn't see his rank. His haircut was within regulation. His days-old beard was not. *This is entirely out of order.*

"Are you a civilian?" I asked.

"Cut!" said Timmons. "It's Staff Sergeant Timmons, but not today."

"Thank you, sir. Here are my—"

"Cut!" Timmons hiked up his left foot on a nearby chair, stroked his chin in skepticism, and evaluated me like a movie director working an actor into shape.

"What'd you bring us, Hlavacka?"

"This is our new hero. Check him in. I want to get out of here."

"OK, Mr. Chisolm," said Timmons. "Here's how we do it here. You listening?"

"Yes sir, Staff Sergeant Timmons."

"Cut! Goddamn it, cut, cut, *cut*! See? There you go again, Mr. Chisolm."

Under duress, my body tensed into its default position of attention.

"Lesson one—this is *not* the real Air Force. Stop playing like it is and we'll all be pals. OK?"

I remained silent. Timmons retained his director pose. I turned to seek help from Hlavacka, but his smirk and lifted eyebrow offered none. I maintained my bearing.

"Lesson two—refer to lesson one for further guidance. Now let's try it again."

"Sir?" I asked.

"This is on you," said Timmons, throwing down a pen and sneering at Hlavacka.

"Yeah," said Hlavacka. "Merry Christmas to you too, asshole."

"Now let's take it from the top, Mr. Chisolm. Ready? *Action!*"

"Timmons, here are my hand-carried docs for in-processing," I said, offering my documents.

"By George, I think he just might work out after all. Well done, Mr. Chisolm."

"Will there be anything else?" I asked.

"Height and weight?" asked Timmons, pressing pen to paper.

"Is there a scale around here?"

"Mr. Chisolm, do you or do you not know your height and weight, *sir*?"

"Seventy-two and one quarter inches, exactly. One hundred eighty-seven pounds, approximately."

"You're a quick study, Mr. Chisolm."

Timmons's directorial guidance and in-processing formalities totaled fifteen minutes. Hlavacka and I left the orderly room and walked back to the dorm.

"What just happened?" I asked.

"Do your time," said Hlavacka as he paused in his tracks. "Nobody wants a showboat."

I locked eyes with him, searching for a reprieve.

"Anything else?" I hesitated to ask.

"You're free until after the New Year," said Hlavacka. "Adjust to the time zone."

My eyes bugged out. Hlavacka shrugged.

"How am I getting to the Bunker?" I asked, breaking the vacuum of silence.

"You probably need that bit of information."

"Could be helpful," I said with a feigned laugh.

"On Monday, take the 06:50 bus right here at the foot of the dorm. If you miss it, there's one more an hour later."

"How will I know I'm there?"

Hlavacka looked back as he walked away.

"You'll know."

7

"Chisolm, call on second floor," someone yelled through my door on the morning of Sunday, January 4.

Except for the dorm manager's office, each floor had one phone placed on a writing desk centered in the hallway. If someone tried to reach you by phone on your floor and it was busy, they could call a phone on another floor. I left for the second floor.

"This is Airman Chisolm."

"Roy, this is Carter."

"Staff Sergeant Carter, hello, sir."

"Yeah, just letting you know to take the 06:50 bus in front of the dorm in the morning."

"Sergeant Hlavacka briefed me on the plan."

"You'll be kicked off at the gate. Dial 396."

"Anything else, sir?"

"Nada. See you then."

Carter hung up before I said another word.

On Monday morning—still dark, overcast, and bitterly cold—I boarded the bus. I recognized many airmen from the dorm. In silence they boarded, though not more than would fit one person per two-person seat. The fan was blowing on high, but I could feel no heat. The side windows remained iced or fogged over for the entire trip. I kept wiping my window with my gloves to clear a hole. No one else attempted to look out a window. Their heads bobbed as the bus hit bumps and took turns.

I monitored the road taken. We passed through two villages so small they had no traffic lights. The chimneys on old-world homes funneled smoke in hand-drawn Christmas card fashion. We'd departed the Brook with only traces of days-old snow. In a little under forty minutes, we'd ascended to a snow depth of at least three feet. A swath of trees had been cut for the road, but it was so narrow that turnouts were required for vehicles to pass. At the end of the line, the bus rumbled to a halt outside a gate, and someone emerged from the compound.

A guard entered the bus wearing an open parka, a conductor's hat, combat boots, and very high torso-fitting overalls. A thick layer of thermal underwear protruded at his wrists. The guard held and checked in detail the security badge for each passenger.

"Ja!" the guard said, as he approved each person allowed to remain in their seat. When he reached me, he scrutinized me from beneath his hairy-caterpillar eyebrows. The sight of his two gold front teeth distracted me momentarily as he motioned me off the bus.

From each side of the gate, a heavy-gauge chain-link fence topped with concertina wire went off in either direction. Outside the perimeter, I was easy to see. Floodlights illuminated everything in front of the gate. I squinted to get my first look inside the compound. I caught sight of a watchtower at the fence line. A guard peered down at me with a machine gun.

I turned away from the floodlights to take in an attempted breakthrough of first daylight. My surroundings came more clearly into view. At this elevation, the firs were enormous. Wind gusts high above blew wisps of snow off the treetops.

Gold Tooth emerged from the bus, motioning me to follow. I walked with him through a personnel gate and proceeded to a small guard building just inside. He pointed to a phone on an outside wall and I called Carter, the watchtower guard scrutinizing me all the while. As I hung up, I saw that Gold Tooth had returned with a German shepherd. Both Gold Tooth and the dog stood motionless, staring at me.

This was an assignment requiring security clearance, same as my prior assignment. I didn't intend to ask anyone anything. In the classified world, you lived a life of split personality. With work, you never asked what you didn't already know or hadn't been told. Why would you? What would you be trying to do? In the classified world it was all routine. Variation of routine was bad. Being unpredictable was very bad.

Each day upon arrival at Strategic Air Command HQ, I had my identification card checked and my security badges checked, then I went through a briefcase check, a coat check, an anything-carried-along check. Living meant being routine, keeping the same routine every day, because losing routine implied something was abnormal, and abnormal meant something was wrong. On assignment to SAC, without fail, every day, I kept quiet. I kept on my current project, whatever that project may have been on that day. I never strayed from what appeared "normal" relative to anything else. Being tight, driven, and certain would have been impossible any other way.

Standing now inside the perimeter of the Bunker, awaiting my next three years, I got my bearings. I looked to the east, locating the brightest part of the sky. I then planted myself facing opposite toward the west. Beyond the trees, beyond the villages and towns and indifference, lay home. *I will get through this, and I will one day go home.* I stood in silence, in bone coldness, intoning that conviction.

8

The crunch of snow signaled Carter's approach.

"Hello, Airman Chisolm."

I interpreted Carter's gray hair to mean a senior enlisted rank. But he was no Sergeant Crowley. Carter's uniform cap wasn't placed on his head with any precision, either. Wearing a standard-issue long blue winter overcoat would be expected, rather than the green parka he was wearing over his blue uniform.

"Good morning, sir," I said while reaching for a handshake.

"Formalities later. Too cold out here. Let's move."

Carter made no attempt to remove his hands from his jacket pockets. Instead he turned, and I followed. From the guard's office, we hiked more than a hundred yards up an ice-covered driveway. Sand had been thrown about to help with grip. At the top, we veered left and walked another hundred yards or so past several dark-green support buildings. Their color meshed with that of the surrounding firs. At the end of the line, and at the base of a ridgeline, was an entrance. A two-foot-thick, car-width, green-painted blast door was open to the outside. We stepped into a confined concrete foyer, all painted green. Underfoot was the same concrete, but with a steel grate laid down for wiping snow and ice from shoes. A floor-to-ceiling turnstile blocked the way.

"I'm escorting," said Carter.

Three uniformed West German guards stared at me from behind multi-inch-thick bulletproof glass. They were armed. They did not smile.

"ID," said a guard.

"Give him your military ID," said Carter. "You'll get it back later."

I slipped my ID through a bank-teller-type slot.

"Sign," a guard said, pushing a registry form toward me.

After working to pry open the edges of my ID, one of the other guards held it up to the glass and compared me to my photograph.

I filled out the form, slid it back, received a temporary badge, and was let through the turnstile, which clanged as it rotated past each locking rung. A similar turnstile was installed perpendicular to the guard post, allowing for exit.

"You have to be escorted until you get your permanent badges, so don't get lost or go crazy," Carter said.

Once inside and past a dogleg, we then marched under the cold lighting of a hardened concrete corridor. The corridor sloped downward and had been painted a dark fluorescent green. Bright glow-in-the-dark arrows at ten-foot intervals on both walls pointed in the direction of the exit. I stopped counting them at ten, which was about half the length of the passage. Continuing through one more dogleg, we traversed through another enormous blast door. If you feared being crushed into insignificance, you would not have done well in this place.

"*Now* you're in the Bunker," said Carter.

We wound our way through a hallway, then up two

concrete staircases. The walls and ceiling were painted sand yellow. Office doors stood eight feet high, each the same green as the concrete entrance corridor.

Numerous steel conduits ran the length of each outer corridor wall. Overhead, a series of cable trays followed the path of the ceiling. Smaller conduits ran from those trays into each office, feeding power and data. With the hardened concrete design, it would be impossible to run this infrastructure any other way. If a direct hit didn't kill us, death from splintered high-voltage wiring might do the trick.

As we walked, I remembered my war effort with Sergeant Clegg. My summer reinforcement runs ended the week he and his family moved away. Once they were gone, I hopped his fence to get a close look into his fortification. Three trenches had been excavated as crawlways, between three small bunkers. The bunkers themselves sat at the corners of a triangle. While on assignment, Sergeant Clegg remained combat ready, steadfastly refusing to be overrun. I can attest to his sworn performance of duty in the face of the enemy.

I remember those days from time to time, of the war in Sergeant Clegg's backyard. Neighbors looked without "seeing." But I looked, and I saw. The last time I spied him, I was on a supply run to pick up my canteen and flag. Sergeant Clegg had left a note within a plastic bag held on to my canteen with a rubber band. I immediately jumped to my command post and looked for him. His eyes were there. He was helmeted as required, stuck down deep as expected, on duty. He held up the palm of his hand to me, as I had done the first time I left reinforcement provisions for him. I held up the palm of my hand in return. He nodded once, then went down for good. For both of us the defense of our posts ended that day. We won. The enemy never materialized, and our clandestine operation was never compromised.

Sergeant Clegg, even down to how we fight our wars, we are one and the same inside our bunkers.

Carter entered a code on a keypad next to a heavy steel door. A release lock clicked. Carter pulled open the door and as we entered, a gust of air rushed in from behind us. The door was hinged with a device to pull itself shut at a normal rate. If not for this device, the low air pressure inside could easily suck the door shut with enough force to sever a hand. Inside, we took two steps up onto a raised floor.

"This is our server room operations area. We call it the OPS floor."

"Got it."

"This is where we do all programming and software work on the system."

"Feels almost as cold in here as outside," I said.

"Yeah, look at the amount of equipment to keep cold. All the AC is routed up through the subfloor."

"These mainframes are enormous."

"Pride of the command," said Carter. "This'll be your second home."

"How does anyone work in here?" I asked.

"You'll need to find a way to keep warm—try a jacket. But the noise, we can't do anything about it."

We walked through this room of large blue mainframe servers. The combined sound of air conditioning and cooling fans would make normal conversation difficult outside of several feet. At the opposite end of the OPS floor, Carter opened another steel door, and we proceeded down two steps into a passageway. At the far end of this passage, there were two steps up into another room. The entrance to that room was open, so I could see several people talking and walking about inside. Between these two rooms, about midway along the passage, stood one more door. Carter pointed toward it as we hung up our coats on a nearby rack.

"Take a step inside. This is the programmer abode. AKA, home."

There were four midcentury steel desks on each side of the room, abutted sideways one next to the other. When seated at any desk, you looked at a wall. The desks ran the length of the room. My rough guesstimate was that a three-foot path would remain if opposing seats were occupied. A partition stood between the last and second-to-last desk on each side. Books and papers comingled with pictures on all eight desktops.

"Thank you, Staff Sergeant Carter."

With Carter's nonregulation coat now off, I could make out his rank. His completely gray hair belied his rank.

"No need to include rank, Chisolm," Carter said. "We're pretty easy like that here."

I could have played connect the dots with the spaghetti splash marks on Carter's shirt. At Strategic Air Command, you were one of two things—shit sharp or fucking booted. Predictable order was what you could rely upon. SAC provided a level of structure and enforcement unseen and unavailable to most people. There would be no wavering dissent, no rogue anomaly at any time on any level—whether in terms of behavior or, worse, of thought. SAC was an easy tour if you could toe the line. For anyone assigned, there stood only one requirement—to follow orders, with conviction.

"Chief," said a senior airman with a country drawl, reaching for a handshake. "How you doing?"

"I'm good," I said. "Chief? You're missing five stripes."

"He volunteered for an extended tour," said Carter. "He'll be here so long that he'll make chief before leaving."

"He's going to be a millionaire," said another voice from the back of the room. A well-kempt master sergeant appeared and greeted me. "Legal. Systems shop."

"Systems" referred to the Systems programmer shop. Just as at SAC, the Bunker had one too.

"Nice to meet you, sir."

"Don't call me *sir*. I work for a living. If you need a read on anything legal, come to me."

"He's our resident counselor-at-law," said Chief. "And I'll make my millions, once I get a real job."

"Yeah, you'll get your millions, alright," said Legal. "Chief is our resident dart champion. Try and make millions on that."

"Why didn't you run, Chisolm? You had your chance."

I turned and saw Hlavacka smiling and throwing a yo-yo at the back of the room. I knew he was in the Systems shop, as he'd mentioned it on our drive to the Brook.

"Airman Chisolm, that's a serious high and tight," said a Mr. Magoo–looking character. He had been reading some sort of report but stood to greet me.

"Good morning, Staff Sergeant Woodard," I said. He was full regulation, rank insignia and name tag all in order.

"Just call me Woody," he said with a firm handshake. "I'm in Apps with you. Good to meet you."

"So, I'm with *you*," I said. "Good."

"You say that like it's a bad thing."

"No, no. Just taking it all in."

"You'll figure it out," said Legal, analyzing me with a skeptical eye.

"How you doing, Schmink?" I asked.

Schmink was a dorm resident whom I had only met in passing, although I had learned that his long eyelashes earned him the name. Schmink hadn't once mentioned that we'd be in the same office.

"What's up?" asked Schmink, giving me a nod. He returned to doing a crossword.

With the close quarters of this office, joining a conversation meant merely chiming in. There would be no need to get up, turn around, or otherwise make eye contact.

"You're gonna *love* this place," said someone entering the office behind me, slapping my back. "How's Omaha, bud?"

"About as cold as here," I said, turning for a shake. "Sergeant?"

"Bucknical Sergeant Treadwell," he replied. "Welcome."

I tilted my head and squinted, waiting for Treadwell to laugh at his self-created rank. Nothing doing.

"Have I got a desk?" I asked.

"Uh, right," Carter answered, "that's a little problem. We hot bunk. You're with Woody."

"C'mon, Airman Chisolm," said Woody, turning to walk out of the office. "Lots to learn."

9

I followed Woody as we began a circuit around the perimeter of our floor.

"You got one john on each deck, four decks in all."

"Like NORAD."

"Kind of, I guess. It's basically a four-story hardened concrete building, sitting on a lot of shock absorbers."

"Shock absorbers?"

"More like huge springs," said Woody. "I've seen 'em. The size of a Volkswagen Bug. They're supposed to help us survive a near miss."

"What about a direct hit?"

"You get two tons per square inch of concrete lunch."

"How the hell did I end up here?" I asked rhetorically.

"Same way we all did."

"Signing our life away," I said.

"No," said Woody. "The world is mad and they're taking it out on us."

"How did you get to see these springs?" I asked.

"The Germans own the Bunker. The building engineers give tours to those assigned here. But be forewarned, they're proud. You'll hear ad nauseam about engineering this and engineering that."

"I'll sign up."

"You don't 'sign up.'"

"Well, then how do you get in on it?"

"You need to have a clearance. *Check!* And you must be assigned here. *Check!*"

"Okay, so I qualify?"

"You do."

"Alright, so now what?"

"It's basically word of mouth. But don't worry, if you miss one tour, it'll come around again. As I said, they love their springs."

"Got it."

"In a direct hit, the Germans say we're goners. But an *indirect* hit, we'll survive."

"Are you even bothered by that?" I asked.

"Do you know where you are, Chisolm?"

"We're down two decks," I said, scratching my head, "and it looks like we're close to the exit corridor."

"No, Chisolm, that's not what I mean. They haven't buried us down here for nothing."

"What do you mean?"

"Castle Bravo."

I cocked my head back and squinted, waiting for an explanation.

"The big one. Castle Bravo. Bikini atoll was blown to hell."

"*What?*"

"Do you know your history, man?"

"You're going off on tangents," I said.

"No tangents. That was our largest thermonuclear test," Woody said. "Think a thousand times bigger than Hiroshima."

"I'm aware of what we've got."

"We're all here, or rather, *down* here, because of that," said

Woody. You would not have entertained a conversation like this in polite company at SAC. "Those commies have the same crowd pleasers pointed at us," he added.

"I don't think we're deep enough."

"Probably not. For sure everything would be vaporized from a direct hit. In fact, they wouldn't find so much as your fingernail." Woody looked side to side, then leaned in toward me. "You don't look shifty. Can you keep a secret?"

"Of course I can keep a secret."

"I've got a hideout within this hideout."

Talk of annihilation could only be withstood for so long, even though annihilation was all we stood for.

"What do you mean?" I asked.

"Lots of nooks and crannies down here, if I can trust you to keep quiet."

"I can keep my mouth shut."

"Then I'll take you on the underground, *underground* tour. Soon."

"OK."

"Stateside, they get to go home every day—malls and home and English everywhere. Not us. They don't even know we're here, and here for *them*."

"They don't even know," I copied, recognizing my true distance from home.

"Any way you look at it, we're dead," said Woody.

"Yeah, any way you look at it," I repeated, dazed.

"What are you going to do, though, right?" asked Woody. "Sometimes hunkering down is all you can do."

Woody and I worked our way to the office where I completed the clearance for my security badges. Then we returned to the programmer office, where access and indoctrination would be granted for my assigned projects. After half a day of being read in, I was anxious to get started.

10

"Your top-line worries." Carter held a report in his hands.

"I'm with you," I said.

"AardVark is straightforward. The All Vehicle report. You just ensure the numbers are accurate."

The term *vehicle* was a euphemism for every type of equipment capable of carrying or shooting any munition except nuclear.

"That doesn't seem complicated."

"It doesn't seem complicated until it is. For some damn reason, the numbers can get out of whack."

"That can't be good."

"Usually a data import failed, or one of our upstream sources fucked up."

"Then what?"

"No biggie," said Carter. "Intel will believe what you send them, or they might ask questions."

"Alright."

"If you notice a problem, or Intel asks questions, just track it down and fix it."

"Understood."

"And then you have your *real* headache," said Carter. "DiAPERS."

"DiAPERS?"

"Yes, DiAPERS. The Divisional Active Personnel and Equipment Reporting System."

"OK. What else?" I asked, fidgeting with a pen.

"AardVark is your 'What have they got?' while DiAPERS is your 'Where is it right now?'"

"Makes sense."

"Intel doesn't use AardVark every waking moment."

"OK."

"DiAPERS, on the other hand, Intel monitors 24/7. It'll be on you to make damn sure it never goes down."

"Or?"

"Or they'll be shitting bricks," said Carter. "Or court-martial you. Who knows? Just keep it going."

I let the weight settle in my mind.

"You think we might be a target?" I asked rhetorically to those present, while taking a break from Carter's tutelage.

"Might, Chisolm?" asked Legal. "*Might?*"

"I hear the Russians have a dozen nukes targeting our asses," said Hlavacka. "To account for duds, they need that many."

"We can't be worse off than SAC," I said. "SAC is top of the food chain high value."

"Yeah, where they actually give a damn," said Schmink. "But they have the button. Here, we're just I&W."

"*Just?*" asked Legal. "SAC and everyone else rely on *us* to tell *them* when to press their sweet red buttons. We're a lot more than *just*."

The Bunker's role in this war was one of Indications and Warning. The Intel group conducted I&W, and our side supported them through computers, systems, and software that we acquired, designed, and maintained.

"If their missiles are anything like their cars, they'd need fifty nukes just to make sure one actually hits us," said Woody.

"No chance we survive," said Schmink.

"We know where we stand," said Legal. "They'll want us off the chessboard."

SAC never spoke about being hit. We would win any confrontation with the Russians.

"Man, are we out there," I whispered to myself.

"Don't sweat it," said Woody.

"Who designed a war where no one dies, until *everyone* dies?" I asked. "No one will even know who wins."

"If that ain't the shit," said Schmink.

"If that ain't the shit," I concurred.

"Much to learn, grasshopper," said Woody, leaning toward me.

"Now what?" I asked.

"No one knows anything about this place."

I allowed Woody's observation to distill in my mind.

Growing up, Mom dreamed I'd become president, or at least go to college—something no one in the family had ever done. Instead, on October 15, 1984, I left a note on the mantle, walked out of the house, and reported to boot camp. On my final day of basic training, a few hours before leaving on a bus to programmer technical school, I got up the nerve to phone home.

"You could have told us, Roy," Mom said, crying.

I choked back tears that I didn't think were in me.

"You did everything right, Mom," I said. "I'm sorry I didn't tell you."

"Oh, Roy, we miss you! When can you come home?"

"I plan to be home for Christmas."

Mom sobbed. "Yes, please be here. We love you, Roy."

"Mom?"

I could hear her swallow hard.

"Yes?" she asked.

"I love you. And Dad. I'm on my way to tech school in Mississippi. My bus leaves in three hours."

Mom was silent for what felt like a day.

"We love you, Roy," she whispered.

"I'll call in a few weeks. I have to go. I love you."

Nothing could stop me—not war, not violence, not illness, not others' certainty of death. That was for "them." I phoned home three more times leading up to Christmas that year. One day before I was to fly home, leave papers in hand, Mom passed away.

Back when I ran my covert operation with Seargent Clegg, on one of those sunny summer California days while on a re-supply mission, I had couriered my plan to him: "As soon as I can, I'm joining."

So here I was. I had no choice.

"No one even knows," I whispered to myself.

"What's that?" asked Woody.

"Nothing," I said. "Just thinking out loud."

"You're going to see things you've never seen before."

"I've seen things before," I said.

"This ain't before."

11

"I count fourteen people on the board," I said.

While leafing through documents for a project, I took a break to scrutinize the contents of a dry erase sign-out board mounted next to the office entrance. Rows and columns had been created with typewriter correction tape. The first column contained last names, mine at the bottom among them.

"It's for show," said Schmink. He continued reading a novel he'd been working on from earlier in the week.

"If that board is right then I've only met half."

"It's *not* for show," said Legal. "It's every billet assigned to us."

"Where are they?" I asked.

"A couple of them are down one deck," said Woody. "The rest are gone. We leave their names as placeholders until replacements show up."

"I told you motherfuckers." Schmink laughed, pointing at me. "He's a live one."

"Steady as she goes, Airman Chisolm," Hlavacka said.

"I get the In and Out columns, but what's the OFO column?" I asked.

"Means 'out f-ing off,'" said Woody.

"Still won't say a swear word, will you, Woody?" asked Hlavacka.

"I've heard enough for two lifetimes," said Woody.

Three people currently in the office were listed as Out, while a few I'd never met were marked as In. Two more I'd met but who were not currently in the office were OFO. The remaining OFOs were MIA. Schmink raised an eyebrow at me.

Thwipit, thwipit, thwipit. Hlavacka stood up and examined his yo-yo throwing technique. He awaited my reaction. After all, the luck of the draw meant he was sponsoring me. I was his problem. Therefore, at least in part, I was his responsibility to stifle, spindle, and mute.

"It's nothing," said Legal. "Some *are* gone. Others might be at Ramstein, or the Brook."

"Too crowded in here anyhow," added Woody.

"Who was that guy they pulled out of here a while back?" asked Hlavacka, changing the subject.

"Some watch lieutenant," said Legal. "Thought the Russians were spinning up."

"Winter Exercise, or WintEx, 1983," said Woody. "The guy broke."

"I heard they pulled him out in a straitjacket," said Schmink.

"Medevaced stateside," said Legal.

"So welcome, Chisolm," said Hlavacka. "Just wait your turn to get out of this joint."

Thwipit, thwipit, thwipit . . .

"What about war games, then?"

"Normally twice a year," said Legal. "We do one. They do one. Cat and mouse. Our next one is in spring."

"What are we doing in the meantime?"

"Waiting," said Woody. "Watching."

"We wait for an outcome where the ending is known," said Legal.

"Honey, I'm home," said Carter as he entered the office. "What did I miss?"

It was lunchtime, though Carter had been signed in all day.

"You missed nothing," said Schmink.

"You did it to yourself, Chisolm," said Legal. "You just had to be a hero, didn't you?"

"You get yourself in the pipeline and this is what happens," said Hlavacka.

"We've got a lot of people leaving the next year or so," said Hlavacka. "You're just one of the first replacements."

I'd be replacing Carter in the Applications Programming, or Apps, section. For the next few months I would shadow him, picking up the intricacies of my projects.

"This place will soon be a distant memory," said Schmink, "when I get back to the real world."

Chief walked up and stood next to him. Since Schmink was seated, his right ear was now about one foot away from Chief and just above dick height.

"Say that again, sweetie," said Chief.

Schmink didn't turn and did not respond to Chief's encroachment on his space.

12

"Spermburper."

"Sosa, why don't you go find someplace to hide?" Hlavacka was practicing intricate yo-yo tricks.

"Go sit on it, Mr. H," said someone I'd yet to meet, and who had been seated with perfect posture at one of the desks.

"I'd say 'kiss my ass' but I'm afraid you just might," said Hlavacka. "We need a new password, and not that one, Sosa."

I looked at Sosa then scanned the room. Treadwell observed me from his desk. Woody turned around to watch me.

"Hello, Staff Sergeant Sosa," I said, reaching for a handshake. "Airman Chisolm."

"Oh, formal, aren't we, Mr. Roy?" Sosa asked while batting his eyelashes at Hlavacka. "I guess you haven't been indoc'd yet."

"No, I've been indoc'd," I said.

Treadwell and Carter laughed and high-fived.

"Someone is falling down on the job," said Sosa.

Hlavacka pulled up the yo-yo, crossed his arms, then cocked his head sideways, looking at Sosa. "I've got this, asshole."

Sosa swiveled around to face Hlavacka. As he turned, he scratched his left and right cheeks with his left and right pinkie nails, respectively. His pinkie nails were substantially longer than his other manicured nails.

"Oh, don't listen to his silliness, Mr. Roy," said Sosa. "Besides, I come up with passwords no one would guess."

"What?" I asked.

"We need a new admin password," said Woody, still watching me. "You got any ideas?"

"That reminds me, Chisolm," said Carter. "Timmons needs you to pick up your NBC gear from the orderly room."

"Alright," I said. "I'll call him."

NBC was nuclear, biological, and chemical protection equipment.

"You're slated for the end of the month, same session as me," said Carter.

"They'll nuke us way before they waste time on that," said Schmink.

"You're an eternal optimist," said Sosa.

"I'm a realist," Schmink said. "Face the facts."

Legal held up a large silver mug. "Survival mode, gentlemen. When all else fails, survival mode."

"Take this stuff seriously, Mr. Roy," said Sosa.

"I'm taking all of this seriously," I said.

Legal then held up a bottle of scotch. "If you want a swig, line up with your mug. You've earned yourself a gulp."

13

As winter hardened its grip, I immersed myself in deciphering the spaghetti code of AardVark. Multiple programmers before had their hands in its design and changes. The embedded notes attested to the FORTRAN code having been worked and reworked dozens of times.

"This is Airman Chisolm," I said, answering the phone at my desk. I'd become de facto office receptionist, as the others refused to answer any phone.

"This is Timmons, Mr. Chisolm. Can you put Carter on the phone?"

"He isn't in right now. Can I take a message?"

"When will he be there?"

"One moment." I put my hand over the mouthpiece. "Does anyone know when Carter will be back?" I asked everyone.

"Who's asking?" asked Legal.

"The orderly room."

"*Who* in the orderly room?"

"Timmons."

"Tell him Carter is at an appointment."

"He's at an appointment, Sergeant Timmons," I said,

maintaining my bearing despite this place. "Can I take a message?"

"I'll call back tomorrow, Mr. Chisolm."

The next day my phone rang again. The other four phones in the office would ring only once, followed by mine ringing until I answered.

"This is Airman Chisolm."

"Is Carter around?" asked Timmons.

"He isn't here right now. Can I take a message, sir?"

"Cut the act, Mr. Chisolm. He's obviously out fucking off. I just need to get ahold of him. Any idea when he'll be back?"

"One second," I said. "Does anyone know when Carter will be back?"

"Who's asking?" asked Hlavacka.

"It's Timmons. Again."

"Tell him he's at Ramstein, Personnel. Back tomorrow," said Chief.

"He's at Ramstein Personnel. Should be back tomorrow. Can I take a message?"

Timmons hung up.

The next day, and about two hours late, Carter showed up.

"Sergeant Carter, the orderly room has been trying to reach you," I said.

"Did they leave a message?"

"They did not."

Schmink and Chief laughed.

"What did you get?" asked Legal.

"My old lady wanted Lladrós. And crystals," said Carter. "Picked up several."

"Did you ever get that cuckoo clock you wanted?" asked Chief.

"Got it on my last trip," said Carter. "All hand carved. That thing is three feet tall with a dozen birds and even more whistles."

"Wow, you're all set now," said Legal.

"Lladrós?" I asked.

"Yeah, figurine collector stuff. Stopped at the Lladró factory. Wife loves 'em."

"Oh, I didn't know you were on leave," I said. "I told the orderly room that you were at appointments."

Chief laughed and picked up his darts, then left for the OPS floor.

"I didn't tell you to say that I was at appointments," said Carter.

"You didn't tell me anything," I said. "You took leave, right?"

I picked up a software change tracking booklet to review and refocus on the real task at hand.

"Airman Chisolm, you need to get wise," said Carter.

I stared like a deer in the headlights toward those still in the office. I sought refuge. I got none.

"You're the one who told the orderly room about appointments, no one else," said Chief. "That's on you, Chisolm."

Now I was a coconspirator to this narrative. My heart raced. I gripped the booklet so hard that I made fingernail marks in the leather-bound cover. I stopped answering the phone. I no longer inquired about absences.

Two weeks later, I attended my first NBC training. A dozen or so others joined me for either their first or their annual refresher course.

"Now listen up, cherry lips," the instructor shouted, "because it might be *you* who keeps your buddy from drowning on his own saliva and blood."

The instructor stood in front of a small stage inside an auditorium on the Brook. Offering Hollywood films on weekends and military training sessions on weekdays, the auditorium would have made for an ideal abandoned structure on a movie set. Inside, the rows of hardback wooden seats arced left and right away from the center aisle. The seats were missing sections of veneer or were otherwise heavily chipped and scarred while years of neglect faded the remaining varnish. The black tile floor was finished to a high gloss. The lamps hanging from the thirty-foot ceiling were woefully underpowered. Side windows painted black had to be opened to allow in daylight. It would have been a proper dungeon otherwise.

"When I'm done, you'll come up one by one while I ensure that you can get your charcoal suit on in forty-five seconds. Then, we're going to verify that you can get your gas mask out, on, and sealed in eight seconds, all while holding your breath. After that, we'll run through your 2-PAM chloride injection sequence. Then you're certified."

I looked toward one of the open windows; it was a drizzling, gray day. Constant rain. Daylight, but no sunshine. Ever. The sun never shined clean through. I hated this place.

"Ivan's got a hard-on for you," the instructor maintained. "If you don't stay vigilant, he's going to give it to you up your cherry ass."

In two hours, I was certified to operate my NBC gear.

"The Bear is hibernating today, but he'll soon be waking from the winter freeze. When he does, expect him to start testing us. Stay vigilant."

The session concluded with a US Army film showing the blood-oozing, blister-causing, and near-instantaneous effects of biological and chemical weapons on lab rats.

"Your assignment here is important. So remember everything you learn, sweet tarts. It'll save your life."

14

January 31st, 1987

Dad,

I made it! One month in country and a wild ride at that. I can see why the Air Force calls us a geographically separated unit. My dorm is located on a tiny military post at what feels like the edge of civilization. Our work, however, is done miles away.

For those assigned to Borlingau, we call it the "Bunker." We're the tip of the sword. That's pretty much all I can say about it. Remember the movie scene from The Shining *driving up to the hotel? We are at the end of that kind of line.*

I'm glad I could take time off before leaving the US, especially seeing you for Christmas. Thank you for taking me to the animal rescue center. I realize now why Mom volunteered,

and why you still do. If not for the likes of you and Mom, I'd hate to think of the alternative.
 I miss home. I'll write again soon.
 Roy

15

It was mid-February when Senior Master Sergeant De La Cruz made his way to the Bunker. De La Cruz was the senior noncommissioned officer, or NCO, of the programmer shop. Because of his rank and lack of Bunker space, he maintained an office at the Brook. Legal advised the office of De La Cruz's forthcoming arrival. In preparation, I double-checked my uniform, triple-shined my shoes the night before, and awaited inspection.

"Are you going to lay off the goddamn book reading?" I asked Schmink.

"What for?" asked Schmink, scowling at me.

"Sergeant De La Cruz coming up. *Hello?*"

Schmink, Chief, and Treadwell laughed. Hlavacka pushed back from his desk to eyeball me.

"Don't worry about it," said Hlavacka. "You really need to chill, Chisolm."

De La Cruz entered the office. I stood. My toes curled. Schmink kept reading fiction. Hlavacka threw his yo-yo. Following a cursory round of greetings, the novels were given a rest, the yo-yo kept rolling, and De La Cruz joined in on a bull-shit session about sports, who would soon be leaving and was afflicted with short-itis, and who'd gone on what trips. There was no discussion of the mission. There was no inspection.

"Roy, we're happy the reinforcements arrived," said De La Cruz.

"Airman Chisolm is going to win us a war," said Chief.

I reached for De La Cruz's offered handshake.

"Your work with DiAPERS is very important to Intel," said De La Cruz.

"I've got it covered, sir."

"I know you do, Roy. How are you doing here so far?"

Hlavacka's yo-yo stopped. The sound of a chair creaking somewhere behind me stopped. All other discussions and sounds ceased.

"He's doing great here is how he's doing," said Carter.

"Yes," I said. "Very interesting assignment, sir."

"Listen, how would you like another project?" asked De La Cruz.

"This is in addition to AardVark and DiAPERS passing off to you," added Carter.

De La Cruz turned to leave the office. Carter looked at me and tilted his head toward the door for me to follow.

"That sounds great," I said.

I followed Carter out of the office.

"It's nothing big," said De La Cruz. "Just something I've been thinking could be useful."

"What is it you want?" I asked.

"We want you to write a programmer-productivity track-ing program."

"Alright. What exactly are we going to track?"

De La Cruz looked at Carter. They nodded at each other.

"Why don't you take a stab at it," said Carter. "Think of

what we could track. I don't know, maybe project start date, end date, hours worked per week or day or whatever."

"When is the deadline?" I asked.

"Take as much time as you need," said De La Cruz. "Three months. This summer. No rush."

"Three months?" I asked. "I can probably do it in three *weeks*."

"Take your time with it, Roy," Carter chimed in. I saw his fists clench. Regaining his composure after a glance from De La Cruz, he added, "Just show us what you have when you're done."

"No problem, sir," I said, looking at De La Cruz. "I'll come up with something."

I returned to the office, sat down, and spaced out. *They're all in on it.*

"*Now* you're getting it, Chisolm," said Chief.

I turned toward Chief without realizing he'd walked up close to me.

"Man, what is your dick fetish?" I asked, standing up.

"It's going to be OK, Mr. Chisolm," said Chief, "so long as you shut the fuck up. I mean settle down."

16

I left for the OPS floor and connected with Woody, whom I had since begun following on occasional Bunker walk-throughs. Any given day, a few programmers milled around the OPS area while others read in the programmer office. Chief practiced his darts on a board mounted behind one of the two mainframes. It would be a rare day when 50 percent of the staff was on station.

Woody was consistent. Unless we were sitting at our desks for lunch, he was most often in the Intel area or on the OPS floor, where, if he wasn't programming, he sat in a chair hidden behind one of the mainframes.

"Why do you come out here to read?" I asked him.

Woody never read anything unofficial in the programmer office.

"To avoid the distraction," he said without looking up.

"How can you think straight with all the noise in here?"

"I use these," he said, pulling a piece of wadded-up paper towel from each of his ears.

"Right."

"At least out here, I don't need to talk to anyone," Woody

started, putting down his book, "at least not anyone without two brain cells."

"Where is the order in here?" I asked.

"You've seen the dorm. You've heard about the Battle Cab."

The dorm resembled a college frat house. I would call it a loose affiliation with the military. Drinking binges occurred frequently inside various dorm rooms used for both bunking and drinking. The hallways were sometimes strewn with broken glass. You damn well couldn't stand in the stairwell, for concern about falling objects thrown by drunkards.

"What about it?" I asked. "We walked through it that one time."

Woody walked me through the Battle Cab during my initial Bunker tour. In the event the Cold War turned hot, the Battle Cab would be the command post for fighting a hot war. Short of a hot war, it was used for war games. Outside of these two uses, the Battle Cab was dark.

"Oh, I guess you haven't heard. That's Ginger's hideout."

"Who's Ginger?"

"Sergeant Reid. Mary, officially," said Woody. "Unofficially, Ginger. The redhead analyst back in Intel."

"What about her?"

"Actually, they're probably hush-hush because they don't want you in on it."

"*What* already?"

"Alright, alright. If she's on mid shift, and if she likes you, she just might do you. Unless you're a pencil dick."

"What in the hell are you *talking* about?"

"A few of the Intel sections do twelves—three on, three off. If Ginger is on mids, and she likes you, you could see action."

"How do you even *know* this?"

"I was in here one night. Saw her come in with one of the OPS guys. You just need to keep your eyes peeled and your ears open."

"You're kidding me, right?"

"If it weren't the Bunker, I might be."

"Jesus H. Christ."

"If you're lucky, you could be first up that night."

"Son of a *bitch*."

Woody broke out in side-splitting laughter. "Yeah, and there are times when someone is gone all day, only to show up at night."

"What are they *thinking*?"

"They don't want you rocking the boat, that's what they're thinking."

"Who actually does work around here?"

"You do. I do. Hell, just a month ago I discovered an incorrect tally in AardVark. Carter messed up a data import. We have to be on the ball."

"Holy hell," I said. "What did he say?"

"Nothing. He's short. But I did slap the back of his head."

"Did Intel say anything?"

"I caught it quickly."

"Holy fuck."

"Holy F is right. If Intel messes up, we're goners."

"I am not supposed to be here," I said under my breath.

"If you'd messed up, they would have washed you out. That's on you."

"Why are the others here?"

"They were once like you. Chief. Schmink. Hell, pretty much most of them at one point gave a D."

"Screwups."

"Yeah, now maybe. But they all showed up once ready to rock and roll."

I clenched my teeth at the monumental disregard.

"Now they're filler," Woody continued, "or fodder. Your choice."

I stared off in no specific thought.

"This is a war of mathematics," said Woody.

"Meaning?"

"Stay with me—you know as well as I do they don't do anything. We just need them now for the numbers."

"You've been stuck down here way too long."

"No, listen," implored Woody. "If you have two thousand soldiers on the line, your enemy will plan one way. But if you have twenty thousand soldiers on the line, his calculations are going to be different. Same with nukes."

"Nukes aren't people," I said.

"Follow me. Think fifty, or even five hundred. Better yet, let's go crazy and have five thousand, or fifteen thousand. Calculations are going to change."

"And *our* numbers?" I asked. "In here, in the Bunker?"

"Kind of like Vietnam and body counts, in reverse. Live bodies. We need all of us. The Russians just need to think that we have a big standing army right on their doorstep."

"Your eyes are bugging out," I said.

"I figured it out."

"Still doesn't explain the dead weight."

"We know that Ivan knows that *we* know what *he's* got. Ivan also knows that we know that *he* knows what *we've* got. So long as we all know that we *all* know, we're golden. And no one better blink."

"If everyone knows everything, then there is no secret."

"That's what I'm saying. Just *being* here is the job. None of us can get out. It would change the numbers. Doesn't matter if we take a first strike, but we hope it doesn't come to this. That's why all the numbers."

"We're prisoners."

"If that's how you see it," said Woody. "Besides, this isn't a shooting war. A real war."

"We're inmates. And worse, on lockdown."

"Just stay focused," chided Woody. "The Intel users are

making split-second decisions to national command. Don't mess up your numbers."

"I feel ill."

"Get sick all you want—just don't blink, or break. We'll all be home for birthday cake in no time."

"This can't end well."

"Makes you wonder what the heck Ivan is doing."

"Like I said, this can't end well."

"Oh, one more word of advice—if you've got a pencil dick, Ginger will let that cat out of the bag. One of the operators found that out the hard way."

"*That's* your worry?" I asked.

"You can't let annihilation worry you. It'd be over in no time. But a pencil dick, that's a lifetime of grief. Nuclear incineration doesn't look so bad now, does it?"

"We're fucked."

17

In the weeks that followed, I stopped using the bus entirely. Secure parking was available within the Bunker compound.

"Zee front-veel drive vill be goods for zee snows," said the German used-car salesman.

I purchased a nine-year-old Audi 100. Gold Tooth smiled at me now when checking my entry badges. I had also discovered a back way to the Bunker. This new route was a logging road, scenic but tricky due to infrequent snow plowing. This became my standard route.

"Why do you keep doing that?" asked Schmink.

"What?" I asked.

"Spanking your chest."

Chief and Hlavacka laughed.

"Yeah, what's up with that?" asked Hlavacka.

"I don't spank anything," I said. "I touch my chest as a reminder."

"Reminder of what?" asked Hlavacka.

"At the moment, just a reminder of why I'm here," I said.

"Who the hell needs to be reminded that they're here?" asked Chief.

"Not a reminder *that* I'm here. A reminder of *why* I'm here." I paused.

"*And?*" asked Chief.

"God and Country," I said. "Something you seem to have forgotten."

Schmink shrugged and returned to reading. Chief stared at me, then retreated to the OPS floor.

The programmers availed themselves of many pastimes, reading and obfuscation among them. I learned most of our operations by shadowing Woody and our users. On rare occasions, I worked with Carter. Since I didn't have my own desk, I spent as little time as possible in the programmer office. I damn well wasn't going to pull phone duty.

I didn't know what work some of those assigned did, and I didn't ask. But "not asking" in the Bunker was different from "not asking" at SAC HQ. In the Bunker, "not asking" was a means to avoid wasting time trying to learn something from those who themselves had no clue what they were doing. At SAC, "not asking" was merely a security protocol meant to protect the country's classified secrets.

In the Bunker, when a user had a computer issue, they wrote a problem report, part of the official record of system or software problems. The reports were used to track the solution performed by the assigned programmer. Since classified information was maintained on the servers, all software changes had to be documented for an audit trail. Once my office received a problem report, a programmer would be assigned to it. This began a software-maintenance activity.

Woody could never sit still for long. Fiction took him only so far. For purposes of enjoyment, he'd sometimes conduct painstaking analyses of intel reports or computer processes that had no problems to begin with. Woody could dredge up "improvements." His problem-resolution count exceeded that of all other programmers combined.

I proceeded in earnest to complete De La Cruz's programmer-productivity tracking program. I could account for each programmer and each project assigned, and report down to fifteen-minute blocks of time allocated to any given project for any given intel user.

I gave an office presentation the morning De La Cruz returned to the Bunker.

"Not needed," said Chief. "Definitely *not* needed."

"We all know what we're all doing," said Carter. "It's probably overkill."

Hlavacka stood at the back of the office, looking at me.

"How can that be?" I asked, looking at Carter. "You're the one who asked me to write this thing."

"Hang on there, Chisolm," said De La Cruz. "No need to be pushy."

"If they don't want reporting, it's because there's nothing *to* report," I said.

"Hey now," said De La Cruz. "That's uncalled for."

"Speak for yourself, Chisolm," said Chief. "You have no idea what I'm doing."

"You don't know what anyone is doing, for that matter," said Schmink.

My logic couldn't wipe the smug from their faces.

"Is Woody around?" asked De La Cruz.

"Ain't seen him," said Chief. "Probably out with Intel."

"Have him call me when he turns up," said De La Cruz. "And Chisolm, I'll take a closer look at your project when I get back up here."

De La Cruz never mentioned my tracking project again.

"I'll go find Woody," I said. I wasn't interested in finding him, but I didn't want to sit around the indifference. I left for the Intel area.

"Good morning, Captain," I said to the watch officer. "Seen Woody, sir?"

"Neither hide nor hair, Airman Chisolm," said the captain. "Give me some of your time this afternoon, will you?"

"Yes sir. Have a time in mind?"

"Fourteen hundred."

"I'll be here, sir."

I swung back by the programmer office, looked in, still no Woody. I proceeded to the OPS floor, no Woody. I headed to Woody's prime hideout.

On the top level on the back side of the Battle Cab, inside a booth that was usually locked, I found Woody sitting in darkness. This booth served as the command room for the larger Battle Cab. Woody had shown me all the spaces and places to hide within the Bunker. I knew this to be his favorite spot. Two safety lights were on at the top corners of the Battle Cab. They barely lit the entirety of the cavern. An ounce of that light reflected off Woody's face.

"Hey. Woody," I said, hushed, "what's going on?"

Woody kept staring into the enormous chamber. I maneuvered a chair up next to him and sat down.

"Mind if I join you?" I asked.

Woody looked at me. His eyes were watery, just shy of full-blown tears.

"This is my place," said Woody.

"Yeah, I know it's your place," I said. "De La Cruz was looking for you."

Woody tensed up in his chair.

"Didn't sound serious, though," I continued. "What are you up to?"

"Thinking," Woody replied, with a tear rolling from each eye. He stared at one of the lights. "This place. Too much like home."

"What do you mean?"

"I'm good at finding places to hide—under stairs, in closets, here."

"I give you that," I said. "But why?"

"Constant war between my parents. That's also why I don't curse. It's all I remember growing up."

"Nothing wrong with that," I said, in a misguided attempt at therapy.

"*Everything* wrong with that." Woody scowled at me.

"I mean the not cursing."

"I'm sorry," Woody added.

"Don't worry about it," I said, attempting to look unfazed.

We sat motionless for about half a minute. I wanted to leave. Something forced me to hear him out.

"I'm my father's son in name only."

"That happens sometimes."

Woody looked at me, then turned back to the light.

"One night, after a hellacious knock-down drag-out, it was over. I'd hidden under my bed and fell fast asleep. Later that night, Mom found me. She whispered to keep quiet as I crawled out. She opened a burlap sack for me to fill with my clothes. We tiptoed out of the house, got in the car, and didn't look back. We drove halfway across the country to her parents."

"Wow, man."

"It was good. For a while. Mom remarried. My stepdad hated me. I wasn't *his* kid. He made sure I knew it. If I was *right*, I was wrong. If I was *wrong*, I got hell for it."

"Do you remember anything about your real dad?"

"All I know is he was one of those passing-through-town types—no history, or none provable, anyhow. He stuck around for a while. I guess Mom tried to domesticate him. But you can't hold down what isn't meant to be held down."

"Ever wanted to find him?" I asked.

"Nope, and don't care to."

Woody's eyes began to well up again. I sat up straight.

"One week from my eighteenth birthday, my stepdad told

me it was time to shove off. I had no one left to know and no one left to care."

"Then?"

"I don't think I had much of a choice," said Woody. "I had to do something, and quick. A recruiter visited my school the same week as my birthday. I turned eighteen and joined that day."

"You went from that war to this war," I said. "All you've known is war."

"*Fear*," said Woody. "Fear."

"I'm seeing that."

"It's why they read their novels," said Woody. "They're hiding. All of them. One way or another, we're all hiding." His tension lifted. He looked at me square on. "A world without fear is a world of fiction."

We nodded. I got up, tapped my hand on Woody's shoulder, and walked out, leaving Woody in peace.

During my back-road drives to the Bunker, the cultural silence became deafening. Sometimes on my morning treks, particularly after a night of fresh snow, I'd stop my car, turn off the engine and lights, then stand on the narrow logging road. Only after every road in the vicinity was cleared did this one garner a plow, and then only maybe. At the early hour I drove it, my tire tracks were often the first imprints. I'd stand there as long as I could, listening to the air whoosh through the tops of the giant firs.

Set back a bit from the logging road was a tiny village carved out of the forest. By virtue of proximity to the Bunker, the villagers had to know they would join us in annihilation. They lived in that village, in that enormous forest, hearing the same wind whoosh as I did, and felt the same chill I felt. They had to know. But if you thought too much about it, about being a target, you might get unwound. So you attempted not to think about it, and almost certainly didn't talk about it.

Everyone just "knew." Annihilation might take minutes, or it might take a lifetime.

Following a night of heavy snow, I stood in that road. The cold didn't bother me that morning as it usually did. I was reminded of Sister Hildegard's words: Sin required thought. Sin required penance. Sister Hildegard always said that one should be locked up in confinement with no daylight to think about one's sins.

A few days prior to this, I had an early afternoon meeting at Ramstein with a counterpart to discuss Project DiAPERS. Following the meeting, I returned for an hour's worth of duty time in the Bunker. I had announced this meeting to the office before I left.

Upon my return, I hung up my coat and noticed Chief getting up from his desk.

"Get in here and sit down already, Chisolm."

"I'll stand, thank you."

Chief looked around the room. Everyone kept their head down.

"What the *hell* are you doing here?" Chief snapped. "You're going to set a standard for all of us. *Cut* it out!"

Those words resonated that morning. The Bunker existed as both ransom and threat from the weapons used, one and the same, for and against us. For the inmates assigned, incarceration was adjudicated as a tour of duty.

I resolved at that moment to comply by not complying. I didn't want to continue down the road. I did, but with a great impatience for summer.

18

My clock read 04:26 when someone pounded on the door.

"Recall!" a voice yelled in the hallway. "Everybody up. It's go time."

"*What?*" I asked, startled, jumping from my bed.

"This is it," said Jensen.

Jensen was my roommate, but a "ghost." He was assigned to shift work on an OPS team. If I was awake, I'd have to keep quiet in our room when he slept. If he was up, he was either at the Bunker or in the room, but I was asleep.

"This is your paycheck, Chisolm. BDUs and chem gear, brother."

This was a blue uniform Tuesday, but I scrambled for my battle dress uniform, then pulled on my boots and jacket. In my haste, I didn't feather up my laces, instead tying them around my ankles. I grabbed my NBC bag and ran out after Jensen. Others were descending the stairs and rushing out of the building ahead of us, then down the steps to a waiting bus.

"Your *hat*, Chisolm," said someone behind me.

I'd forgotten my hat. "*That's* what's important?" I asked, looking back.

I noticed Schmink laughing behind me. The sound of heel beats echoed from the dozen or so pairs of boots in a hurry.

"What in the *hell*?" I mumbled to myself once seated.

"It's Ivan's turn to be an asshole," Schmink said, sitting across the aisle from me. "They've obviously done something stupid."

My eyes bugged open the whole drive to the Bunker. Once we arrived at the gate, two uniformed German guards entered the bus with machine guns. They quickly checked badges and exited, waving us through. Gold Tooth was nowhere to be seen. Instead of stopping at the turnaround at the top of the hill, the bus proceeded all the way to the Bunker entrance. We filed out in rapid succession. The entrance turnstile did not clang, as it had been reset in a position allowing quick entry. Our badges were once again checked, then each of us proceeded to our respective duty location.

"How did you guys all get up here ahead of us?" I asked.

Chief, Treadwell, Hlavacka, Legal, Woody, and Carter were already present and in BDUs.

"Recall roster," said Legal. "We're picked up at specific meeting points. Dorm residents are all in one place."

"What is going on?" I asked.

"Russians have lit up their air defenses like a Christmas tree," said Hlavacka. "Nothing unusual, except Intel says they've also spun up a lot of aircraft."

"Is this it?" I asked. "Are we fighting?"

"Goddamn it," said Legal. "There go the doors."

"The doors" referred to the blast doors being shut. Air pressure pushed into my ears.

"I hope they get a read on it soon," said Carter.

"Ivan's about due for his winter exercise," said Legal. "We can't take it for granted. Could be a ruse for first strike."

"What now?" I asked.

"You make goddamn sure DiAPERS doesn't go down, Chisolm," said Treadwell.

"Or if you're religious, you might pray," said Chief.

"Yeah, like that's going to solve anything," Schmink said.

"Seven minutes by airmail," said Hlavacka.

"Let's go out on the Intel floor, Chisolm," said Woody. "You're going to be their best friend for a while."

The Intel commander, a colonel, presided from an elevated seat toward the back of the room. This allowed for oversight of all operations. Intel comprised five sections. I supported two of them. The floor was a hornet's nest of activity.

In one section, there was a large rectangular table surrounded by three NCOs poring over documents. Two lamps hung low and bright over the table. This was the AardVark team. They worked only days except for war games or Ivan being an asshole and getting us recalled. Above the table, centered between the lamps, was the team mascot painted on a canvas. The painting depicted an aardvark driving a tank and smoking a corncob pipe, à la General MacArthur.

Adjacent to AardVark and directly in front of the commander was the DiAPERS team, or person. This role required a commissioned officer. Intel had a four-person shift-work team to staff this watch officer position 24/7. DiAPERS ran on a powerful computer workstation with two large monitors and was linked to the mainframe.

The DiAPERS mascot was painted on a two-foot-square piece of plywood and hung from the ceiling above the workstation. It was a sitting baby looking backward, wearing a shirt with the Soviet flag emblazoned over the back and a diaper with a sticker of a mushroom cloud. Covering the baby's face was a picture of Mikhail Gorbachev, the current Soviet leader. Frayed edges of pictures protruded from underneath Gorbachev's. The names Brezhnev, Andropov, Chernenko, and

Gorbachev were written on the plywood to the left of the baby; each of the first three names had a line drawn through it.

Woody and I took up a position next to the watch officer in DiAPERS. The captain wore a headset and was giving out constant updates to forward operators about the movement of Eastern Bloc assets. All the while, information scrolled rapidly down one of his two computer screens. The captain paused one of his screens at various times to read some of the traffic in more detail. On the other screen, a map displayed Europe, serrated north to south by a jagged red line marking the Iron Curtain.

"He is toggling fast through the overlays," I whispered.

"He's comparing historical activity," said Woody. "If it doesn't match, it might be a preemptive strike. Hell, even if it does match, it might still be a preempt, commie bastards."

The captain zoomed in and out for detail and could toggle between views of military equipment, known weapons locations, troop strength and locations, civilian aircraft, or any combination. Green and red aircraft icons—representing us and them—circled within narrow bands on either side of the Iron Curtain.

"That is a lot of equipment," I whispered to Woody.

"Especially tank regiments. Like they're stuck in World War II."

Moving west or east from the curtain, traffic movement and symbols thinned out.

"What's that lit up way east?"

"Their forward HQ. They're running the show from that place right now. Unbelievable ring of SAM sites, eh?"

Their surface-to-air missile sites lit up in pockets all over the place.

"What are we waiting for?" I asked.

"Looks to be the Bear's wakeup from hibernation. His winter war game gives us a chance to watch what he does, and to hone our own countermeasures."

"But this could be a ruse," I said, as though I were an expert at this game.

"What are those bastards doing?" asked the captain.

An Intel NCO rushed by with a thick report. Three others joined him at a table, where they pored over the pages.

"Red Eight Corps, twenty heavy-track vehicles two clicks closer to the line. Red Eight Corps, twelve artillery pieces also two clicks closer to the line."

"Roger that," said the colonel. "Notify forward commands of movement."

"Now we're going to have to move our stuff," said Woody.

The captain panned the map east of the curtain.

"All fivers, Colonel," said the captain. "All required aircraft now in orbit."

Communications from the Bunker were on classified and encrypted frequencies. No civilian would be aware of what was going on, save for aircraft flying unusual routes and elevations.

"We're balls to the wall on the curtain," said the captain. "Don't fail me now, Airman Chisolm."

"Yes sir. No," I said.

"Is that a yes or a no?" whispered Woody. "Be firm next time."

"We've got Ivan by the tail," said the captain. "Just no one blink, and Daddy gets home to Momma safe and sound."

"We've met our scramble time with all but one squadron, Colonel," said a major standing in front of a large display screen.

"If you want dinner, Major, you better figure out who failed what and why they weren't on station on time."

"Yes sir."

I spoke not a word, sitting at attention and observing for about half an hour.

"All our bases around Europe stand ready for just this kind

of moment," whispered Woody. "Spangdahlem, Zweibrücken, and Bitburg are a few of them."

"Understood," I said.

"Looks good, Captain," said Woody. "We'll be on the OPS floor if you need us, sir."

I stood up to follow Woody.

"That place is really lit up," I said, looking one last time at the map. It had been zoomed in too close to identify any geographic reference point.

"Oh, that's us," said Woody.

"Us?"

"Sergeant Woodard, don't make me have to hunt you down," said the captain.

"We're here, sir. Let's go, Chisolm."

An ice-cold feeling descended from my neck, down my back, around my arms, then to my hands. I followed Woody.

"We're ringed by SAM and triple-A sites," said Woody.

"What the hell? *Us? Here?*"

"Welcome to the Cold War, Chisolm," said an Intel NCO in passing.

"I've seen nothing outside," I said to Woody as we departed the Intel area.

"And you won't see anything. Not from the ground, anyway. It's up on the hills around us. That's our insurance policy, a defensive ring, last chance at life—call it what you want. It's all the same thing."

"How much do we have up there?"

"Heck if I know. That's classified. But as you saw, we're lit up like a Christmas tree."

"Goddamn," I said. "We're painting a bull's-eye on our heads, for Christ's sake."

"That seems counterintuitive, but if we know that they know where we are, and they know how important we are, then we need the firepower."

"With that logic, we would need everything!"

"It's all in the numbers," said Woody.

"What's your guess on how much we need?"

"That's the point," said Woody. "No one really knows. But we're not entirely leaving it to chance. We can at least go by how important our survival is down here. And we can go by how important the Russians *think* we are, and the answer to that is *very*."

"Basically, what we've done is arm ourselves to the teeth, but all that does is tell Ivan that we know we're important. Ivan then aims all kinds of warheads at us, so then maybe we need a little more equipment up there. But for good measure, since no one is *really* sure who has how much, we'll add even more?"

"Yeah, that's pretty much it."

"You enjoying this, Chisolm?" asked Hlavacka, who had walked in behind me and listened in on Woody's and my last exchange.

"Enjoying?" I asked. "Yeah, that's what I'd call it. What are you doing in here?"

"Making sure the servers don't die. Legal and I swap each hour out here."

"Breathe the fresh Bunker air, Chisolm," said Woody "Let's monitor DiAPERS from here."

I sat alongside him at a mainframe terminal.

"Hey AC, make sure the reports are folding correctly as they come out," he said. "Intel's going hot and heavy back there."

AC was a computer operator on one of the OPS floor shifts. He was preparing reel-to-reel data tapes for mounting.

"Already on it," said AC. "All nice and pretty for them."

For two hours, Woody and I read a copy of the same information disseminated on the Intel floor. Chief honed his dart game all the while. A high pitch from the large-format printer irritated deep in my ears as output ran nonstop. Intel users retrieved each new stack of reports about every fifteen minutes.

"We'll know if someone blinks," said Woody. "We'll know if it hits the fan."

"I don't like blinking," Hlavacka chimed in.

"Yeah, we'll know," I said. "But what good will that do us?"

"Good question," said Woody. "Do you want to know if we've got incoming or not?"

"Can I do anything about it?" I asked rhetorically.

"You can pray," said Hlavacka.

Tired, I returned to the Apps office. Diesel engines in the bowels of the Bunker had been turned on in case of power-grid loss from an attack. This caused a low-grade vibration through the floor. The air vents had been sealed against any chemical or biological attack. The filtration system added a burning-oil smell to the air.

Legal and Carter played poker. Schmink and Treadwell read. Everyone else listed on the roster board was signed in, though their whereabouts were unknown. The blast doors remained closed for seven more hours. Then Ivan pulled back his aircraft, our aircraft returned to their bases, and both sides spun down their SAM and triple-A, or antiaircraft artillery batteries. We found peace, after all, under the certainty of annihilation.

Following another two hours of debriefing and forwarding data from my programs to Ramstein by courier, my work was done. I palmed my chest as I walked out of the Bunker and boarded the return bus to the Brook.

19

"Have you seen those cats out there?" I asked.

I sat down at one of the mainframe programming terminals on the OPS floor.

"Definitely good mousers," said Wagner, one of the OPS floor NCOs. He walked past me to pick up a logbook.

"Those support buildings must be home to a lot of mice, what with how cold it is out there," I said.

About half a dozen feral cats inhabited a crawl space under one of the Bunker support buildings.

"Only serves to make the cats fat, stupid, and careless," said Wagner. "They're setting themselves up to be someone else's lunch."

"Two weeks ago, I saw the moment of catch," I said. "I didn't know mice could screech so loud."

"A pleasant outcome indeed."

"Yeah, real pleasant."

"What else should they do?" asked Wagner. "It's in their nature."

"OK, so are you Chinese or what?"

Wagner chuckled. "Do I *look* Chinese?"

"You're some kind of Asian. I just can't figure out what. But if you think fat cats are pleasant, you got me wondering."

"Very funny. Mom is Japanese. Dad was American GI, but German descent."

"How did *that* happen?" I asked.

"How did *what* happen?"

"Your parents meeting."

"The same way everything happens—chance. Dad was assigned to Yokota Air Base when he met my mom."

"Your dad speaks Japanese?"

"Didn't need to. My mom spoke pretty good English. She had to."

"How's that?"

"Because of August 9, 1945."

"What do you mean?"

"If that day had gone according to plan, my parents never would have met. August 9 was the second bomb, the one that hit Nagasaki. No one talks about Nagasaki. Hiroshima gets all the fame."

"If the bomb hit Nagasaki, then it means that day *did* go according to plan," I said.

"The primary target that day was Kokura, but it was socked in. So they flew on to Nagasaki. My mother and her family lived in Nagasaki."

"But you're here, so she made it?"

"In the last months of the war, many cities were fire-bombed. However, there were a select few that were untouched. These few had to remain pristine."

"For what?"

"Children had been sent out of the bigger cities. Most mothers went with them. The workers remained. Everyone knew it was only a matter of time before their city would be bombed. But Nagasaki, and Hiroshima for that matter, had to remain unscathed."

"OK. For what?" I asked again.

"They needed to see the effects of the bomb. The only way to know what the bomb could do would be to start with a clean slate. Hiroshima was one of the untouched. So was Nagasaki."

"Where does your mom fit into this?"

"My grandfather remained in town because he worked as a metal fabricator. He was never found. My grandmother returned to Nagasaki for an overnight on the eighth to pick up clothes and a doll for my mom. Their house was up an embankment on the outskirts of town. That next morning, my grandmother closed the front door and took just a few steps toward a bus stop. As the bomb exploded, my grandmother turned toward it. The flash nearly blinded her. As my mom told it, the colored patterns and fabric weave in my grandmother's clothes left unusual burn marks on her skin. The bus never showed up. It was only a one-hour drive to the village where my mom was staying. My grandmother walked, rode in carts, and slept along the way with countless others. It took her three days."

"No way!"

"My grandmother arrived empty-handed, as the doll was lost, and her suitcase was too much to carry. But she was lucky. She survived, if you could call it survival."

"Jesus. What happened then?"

"She clung to life. As the years went by, the survivors were made fun of, or worse, couldn't find work. They had a name for them—*hibakusha*. It was bad enough if you somehow survived unscathed, but much worse if you were maimed or disfigured, as was my grandmother. No one talked about it. All that would do was bring ridicule. My grandmother never remarried. Instead, my mother cared for her in a life of seclusion. But even my mother, by virtue of connection to that city and my grandmother, found her work and marriage prospects limited. She moved to Tokyo. The Americans on Yokota Air Base hired her to do translation. That is when she met my father. The Americans did not stigmatize the survivors."

"Why in the hell would you join the military after *that*?"

"Dad didn't want me to," said Wagner, with a look of grief that I could relate to. "But my mom and grandmother survived because of Americans."

"They almost died because of Americans, and you say they survived because of Americans. That doesn't make any sense."

"This was war, Chisolm. See it for what it was. It only depends upon which side you stand on."

I nodded in agreement.

"We started with two bombs," said Wagner. "How many do you think we have now?"

"At least ten thousand," I offered.

"Not even close," said Wagner, shaking his head.

"Fifteen thousand?" I suggested.

"Try twenty thousand, give or take, but Russia's got us beat about two-to-one."

"That has to be enough to hit every square inch on the planet, multiple times."

"It is," said Wagner. "But that isn't the strange part."

"If that's not strange, nothing is."

"No, the strange part is that back home, people wake up every day knowing what these things can do yet live like they don't exist."

"It's not like they can do anything about it."

"I thought the same thing. So I asked myself, how can I remain on the outside when the ones who control these things are on the inside? I came in to help make sure our i's are dotted and our t's are crossed."

"You're right," I said. "No one talks about it."

"Got to be careful," said Wagner. "Last thing anyone needs is some asshole on our side being sloppy. Basically, I'm here to keep you and me alive."

"What's more insane, you thinking you're preventing a war or the idea that we're sitting in here, waiting for death?"

"You missed the whole point of the exercise, Chisolm."

I hadn't typed a keystroke since Wagner walked by.

"Why do you think they've got twice as many as us?" I asked.

"Duds. They need twice as many to account for duds. And misses. They're Russians, for God's sake. They copy everything we do but do a shitty job of it. Everyone knows that."

"Can't be that bad," I said, playing devil's advocate. "And we better hope there is someone like you on their side."

"I mean, how good could their science be if they can't figure it out on their own? Basically, their shitty work fucks us even more."

"Very logical, sir," I said. "A hell of a lot to think about."

"You've got all the time until doomsday."

"Yeah, right now I can't get into the tape repository," I said. "Did you guys change the password?"

"Spermburper."

20

February 22nd, 1987

Roy,

It was so good seeing you.

Your mother and I never needed to forgive you. She would be proud of how you've turned out. We gave you a moral compass. How you use it, that's all up to you.

Tell me about what sort of job you'll be doing. It sure sounds like an important place. Just keep your eye on the ball and you'll do fine.

I'm going to stop by the library and pick up some books on West Germany and at least find you on a map.

The animal rescue center is keeping me busy. Just last month we took in two horses. A good Samaritan brought them in—found them starved and near death on some foreclosed and

abandoned property. If I didn't know any bet-
ter, I'd think your mom sent them my way.
I'm saying my prayers for you.
Dad

21

I kept Dad's letter in my breast pocket and used it as a compass. I needed Dad's prayers like I needed the refuge of warm memory from my third-grade classroom. In moments of doubt, I would turn to both.

I had a read on the inmates, single or otherwise. For those married and accompanied, family housing on the Brook was located at the opposite end of the post from the dorm. If an opening existed, an inmate would be assigned on-post military housing. For singles, they could double-bunk dorm rooms if necessary. When family housing was fully utilized—a 100 percent certainty—married inmates were required to temporarily live on the economy. That could be a bitch. The norm was to sign up immediately upon arrival in country for on-post housing, then move on post once a housing hole opened. Those holes always got filled.

To be sure, the inmates encountered the economy—like me, for instance, when I bought my car. We could extricate ourselves from the post if desired. A passing knowledge of German helped but wasn't required. Just about every German near an American base spoke some English.

However, we could just as well commute between the Brook and the Bunker and never be required to deal with anything out of bounds. Everything necessary and needed could be found in bounds. But "needed" was the key here, as anything superfluous went by the wayside. What missed the lading bill forced inmates to contort their requirements into what they could get.

Access to everything "American" was gone, but my memories remained. I instead made the daily ascent on roads absent streetlamps, through snow-covered forests with windswept treetops.

I'm not supposed to be without the fitted shirt of America enveloping me. I've slipped some straitjacket. I knew what I was told "back there." I conformed, just like everyone else. The culture is. *It isn't assumed to be, it just* is. *I conformed without even realizing that conforming was what I did. On the inside, I couldn't see it. But now is my chance. I'm falling out. I took shelter, deep down.*

The inmates are correct. This is not "real."

On the evening of my three-month anniversary and on my way to the first floor in the dorm, I passed AC's room.

"How you doing?" I asked, leaning against his doorway.

"Same old same old," said AC, handing me a glass. "It's a clean one. Join me for a drink?"

"Sure," I said. "What the hell."

I sat down and poured myself a shot of his whiskey after cleaning the "clean" glass with my shirt.

"Where's your posse?" I asked.

"Assholes left without me."

"Where'd they go?"

"Town, I guess."

"So, what's your story?" I asked.

"How much time do you have?"

"A drink's worth."

"Shameful," said AC.

"What's shameful about that?"

"Everyone is impatient."

"Or busy."

"Your drink is finished," AC said, pointing to the door. "You must be going."

"I chugged it. Sorry. I don't mean to drink you out of house and home."

"Not possible," said AC, pointing to a shelf of liquor.

"Sure, I'll have another," I said, pouring another shot.

"So, you *do* want to hear?"

I set down my drink so I'd pace myself, then leaned back in the one "clean" chair in his room.

"I'm listening," I said, "but you probably could have finished your story by now."

"No one ever asks," said AC.

"No shit, if you take this long to tell it."

"I never learned music. Never joined sports. My school had neither. But, in all honesty, I had no time."

"*That's* your story?" I asked, leaning in, sipping my drink.

"We didn't live on the wrong side of the tracks. The tracks didn't run out as far as we lived."

"Where the hell was that?" I asked, sitting back.

"Yazoo City."

"You're fucking with me."

"Dead serious. Mississippi. It's the rural area for the rural area."

"No shit?"

"No shit. Never fit in," said AC. "But, never had anything to really fit into."

"Sounds like a *Deliverance* kind of place."

"Not really. Just dirt, dirt poor."

"Was there anything to do? *Anywhere?*"

"Sure, if by *do* you mean being pulled from school to work

in the afternoons. And if not pulled from school, then the last man picked for lunch-break teams."

"How do you get pulled from school to work?" I asked in disbelief.

AC poured himself another drink.

"Do you need to go, Chisolm?" AC asked, nodding at the door.

I put my hand over my glass. "Keep going."

"No choice. My parents needed all hands to work their small plot of land to survive."

"Ah, farmers," I said.

"Don't look down on us."

"I'm not looking down," I said. "I'm just knocking that option off my list of long-term careers."

"Yes, farmers," said AC. "And field labor, shoveling manure, anything backbreaking. They never complained."

"How the hell did you get here?"

"Not complicated."

"Go on."

"If you forget where you come from, you forget how you got here. I don't forget. Poverty can help you focus. I found the fastest way out, which is how I got here."

"I wouldn't have guessed," I said.

"Everyone I know is still in that town."

"Everyone?"

"All of 'em. I send home all I can to my folks. We were outsiders."

"I know outsiders."

"Why don't you tell me about you?"

"How about a top off?" I asked, reaching for my glass.

22

If I went by what the SAC old-timers said, working in the HQ was not the real Air Force. That, they told me, was something I had never known—flying jets or flying bombers. Then there were the missileers, a small fraternity of ICBM launch officers occupying a different but no less lethal means to deliver annihilation. Anyone who held a "real" job before assignment to SAC HQ could be identified by a wings or missile badge on their uniform. Basically, anyone directly tied to shooting, blowing up, or flying was part of the "real."

The old-timers didn't much like HQ desk duty. But they knew their work was important. Because of their experience, they knew how everything downstream worked, and it was they who told everyone else where to go, when to go, and what to kill. In the name of SAC HQ, no one would make the mistake of questioning anything but that which required a question. In the Bunker, I asked questions. It grated on some people. OK, maybe many people. But, in my defense, I listened so that I wouldn't draw wrong conclusions or paint inaccurate pictures.

I pressed on back to my room. The third-floor drinking had turned ominous. And by ominous, I mean typical and very predictable. I pored over the Sunday *New York Times*, which I snatched up when it arrived, three days after its print date. You could get American periodicals and newspapers, as long as shelf life didn't matter to you. You could also get books. Lots of paperback fiction arrived at the exchange. This was the source of reading by the inmates during duty hours. *Goddamn, they kept those shelves filled.*

While reading this particular *New York Times*, I enjoyed a report about the state of American relations with third world nations. We, America the great and bountiful, the story went, ought to be offering our expertise and support to aid those underprivileged abroad. Not two pages later, in the same section of the paper, another writer condemned the horrible fact that we, as a country, weren't taking care of our inner cities. Our inner cities, deteriorating and collapsing from failing infrastructure as they were, required money and lots of it. In neither story did the author place responsibility on those who lived in either locale, at home or abroad. It was someone else who should handle the solution, and that someone else was you and me, and our government. The same government that fielded the military units assigned to the Bunker.

I had since picked up full-time effort over AardVark and DiAPERS. Carter didn't have an imminent departure, as he had about two months left. But in Bunker time, two months remaining meant imminent. I honed my skills and stayed focused on the mission.

"Carter around?" asked Sergeant Reid.

"He's got an appointment," Legal yelled from behind the Systems partition.

"I need some help, please."

"I can help," I said. "What's up?"

"Can I show you?"

I got up to follow Reid into the Intel area. "Sure, happy to help."

Reid sashayed in front of me. She must have had a long mane, because her hair was spun into a substantial bun. Her fitted uniform hugged a svelte figure around every curve. I failed to notice her looking back at me until too late, when my eyes were on her ass.

"Airman Chisolm?" she asked in a hushed tone. She kept her rear end toward me while looking back with wide-open bug eyes.

"Yes, Sergeant Reid," I said. "There is a problem."

"I know that. It's what I came to tell you."

She continued to her desk, sat down, and crossed her legs. She didn't scoot up to the desk, but instead twitched her foot with her pump dangling from it. *Goddamn that tight skirt.* Her hands were sitting one over the other in her lap.

"Yes," I said, regaining my focus. "When did it start? I mean, what's the problem?"

"About a week ago. Look here."

"This is the first I've heard of it," I said, reading the report. "What are you seeing?"

"Here. This column. These numbers are a big jump over historical. We need to run these numbers up the chain by Monday. It's important we get this rectified."

"I'll get on this right away."

"I told Sergeant Carter," said Reid. "He said he'd fix it, but I never heard back."

"Understood. I've got this now."

"Thank you, Airman Chisolm. And one last thing."

"Yes, Sergeant Reid?"

"It's OK to lighten up a little, at least when it's not balls to the wall."

I hid my boner behind my notepad.

"Very well," I said. "Thank you."

The numbers appeared accurate, at least how I knew the software would tally them. But to the Intel world, when numbers look suspicious, people get nervous. The numbers just might be wrong. I wasn't about to compound the suspense by appearing nervous, worried, or questioning, even if I did sport a boner. I decided to take it up with Carter when I next saw him.

"Hey, you got a minute?" I asked Carter, upon his return to the office the next day.

"You bet. Whatcha need?"

"I tracked down a problem for Sergeant Reid. I'm a little worried."

"She's got some big tits."

"Not her tits, you moron," I said. "It's one of our reports. She says the numbers don't add up."

"And?"

"The report itself pulls from the correct data fields, but some of the counts seem way off—like 'the Russians are planning something *preemptive*' way off."

"Oh, hell," said Carter. "I know the report you're talking about. The update I ran crashed on the first attempt. I forgot to roll back the changes before I ran it a second time. Oops."

"Do you think you need to tell them back there?" I asked. "Like *now*?"

"A count is a count, and I didn't write the report. Neither did you."

"You idiot."

"Careful. I outrank you."

"*Now* you want to play military?"

"Pipe down, man. I've got your count right here," Carter said, grabbing his balls. "Just fix it."

"I decided to check the other database-update logs. Two full updates haven't made it into the database over the past six months. I applied them. This corrected two other reports."

"You're a war hero, Chisolm," Carter said, as he punched my ribbon rack. "Here's your medal."

"The original database in question still needs to be fixed," I said. "And I don't need a medal. The numbers just need to be right."

"You're lucky. I've got nothing planned for the afternoon."

23

"What's it say?" I asked, leaning against the printer on the OPS floor. I was waiting for a job to complete.

Wagner cracked open a fortune cookie as he sat looking out of his office.

"Says 'Happily ever after does exist.'"

"Well, we know it isn't here," I said.

"Not hardly."

Wagner had built himself an "office" on the OPS floor. You could enter it through a narrow passage between two refrigerator-size mainframe auxiliary CPU boxes. Wagner's desk was up against one of the concrete walls, which did double duty as the back wall of his office. On either side of the desk stood a seven-foot-wide partition, giving him a good twenty square feet of privacy.

"Where did you get all those?" I asked. A one-gallon container filled with fortune cookies stood on his desk.

"Mom sends them. It's my care package. How you been, Chisolm?"

"God and Country, my friend. Any news?"

I always looked forward to seeing a select few inmates,

and Wagner was one of them. Whenever I had something to talk about, he was ready to go. Wagner's uniforms were neatly pressed, and he arrived on time and remained awake all day. But his diligence got the best of him.

One Monday morning, the OPS senior NCO asked Wagner why he hadn't signed off on completion of the weekend's backups. In fact, under Wagner's inquisition, the shift responsible for doing the backups noted they were overcome by events and therefore the backups were missed. These "events," as Wagner's sleuthing uncovered, meant sleeping through the time to run the backups. With his uncanny eye for correctly dotted i's and crossed t's, and his perverse interest in evaluating the facts, Wagner, damn him, would not pencil whip any document, even if a signature was all that was required to "prove" something. He also wouldn't rat out the shift on sleep detail. Since backups always had to be proven as done, this was a problem for the OPS senior NCO. He had his own superiors to answer to. For his attention to detail and unwillingness to waver, Wagner was fired. But not "fired" in the truest sense, where one would be kicked out of an organization.

In the Bunker, logic dictated that we never willingly gave up a body. The concern at the Brook was that Air Force HQ might take away a slot entirely if we could afford to lose anyone. So our only recourse was to keep every hole filled. With smart and strategic thinking, a Bunker firing meant promotion into a position of insignificance. In Wagner's case, this meant an all-new role—Time And Daylight Position Lead, or TADPoLe. In some ways, the inmates were brilliant.

"I'm on sixty-three."

Sixty-three referred to the number of books Wagner had read since his arrival at the Bunker. For him, this amounted to fifteen months. The rules of the game were the same for everyone. The calculus dictated that only those books completed during duty hours could be included in the official count. This gave every inmate a level playing field. This rule was adhered to by all, and no one fucked with it.

"That's impressive," I said. "What was it, fifty-seven last month?"

"Fifty-five. Would have been more, but the exercise crimped a few days."

"That's a record."

"Goddamn right it is."

Wagner originally began his Bunker tour as OPS "B" shift supervisor. That lasted over a year. In his new position, he led no shift, had no direct reporting staff of any kind, and worked only weekdays. Wagner's job was to regularly check the OPS wall clock. At the top of every hour, he entered the time in a logbook. This proved neither that the clock told accurate time, nor that Wagner could tell time. It only proved that Wagner could tell when the big hand was at the top of the dial and that he could follow orders. Wagner could never prefill or backfill the logbook, as the OPS senior NCO would randomly appear throughout any given day to check it for accuracy.

"I'm sick of the fluorescent lights in this joint," he said.

"*That's* what bothers you?"

"A lot of things *would* bother me, but I don't *let* them bother me."

"Do you find it odd that in spite of everything around you, it's the lights that bother you?"

"These lights are a nice little problem to have," Wagner said. "Got to bitch about something, right?"

"When do you even see daylight?"

The "Daylight" euphemism in Wagner's position title was intentional. It was a constant reminder that, while his duty hours might have been during daytime, Wagner rarely got to enjoy a sunny day. In winter, he did eight-hour shifts. In summer, he would be on twelves.

"Off days only. I eat lunch at my desk. But hey, I'm breaking records."

"Yeah, at least you're breaking records."

It would prove far easier in the Bunker to assign someone responsibility over nothing and have them reporting daily for no reason. The slots had to be manned, and it had to be called a "promotion," because who could argue with being promoted? Wagner's reading would be no different from what was already being done by every other inmate, except now everyone knew who had clock detail.

A few weeks prior, entering the Bunker on a rare sunny morning, I had a clear view of jets overhead. Contrails swept the sky within predefined routes. On one particular route, all aircraft went west. The deep-blue early-morning sky stood in stark relief to the white jet contrails. I observed a few aircraft before pushing the turnstile and exercising its clanking metal gears. The air that rushed past me felt warm and inviting, especially leaving the coldness of that winter day.

24

"Sorry I didn't ring the office that I'd be late," I told Carter. "Wasn't sure anyone would be in to leave a message."

"Not a problem. I think we had it covered."

I'd arrived two hours late. On this day, I marked the moment I began my effort to conform by not conforming.

"I'm actually moving to an apartment off base."

"Why would you *do* that?" asked Carter.

"Dorm is full, and I volunteered."

"OK, and so *why* would you do that?"

"I don't want to stay locked in."

"Suit yourself," said Sosa. "But everything you need is on base. Well, almost everything." He winked at me and cocked his hip.

"I'd like to request a day or two of leave to find an apartment."

"*Leave?* You don't need to take any leave, just *go*," said Carter.

I looked around the programmer office. No one flinched or looked up. "But I'll be out for a few days finding a place."

"That's official business," said Carter. "No leave required. Take as long as you need."

"I'll let you know when I'll be out."

"You just told me that you'll be out. You don't need to tell anyone again."

"Fair enough," I said.

"Be advised, I'm off on a crystal tour later this week," added Carter.

"What's that all about?" I asked.

"Yeah. The wife and I are packing in more tours before we leave. She needs more crystal, and Lladrós."

"How about a bit more time with me for software continuity?" I asked.

"I'm also out-processing in the meantime."

"Who runs this place?" I asked.

"You do, Mr. Chisolm," said Sosa. "Take charge."

Treadwell walked in.

"Dude," he said, pointing at me. "I hear you're moving."

"I'm outta here," I said. "My orders were screwed up, and instead of coming here I should've gone to Ramstein. I'm gettin' the hell outta here."

"You kidding me?" asked Treadwell.

"Of course I'm kidding you," I said. "I'm moving out of the dorm."

Schmink surreptitiously listened in with his back to us, as he sat up perky and straight in his seat.

"Need a roommate?" Treadwell asked.

I wasn't certain that I wanted another roommate, but for affordability, I had little choice.

"You interested?" I asked. "I mean, I haven't even begun looking for a place. But yeah, if you're interested, I think we can work it out."

"I've got about fourteen months left, but getting out of the Q would be nice."

"The Q" was the NCOQ, a dormitory in Ostenhof used to house a number of more senior NCOs. The remaining NCOs lived on the first floor of the dorm at the Brook. Treadwell had the rank necessary for entry into the Q, but he quickly discovered one of its drawbacks: the lifers there—middle-career conformists—existed in a state of silent, sedentary death.

"Let me find a place first," I said. "If it's big enough, then we can do it. In the meanwhile, you probably need to check yourself with the Shirt."

Squadron first sergeants, or "Shirts," as we called them, held part of their role and power by advising a commander on the morale and welfare of a unit's enlisted force. They could also stick a boot up someone's ass, if called upon to do so.

"So, no problem with me being gone?" I asked.

"No, uh-uh," said Carter. "Do what you need to."

"Alright."

"I'm so short you'll barely see me after today, Chisolm."

Maybe it was the culmination of guilt for all the time he'd been gone, or maybe Carter just didn't give a shit. I left the office to do my rounds, which kept me up to date with the rumor mill. This was a plus. My rounds also meant I had to subject myself to inmates' gripes and complaints, much like a grief counselor. This was a minus. I could take stock of their grievances but offer no relief. I had no choice. The only solution to their pain would be a one-way westbound journey.

The inmates were locked into something from which they could not extricate themselves. If there was a problem that could be put off till the next day, reading of fiction and lengthy debate ensued. Often these were one and the same. That, or they were OFO. However, at no time could a debate center on any aspect of the mission, as this would be absurd.

When proposing an office discussion topic, I carefully observed for a quiet stillness. Everyone present had to appear rested. You could learn a lot about the world from the other inmates. But this could not happen if they were already burned out from something else. I therefore did my due diligence. Yet there was one problem when postulating a thesis. If you were genuinely interested in a conjecture, you had to remain vigilant. Someone might try to hijack the debate. This wouldn't happen to me. I was focused. No one would stray from the lane.

I sometimes aligned myself with the minority, whether I accepted that position or not. Other times, I staked my ground on firm beliefs. At all times, everyone girded their loins for methodical and slanderous attack from the opposition. Beliefs or statements might be recanted if it appeared the group had been swayed in one direction. It was part and parcel of inmate logic. The whole goddamn thing might hinge on a single belief, real or imaginary.

"I know those assholes want to take our machine guns," I interjected, reading an opinion piece in a paper about the Firearm Owners Protection Act of 1986—specifically, its provision outlawing the future transfer of certain machine guns.

I furrowed my brow and eyed each inmate. The books went down. Ears perked up.

"Why is this even a debate?" asked Chief.

"That's what happens when idiots make decisions," Legal said. "Lay off my guns."

"What happens?" I asked.

"They try to take what's yours," said Chief. "They'd have to kill me to take what's mine."

"If only cops can have guns, then you're a half-ass criminal if you obey that law," said Legal.

"That's the point," said Chief. "If good criminals—and by *good* criminals I mean *successful* criminals, good at ruthless and senseless violence—have guns, then everyone ought to have a right to arm themselves against the good ones. I mean criminals."

"I have to agree with that," I said. "Besides, it's our job to kill."

"They just need to keep their slimy mitts to themselves," said Legal.

"Maybe they're right to take away some of them," I said. "I mean, who needs a machine gun in the goddamn suburbs?"

I had no horse in this race. I'd never even owned a gun.

"Chisolm, what side are you on?" asked Hlavacka. *Thwipit, thwipit, thwipit.*

"Pick a side, dick breath," said Chief.

"Why does everyone always have to be pinned down?"

"Chisolm, which side?" asked Schmink.

"You assholes ought to know by now," I said. "I'm for Life, Liberty, and the Pursuit."

"There you go spouting bullshit again," said Chief.

"Whoever *they* are, we've got to listen to them," I said. "They're a part of who *we* are—as a country, anyhow."

"What the fuck?" asked Legal.

"*They, them,*" I said. "Our fellow Americans. The ones who want to take our guns. *They* are part of *us.* They've got a right to state what they think is right, even if it's wrong."

"Twisting words," said Legal.

"Hell, you're supposed to be the legal expert in here," I said. "I'm doing *your* job."

"Run that by me again," said Legal.

"Have all the guns and ammo you want," I said. "I'm just an advocate for the First Amendment."

"Yeah, yeah," said Schmink. "You're changing subjects."

"I'm on the same subject," I said. "They're saying they want to take some guns. I'm only saying they have a right to *say* they want to take our guns, right or wrong."

"And it is wrong," said Legal.

"You lost me, Chisolm," said Schmink.

"That doesn't surprise me," I said.

"Hell, even *I'm* lost," said Hlavacka.

"Chisolm, you are out of your mind," said Chief.

"Look, one of us is right, *right*?" I asked.

"Don't touch my guns," said Legal. "You may be right, but on a technicality."

"Of course I'm right," I said. "But you're also right for saying that I'm right. You're today's winner and master debater. Congratulations, master-bater."

"Fuck off, Chisolm," said Schmink.

"Shhh shhh shhh, easy there now, big fella," I said.

"Chisolm is actually right," said Legal. "On the free speech count *only*."

"I concur, master-bater," I said.

"I ain't no goddamn homo," said Legal.

"Double negative," I said.

Legal looked at me cross-eyed. "Fuck you, Chisolm."

"I just agreed with you that I'm right, which means *you're* right."

I didn't care about one side or the other. I just wanted a proper debate. You had to be fully vested in substantive speculation, as it might go on for hours. On any given day, inmates could enter and leave discussions along the way as we veered into many important subjects—other perennial favorites being who was fucking whom and how those assigned to the Bunker got away with murder. On this day, the debate would have gone longer except for the impending lunch break. After all that work, the inmates were famished.

25

"What's with your ship, Woody?" I asked.

Woody stored a ship-in-a-bottle project in one of our desk drawers.

"It's Shackleton's *Endurance*."

"You won't finish that thing before you leave," said Chief.

"This won't take me but another few months, tops."

"How do you figure?" I asked.

"It's four hundred pieces."

"You've got all the time in the world down here," I said.

"But I only do the work on my lunch breaks."

"Why handicap yourself," said Legal, "by limiting yourself to lunch breaks or building it inside a bottle?"

"You say handicap," said Woody. "I say challenge."

"Not going to make it," said Schmink, snickering.

"It's high detail, but I'll make it," said Woody.

"Why do you put a bottle in the way of building a ship, anyhow?" asked Hlavacka.

"I like the high focus," replied Woody. "It's calming."

"Calming would be getting my dick sucked," said Hlavacka. "Putting a boat together in a bottle would be frustration."

"Six of one, half dozen of another," said Woody.

Woody had the skill of a surgeon and took his time planning each move. Not much got done on any given day, and occasionally parts fell off. Of course, as the project was stored in one of our desk drawers, I was always careful not to bump the desk. At lunchtime, Dr. Woodard would retrieve his bottle. The inmates often took breaks from what they were doing and stared while he worked.

"I like it," I said.

"If it will hold together," said Woody.

I enjoyed the zeroed-in, concentrated reactions of the inmates when Woody had ship-building duty. They maintained vigilance, anticipating a complete collapse of his efforts, and their subsequent winning bet.

"I say you complete it in under three months," I said.

"You're the only one," said Woody with grim determination, setting another piece.

Every inmate had the potential to be odd man out. It was a matter of relativity. With regular turnover in the Bunker, time dictated the players involved. In its current form, Woody was the odd man out. But if not him, it would have been someone else. Like the kid's-game version of the same name, when you were *it*, you had to tag someone else to be *it* so you weren't *it*. But this was no game in the Bunker. It was real life. If you called it a game, that would never do. After all, you couldn't be sufficiently ostracized if it were just a game. For me, this was a game of destiny, since it was destined that we were each selected for assignment here.

In the Bunker, three rules existed for this game—the game was covert, there were weighty consequences once the game was underway, and the game was always underway.

An inmate could elect not to play, declaring themselves a disinterested third party. But even if an inmate thought they'd opted out of the game, that wasn't always the case. They may only have opted out from their perspective. To the other inmates, they may still have been in, or rather *it*.

To have any hope of opting out, an inmate had to declare themselves out of bounds up front. Upon arrival at the beginning of a tour, a newbie had to remain distant from the inmates, only close enough to be cordial. They couldn't sever all ties, of course, because we were not islands. Besides, severing all ties would have been abnormal, and in a classified environment, it would have been flat-out weird, even in the Bunker—interpreted, of course, as not right, likely requiring a criminal investigation or something like that.

Now we had someone who wanted to be *in* but not *it*, while all other players wanted them to remain *out* and *it*. No matter who *it* tagged, it wouldn't matter. The inmate would always be *it* whenever they were around anyone else. That inmate was always and forever out, and *it*. Such was the case with AC.

By May, I had taken the inmates up on their word. It had become customary for me to arrive at my leisure. On one of those days, I arrived late and entered OPS. As I did, a shriek pierced the server room noise, then several people laughed. The voice was distinct enough that I knew it was Hlavacka and that he was enjoying himself. I rounded the corner, past a row of computer-tape storage racks, and saw that Hlavacka had AC in a figure-four leg lock. AC lay face down and clamped in place.

On occasions when the OPS floor took on the guise of a wrestling ring, it was always a two-man event—AC versus some other inmate. The inmates took turns venting their frustrations at him. Not that AC wasn't likable, but he was no match for an assignment to the Bunker. The inmates harbored aggression that AC attracted with a vengeance. He was too goddamn nice.

"You like smelling his balls, Hlavacka?" I asked.

Hlavacka let go of AC at that point. "I'm nowhere near his balls."

"How old are you, and hugging other men on the floor?" I asked the group.

AC had no means to defend himself. He couldn't. He wanted to be *in* even if it cost him his pride. He had to be *it*.

"AC loves it," said Hlavacka. "Don't you?"

"It's good," said AC, his face beet red from gut strangulation. "You can't beat me."

At that provocation, another operator tried to headlock AC to the floor.

"Hey, moron," I said, swatting the head of the operator trying to grab on to AC, "go find some dick that wants you to suck it."

"Go suck your own dick, Chisolm," said the operator as he let go of AC.

"All pussy for me, sweet cheeks," I said. "I ain't the one grabbing man ass."

Hlavacka walked out of the OPS area, chuckling. The other operators dispersed.

"AC, sit down here, will you?" I asked.

AC took a few deep breaths and readjusted his gig line. "I beat 'em," he said.

"You'll never beat them," I said. "They'll never stop."

"Better than doing nothing."

"You're going to break another tooth. Besides, they're only doing this because you let them."

"How do you get away with it?" asked AC.

"Away with *what*?"

"You do what you want."

"I do what I need to do in order to do what I *want* to do. That's what that means."

"This isn't too bad," confided AC. "I've known worse."

"Just curious," I said. "Why'd you join? I mean, I know why you joined, but you don't exactly strike me as the military type."

"Compared to where I come from," said AC, "this is paradise."

"I'm not exactly sure you can call this paradise."

"You don't always have a choice."

"Yeah, maybe," I said.

"I got my GED so I could get into the Air Force. It might as well be a PhD, compared to what my parents ever got."

"I can appreciate that."

AC's eyes welled up. "Yes, it's paradise."

I listened.

"It's weird, right?" asked AC. "We get paid for sitting around here. And we have all we can eat." He pulled an apple from a bag and took a bite.

"It may be insane where you come from," I said, "but it's equally insane here, just for different reasons."

"Why do they not fuck with you?" asked AC.

"You want my advice?"

"OK."

"I learned a long time ago that there are insiders and there are outsiders," I said. "You may have no choice in where you stand."

"I'm standing here, now."

"Stop trying to join their club when their rules are designed to prevent you from joining."

"There is no other club," said AC.

"Isn't there?" I asked. "You're looking at a one-man club. *This* is how I don't get fucked with."

"Maybe you have a point."

"I ought to be the one asking *you* for advice. You should know that better than I do."

"Maybe."

"Just stop allowing those assholes to break your teeth and tear your uniforms."

26

The inmates had no familiar avenues onto which they could rail their minds. The anxiety of the painstaking wait for their final departure was pent up inside them. There was no total and comprehensive "America" to prompt their psyches to act in a predictable way. Their minds regressed backward in the days and months and years of Bunker confinement. They clung to the lowest common denominators, and then—saddled with so much energy—they had time galore to search for restitution.

In late spring, another software development opportunity came up. I wanted to take it on, except it turned out to be in Schmink's area of expertise. You could call Schmink's area whatever you wanted, just not "expertise." He protested the project. Not that time was a factor, as he still had over a year left. But this project would negatively affect his contribution to the book club.

While the inmates spent their time decrying their incarceration, I spent the next few days looking for a place to live. I viewed residences that were substandard by any measure. One place had a hole in the roof big enough for snow to build up inside one of the rooms. It was goddamn early May, and I didn't know what was worse, that apartment or the continuing snow season.

German civilians operated the military-housing referral office on post. These agents acted as intermediaries between German landlords and the GIs who sought to rent from them. The agents coordinated all viewing appointments with the landlords, since the housing office hid all landlord contact information until appointment time. With a few contacts in hand, I left the housing office. On my way out, I was handed a note.

A tall, slinky brunette slipped a piece of paper into my hand as I passed. It had a handwritten address and message: "This is a good one. Go here." After my three official viewings that morning, I drove to the address listed on the note. A grandfatherly man exited the house with papers in hand as I drove up.

"Rachel say you are comings," said the old German man.

"Rachel?" I asked. "She is the girl at the housing office?"

"Yes, she. Come. You looks now."

The man led me into the large house and we entered one of the two second-floor apartments. It was empty but had new carpet, and the smell of freshly painted walls was heaven.

"I'll take it."

"You like?"

"Yes, I like."

"Come. We call Rachel now."

I followed the man to a house next door. He placed a call, then handed me the phone.

"Hello?" I said.

"Airman Chisolm?" asked the girl.

"Yes, this is me. I'm here with a gentleman who will rent me an apartment."

"Yes, I know. I'm the one who gave you the note. He was waiting for you. I told him you would be coming."

"Ah, OK. So, you are Rachel?"

"Of course."

"Alright. What now?"

"He already has a contract filled out with his part. Bring it back and we get you this place."

"I'll be right there."

Carter departed the Bunker in late May. His replacement was already in town but had yet to make his way to the Bunker. Who he was and what he represented was pure speculation. Of course the office dutifully weighed every variable. I maintained the hope that the replacement, one Technical Sergeant Hancock, would be a regular who would want to fit in. No changes, please.

On the first of June, Treadwell and I moved into our apartment. The village of Aufregend was set among giant firs along the road to the Bunker. Except for a butcher and baker, there were no shops in the village. The next day, I returned to work and pressed on with my rounds.

"What up?" asked Wagner.

"Passing through," I said. "It's quiet today."

"It's quiet every day."

"Give me a cookie?" I asked. "I need some guidance."

Wagner reached into his cookie container and threw me one. I cracked it open.

"And?"

"'Yes.'"

"What's it say?"

"It just says yes."

"Bullshit."

I showed Wagner the fortune.

"No way," he said. "I've never had that one. If I had that one eight months ago, I wouldn't be stuck here now."

"But yes to what?" I asked.

"There's your conundrum, Chisolm."

"I'm pocketing this one."

"Luck of the draw. It found its way to you." Wagner came out of his office exile to stretch. He held a fortune cookie in each hand but did not open them. He swung his arms like propellers. "You want another word of advice?"

"I'm good with my yes already."

"Seriously, you want to make it to the end?"

"Not if the *end* is anything like this cluster you're in."

"Well, whatever your *end* is, keep your head down and remember one thing."

"What's that?"

"The nail that sticks out gets hammered down, and they are going to try and hammer you down."

"So, I'd be due combat pay?"

"What?"

"For doing my job while under attack," I said. "If you're assigned to a combat zone, you're due combat pay. If they try to hammer me down, all while I keep the mission going, I'll end up being due combat pay."

"Hardly," said Wagner. "For making them look like frauds, they'd probably 'promote' you."

"Who are they to hammer me when I'm doing what is needed to win this war?"

"You're not winning any hearts, Chisolm."

"The only thing I want to win is this war."

"I&W isn't just for Intel back there," said Wagner. "It's also for us. Life is an exercise in I&W."

"What's your cookie say?" I asked.

"I haven't decided righty or lefty yet. Which side would you take?"

"Go left," I said. "Through the cross traffic."

"Left, you say? Left it is. I'm counting on you, Chisolm. You got the only yes I've ever seen." Wagner pocketed the other cookie.

"OK, what?" I asked.

"'Beliefs are not always truths.'"

"That's genius."

"This one's a keeper."

Wagner retreated to his exile and took out a five-by-seven-inch leather-bound notebook from his desk. "I keep the good ones right here," he said. Nine fortunes were tucked into three pockets. He pulled out one of the fortunes.

"Why did you take that one out?"

"It's a dud now. This goes into the top nine."

Wagner placed the dud with hundreds of others in a wooden cigar box that he kept in the same drawer as his notebook.

"But you keep every one of them all the same?"

"Have to," he said. "Bad luck to throw them out."

"How do you rank one over another?"

"You know it when you feel it. Besides, I might change my mind later, so I keep them all just in case."

Like many Bunker days, except for the whine of the mainframe servers and heavy-duty air conditioners, there was little noise or movement today.

"Where the hell *is* everyone?" I asked, feigning surprise.

"When the cat's away the mice will play."

27

"You've got a thing for tables," I said to Rachel.

"You don't like tables, Roy?"

When I returned my signed lease to the housing office, Rachel asked me to give her a call. I asked her out for dinner. She asked me back to her place. Then she asked me out another time for dinner, and I asked her back to her place. Her place was nicer.

"Oh, I like the table. I'm just curious why you like to have sex on the table every time I'm here."

"Every time I have breakfast, I know we had sex right here."

"We fuck in your bed too. Why don't you just eat in bed?"

"Oh, no. That's for grandmas."

"Thank you for giving me the address to my new apartment."

"I wanted you to have first choice on something I knew was better than the trash we had in the books."

"You do this for every guy who comes along, huh?"

"Of course I do. Every guy with blue eyes and a smile like yours."

We smiled at each other.

"Were you curious about me?" she asked.

"From the minute I saw you."

"I was so excited when you called back."

"I can't believe we met."

"Kismet."

"What's that?" I asked.

"Destiny."

Our magnetism locked us together without words.

"Yes. Destiny," I said. "You look cold."

"Why do you say that?"

"Your nipples are saluting me."

"Maybe you can help me with that?"

"Yeah, I can help with that. But in bed."

For the month of June, I spent many evenings with Rachel and never left her place in under five hours. I couldn't. After sex, she always fed me. Rachel made time for me, and sometimes time is all you've got.

28

"Hey all, this is Tech Sergeant Hancock," said Treadwell.

Hancock would take over Carter's supervisory role. His jet-black coif, professionally pressed uniform, mile-high ribbon rack, and polished shoes came from a place of order. His poster-perfect military recruiter hands, face, chin—everything on that son of a bitch—screamed real Air Force. As for Carter, the *real* had long since been spanked out of him.

I had since discovered a few corollaries about Bunker newbies. Speculation held that the higher the rank, the greater the potential for changing the status quo. More importantly, if the status quo had value, and it damn well did in this place, then whatever had to be done to salvage the status quo would be done. No one in a classified world liked unknowns, least of all the Bunker inmates. We were at war, for Christ's sake. We couldn't live with unknowns.

On this early June day, Treadwell drove Hancock to the Bunker for his indoctrination and tickets.

"Hey, guys," said Hancock.

"Welcome," Legal said, standing to greet Hancock with a

handshake. "Be right back." Legal just as quickly departed the office.

"How's it going?" I asked, introducing myself. "Roy Chisolm. I believe I'll be working for you."

"It's good. Pleasure to meet you, Airman Chisolm."

"Where you from?" Schmink asked, leaning back in his chair.

"Dover."

"Dover?" asked Sosa. "How did you end up here? Welcome, by the way."

"Small shop. Worked on avionics programs."

"Yeah, well, don't regret leaving that," Treadwell said.

"I'm easy. I'll make the best of wherever."

"Did you have windows where you were?" I asked.

"I had windows."

"I miss windows," I said.

"Don't worry," said Treadwell. "You're going to love the Bunker."

"Yeah, there's a lot to love," said Schmink. "Let me know when you find it."

"I couldn't find out anything about this place before I left," said Hancock. "It's not what I expected."

"No one finds out anything before they get here," Chief said.

"Listen, I'm going to run Sergeant Hancock around," said Treadwell.

"Great meeting you, sir." I stood to shake Hancock's hand once again.

"Good meeting you, Airman Chisolm."

"We'll be back later," said Treadwell.

Later would be two days.

I hung around the office to get in on the ground-floor appraisal of Hancock. The ground floor was where the dynamics of inmate self-interest manifested themselves. It was always and only about the math.

If the addition of a new personality would not subtract from the good of the current operation, the result was a positive, or at least no less than zero. Otherwise, the inmates had to determine if the multiplicity effect of all inmates ganging up could reduce the new person to insignificance. We sure as hell weren't going negative. To determine the value of the unknown variable, the newbie, everyone got in on the discussion at the ground floor. The inmates had the process nailed down. It even had a name.

"Will we need to employ Operation Gangbang, gentlemen?" asked Legal. "And I use that term loosely."

"I vote for full-on gangbang," said Sosa, perking up and clapping his hands. "A nice, big, hard one."

"Fucking-A, Sosa!" Chief slapped his desk. "Get your ass out of here, why don't you?"

"Everyone's got a say in this," said Legal. "He stays."

"Why don't you take him, Sosa?" asked Hlavacka.

"He's not my type."

"You're a sick fuck, Sosa," said Hlavacka.

"You have *no* idea, Mr. Hlavacka."

"Please stay focused, you assholes," chided Legal.

"Treadwell should handle it," said Chief. "And you can bribe him with rations, Legal."

"I'll talk with Treadwell," said Legal. "But you dimwits better look alive in here while we run this to ground."

I think I could safely speak for the inmates in that they all had high expectations of Hancock coming in with low expectations. The inmates were always careful with newbies. They had a lot to lose. As you might imagine, they took these analyses quite seriously.

"He's going to jack it up in here," said Schmink. "He's got too much rank and too much haircut, I'm telling you."

"Schmink, have some optimism, sir," said Legal.

"I think we can manage it," said Hlavacka.

"Define *manage*," said Chief.

"He's from Dover," said Legal. "That's one thing. How important can that place be? And two, he looks too gung ho to keep that charade going for long."

"What's the scoop?" asked Woody, entering the office to retrieve his ship.

"Hancock. Is he going to fit or not?" asked Hlavacka. "I say yes."

"What do you have against doing some work around here, anyhow?" asked Woody.

"I didn't get my knees blown out for this," said Legal.

"What do you mean?" I asked.

"*This* place," said Legal. "I didn't get my knees blown out to be thrown down in this bitch as a reward for my service."

"I'm leaving," said Woody. "I've got real work to do."

"Go sit on a dildo, Woody," said Schmink.

"Wow," I said. "The manners on you, Schmink."

"Blown out from what?" asked Chief. "Vietnam?"

"No," said Legal, painting his lips with ChapStick. "From going down on your wife. Of course Vietnam, you moron. Shrapnel. I did a tour as a FAC." Legal was a former forward air controller.

"Hey, I didn't know, man," said Chief. "Sorry."

"I know someone who was over there too," I said. "But I don't think he got hit by anything."

"We all got hit by something," said Legal. "Just some got it worse than others."

"What *exactly* were you doing?" I asked.

"Calling in air strikes from places we weren't supposed to be."

"Thank God," I said.

"What do you mean *thank God*, asshole?"

"I mean in a good way. You were in the real Air Force. But it is a bad thing about your knees."

"He's got a Purple Heart," said Hlavacka.

"I did not know that," said Chief.

"It's on his ribbon rack that he wears half the time, you idiot," said Hlavacka. "Open your eyes, why don't you?"

"You have new knees?" I asked.

"One hundred percent Uncle Sam metal, bought and paid for," said Legal, tapping one of his knees with a pen.

"How long before you could walk again?" asked Schmink.

"Laid up for a good three months during the rebuild, but they gave me off six."

"So it isn't that bad?" asked Chief.

"Of course it's that bad. They're my knees."

"How did it happen?" I asked.

Legal paused, looking toward the ceiling. "God, that's a flashback. We were on the fifth of ten days clawing through the bush. I was part of a field test that embedded FACs with Marine patrols along the Ho Chi Minh Trail. Officially, we weren't there. We were searching for any NVA underground weapon caches or ammo dumps hidden in villages. Things had been quiet up to that point. We were waiting for a resupply drop."

Legal didn't make eye contact with any of us, instead choosing to stare over our heads.

"A supply chopper approached to make our drop. Then all hell broke loose. The chopper retreated. He couldn't make the drop with all the flak. I called in air strikes. Then one of those NVA bastards got through our perimeter. I was in the middle of a reload. I grabbed my knife. Everything slowed down. I'll never forget Charlie's angry face. For some reason his handgun never went off. He jumped onto me, and I got him right in the gut. I didn't realize how far I'd slit him open until his intestines came out with my knife. I wasn't thinking right. I pushed him off, then jumped up. I wanted to get his guts off me. I got hit in the knees. I don't remember too much after that. When it was over, we had lost two, plus four wounded. How the hell my knees got hit and not my head, God only knows."

The room fell silent.

"That chopper also carried mail. Because I landed in the hospital, it took another month for a letter from my wife to find me. Had Charlie not been there, had that chopper gotten to us, I'd have been out of the country on emergency leave. Instead I received the letter one day after my father died. There wasn't a damn thing I could do about it at that point. I couldn't very well walk home. I healed up and never returned to that death sentence."

29

It was a Thursday in mid-June, and the weather was clear and calm. The week prior, Treadwell had asked if I was interested in a weekend trip somewhere and I'd accepted. Timmons picked us up in a rental car. I took no leave days. Neither did Treadwell. Timmons signed out of the orderly room for two days of "training."

"Here's good," said Treadwell. "Let's grab a coffee."

After six hours in thick but very fast-moving autobahn traffic, we arrived in Amsterdam. Timmons had booked us three nights at an inexpensive hotel in town. We parked on a main thoroughfare just inside the city limits.

"Let's do it, man," said Timmons.

"You know this place?" I asked.

"It's a coffee shop," Timmons replied.

The store's sky-blue facade was edged in bright yellow. A blinking green-and-red neon sign said Scoobie Doobie Coffee Shop. Five small café tables stood on the sidewalk in front. Two were occupied. Treadwell and I sat at one of the tables.

"What do you want?" asked Timmons, heading for the entrance.

"Usual?" asked Treadwell.

"Yup," agreed Timmons.

I picked up a laminated menu from the table. Listed on the bottom-right corner were a few types of coffee. The few dozen remaining items on the menu were variants of marijuana. Out of the corner of my eye, I noticed that Timmons had been staring at me since we arrived. I looked both ways down the street, then looked at Treadwell.

"What *is* this?" I asked.

"Coffee shop," he replied.

"There's a lot of smoke in there," I said, turning to look inside. "Am I missing something?"

"This is a coffee shop, Chisolm." Treadwell slapped me on the back. "Relax. That's all we know, right?"

"Tell me you guys aren't buying this stuff?"

"A couple of joints, no biggie. It's not like we're dropping acid."

"Three," said Timmons. He held up three joints as he returned. "Let's go."

"You said you wanted to come," said Treadwell. "Now what are you going to do, Scoobie Doobie Doo?"

"What about a random drug test?"

Timmons and Treadwell glanced at each other.

"We're taking our chances," said Timmons. "You in or out, Mr. Chisolm?"

"Alright," I said, without a choice in the matter. The moment required compliance. "I'm in."

"There is no *chance*," said Timmons. "Guess who arranges our *random* drug tests with Ramstein? *Me*, that's who, and there won't be any arranging after this weekend."

"You're *kidding* me."

"See?" asked Treadwell. "You haven't got a care in the world."

"It's legal here in Holland," said Timmons. "Besides, you're a civilian for the weekend, Chisolm."

We continued to our hotel. The car would be parked until our return journey on Sunday.

"Two singles," said Timmons. "You have couch detail, Mr. Chisolm."

The tight room forced us to maneuver sideways around the beds. The wallpaper had been worn away at ass height from years of guests in this room. Ten-foot ceilings kept the room chilly, and it didn't help that we wouldn't receive direct sunlight. Our two windows opened into an alleyway and a brick wall several feet away.

I showered and changed for the evening. Timmons did the same. Treadwell lit up a joint.

"You're going to need to join us," said Treadwell, handing it to me. "You agreed to come along. Now you're along. Take a hit."

Treadwell and Timmons expected compliance. The circumstances required compliance. Secrecy required compliance. In the interest of freedom, in provable measure that I could hold secrets requiring secrecy, as a key to ensure compliance, they needed me to demonstrate that I could comply. I didn't want to take a hit, but in the interest of proving that I could keep secrets a secret, I had to take a hit. Solely in support of the mission, I had no choice but to take that hit.

We chilled and smoked up for the life of the joint.

"What's our first stop?" I asked.

"For one thing, stop laughing," said Treadwell. "That goes for you too, Timmons."

"What I want is to eat," said Timmons. "This is a cockamamie bockamamie lockamamie."

All three of us laughed.

"I'm hungry too," said Treadwell. "Let's jump on a tram and go someplace."

"OK," I said. Then I couldn't stop laughing.

Timmons rolled over on his bed, laughing so hard he had tears.

"I need to sit down for a minute," said Treadwell. "Let me figure out where we're going so we know where we are."

Five minutes went by that felt like hours. Treadwell hadn't moved an inch. My buzz had kicked in deep, which led me to believe that he knew what he was doing, and doing something about where we would be going.

"OK. Where are we?" he asked.

"What do you mean 'Where are we?'" asked Timmons. "You just said you're going to figure out where we're going."

"That don't make sense," said Treadwell.

I lay down and fell asleep. Timmons and Treadwell followed suit. We slept for just over an hour.

"Wake up," said Timmons, shaking my shoulder. "I'm hungry."

"More coffee, right?" I asked.

"More a lot of stuff," Timmons replied. "Just keep your eyes open and a handle on your wallet, and don't act like a tourist."

"Alright," I said. My buzz was fading, but the four hits had knocked me out up front.

We exited the hotel. Amsterdam was crawling with people. The clear sky at this latitude meant that we would see a late sunset. The humidity made the day feel like high summer. *At last, summer!*

"We'll catch the next tram," said Treadwell. "Keep up, Mr. Chisolm."

"I'm behind you," I said.

We rode for a mile in a standing-room-only tram.

"This is our stop," Treadwell said. "That's the main train station at the end."

"At the end" was a quarter mile away, where an ornate building stood.

"This is Dam Square," said Timmons. "The obelisk is their Washington Monument sort of thing."

"This way," said Treadwell, leading us away from the tram-line and main boulevard.

"Why didn't we stay there?" I asked. "There" was the Grand Hotel Krasnapolsky overlooking Dam Square.

"Yeah, what do you think that would set us back?" asked Timmons. "No way we can afford that place."

Throngs of people filled the square, as did pigeons. Many people rode bicycles. We pressed on and passed souvenir shops hawking useless trinkets to visitors. Two blocks later, we hit a canal and turned left. Numerous small boats were moored along the canal, with a narrow lane on each side accommodating one-way automobile traffic. A few meters away, hundreds of people shopped, dined, or ogled the storefronts on the ground floor of unending townhomes that abutted the walking paths.

"We made it," said Treadwell.

"This is the Oude Kerk," said Timmons. "Means 'old church.'"

"Have we come to pray?" I asked.

"Yeah, that's what we're going to do," said Treadwell.

"Or shop, apparently?" I asked, looking around at the retailers of all sorts.

"You could say that," said Timmons.

"This is it," Treadwell said, high-fiving Timmons.

"You made it, Mr. Chisolm," said Timmons. "Watch yourself."

"For what?" I asked.

"From here on out, don't gawk like a tourist," said Treadwell.

30

"I'm telling you, dude, keep your eye on everything in here," said Timmons. "Pickpockets, thieves, you name it."

I put my wallet in my front pocket and kept my hand in my pocket over my wallet. We threaded our way over a canal bridge and into a quieter part of town. Sidewalk dice games were played. Street dancers distracted tourists while pickpockets worked the crowd. Two men ran off in different directions, yelling for help in stopping runners ahead of them.

"*This* is where you take me?" I asked.

"All legal, dude," said Treadwell. "It's all legal."

"I'm starting to wonder how Legal got his name," I said.

"All you'll do is wonder," replied Treadwell, "because that son of a bitch keeps his mouth shut. He doesn't say anything about what he does and where he goes on his time off."

"Probably for the better," said Timmons. "For all concerned."

On the ground floor of countless townhomes, behind plate glass windows, sat girls for sale. The sales pitch for each girl was a silent movie, their rooms decorated to advertise their innocence, sensuality, or nastiness. They were packaged as competitively as boxes of cereal in a supermarket. I found it strange to make eye contact with an entrepreneur for sale behind a plate glass window. There was no advertising otherwise. There were no price lists. Drunks and horny men gawked. Pretty college-age girls negotiated with those who knocked on their doors. Terms of engagement would be concluded verbally, with winning bidders allowed entry. The businesses operated under the presence of a police station located near the Oude Kerk.

"Want an older slut?" asked Treadwell. "They have those too, but over another street."

"I think the proper term is *whores*," I said. "*Sluts* fuck for the sake of fucking. Whores do it for the money."

"For Christ's sake, Chisolm, you're splitting hairs," said Treadwell.

"I'm not paying," I said. "Not directly, anyhow."

"Way too much thinking for the task at hand, Mr. Chisolm," said Timmons.

"If you want weird, you have to go over a few more streets, though," said Treadwell.

"*Weird?*" I asked. "*This* isn't weird?"

"You ain't seen weird," said Timmons.

"This is the center of the red-light district," Treadwell informed me.

"These are your wholesome girls," said Timmons. "They're just trying to make an extra buck to help pay the bills."

"You want deviance?" asked Treadwell. "We've got to go to the fringe."

"Let's walk," said Timmons, leading us.

My buzz had worn off. I didn't want to look like a tourist, but I couldn't stop looking.

"This is crazy," I said.

"Want to see crazy?" asked Treadwell. "Buckle up."

"Check this out," Timmons said, looking back and smiling at me.

This referred to an area where porn shops were interspersed with storefronts behind which were live sex shows. Outside these storefronts, monitors televised the action inside.

"Here's one," said Treadwell.

"You got to be kidding me," I said. "What *is* that?"

"It's the gorilla show," said Treadwell. "Says right there on the marquee."

The "gorilla show" was some dude dressed in a gorilla outfit fucking a girl on a sawhorse.

"There is no need for imagination," I said.

"Why would there be?" asked Treadwell. "Just think it and do it."

Timmons walked ahead of us.

"OK, boys," he said. "This is what I'm talking about."

The marquee said Banana Show. The television displayed a girl in soft purple-and-red lighting. She certainly had a comfortable bed. The camera zoomed in on her pussy as she stuffed it with a banana.

"Yeah, this could work alright," said Timmons.

"Goddamn, they think of everything, don't they?" I asked rhetorically.

"Bizarre," said Timmons. "Very bizarre."

"Excellent word choice," said Treadwell. "Let's see some bizarre."

I gulped. I was drawn in by curiosity. I followed Timmons and Treadwell.

We walked another block. The crowds thinned. Determination filled the faces of those around me. These weren't gawkers. They didn't look around. They didn't make eye contact. Their gait wasn't hesitant. One sensed in them a serious-minded conviction.

Traffic trickled by as those present scanned through racks of videos, magazines, and books. Carts of VHS tapes spilled out in front of each storefront. There were no placards listing what was for sale, so one was forced to rifle through the lot. As with the live sex shows, television monitors in front of each store offered a general idea of what could be bought inside.

"Oh my *fucking* God," I said as we passed a shop. "Is that a *chicken*?"

Timmons and Treadwell did a double take.

"Son of a *bitch*," said Treadwell. "That *is* a chicken."

"Wait, *what*?" asked Timmons. "Am I seeing this right?"

"I've seen a chicken before," I said. "That's a chicken."

Treadwell walked ahead to the next storefront.

"Look at *this*," said Treadwell.

Timmons and I caught up with him.

"That's a trick shot," said Timmons. "That is not real."

"She's got no hands," I said.

"She does," said Treadwell. "I saw them a minute ago."

"No way," said Timmons. "That chick has one fist up that other chick's pussy and one up her ass."

"Holy hell, what *is* this place?" I asked.

"This is our NATO partner, boys," said Timmons.

"Ain't that the shit," said Treadwell.

"Anyone hungry for chicken?" asked Timmons.

"I'm never eating chicken again," I said.

We left the red-light district and caught a tram back to our hotel in the Leidseplein district. The concentration of nightclubs, restaurants, and cafés in this area precluded the need to drive before we left town. Many nightclubs were open until four in the morning, if not later. A few remained open through to serving breakfast. The Dutch might have been deviant bastards, but they were business geniuses for employing such an efficient use of space over a twenty-four-hour period.

Treadwell and Timmons knew this area and had booked

our hotel because of it. That evening, we conducted a walk-through of several clubs, taking turns buying a round at each stop. We slept in late Friday, then did the same thing all over again Friday night.

Saturday began differently. We shared our third joint after breakfast, sitting on a bench in the Leidseplein.

"Fuckable?" asked Timmons, nodding toward a girl walking by. The girl wore knee-high boots and a miniskirt, with a tight shirt that followed the contours of her small tits. Her long, swaying ponytail worked in her favor.

"Hell yeah," replied Treadwell. "Small titties and all."

"That is some gorgeous ass," I said.

"That one would do too," Treadwell said, tilting his head sideways in the direction of another passing girl.

"Lot of brunettes here," I said. "Reminds me of Rachel."

I missed Rachel. But even if I didn't have Rachel, I wouldn't pay for sex, just on principle.

"You are fortunate, Mr. Chisolm," said Timmons. "All you gotta do is all you've got to do."

"Smoke up, boys," said Treadwell. "Let's go sightseeing. Timmons, you lead?"

"Anne Frank House and Middle Ages Torture Museum still good?" asked Timmons.

"All good," I said.

"Yes sir," said Treadwell.

"Hang on," said Timmons. "Buzz is hitting."

"Timmons, goddamn it, all you do is laugh when you're on this," said Treadwell. "Can you get us there or not?"

Timmons tried to contain his laughter.

"Now *you*, Chisolm?" asked Treadwell.

I'd joined Timmons in the pleasure of a good buzz, pretty girls, and laughter for no obvious reason.

"OK," said Treadwell, "that *is* some strong herb."

We remained in place and spent another hour watching

girls go by. And laughing. When we finally got up to catch the tram, a guy approached us.

"You look like some nice gents." He had a British accent and was dressed in black, punk-rock style. "Want some tix?"

"To what?" asked Treadwell.

"Show tonight," said the punk. "It'll be a goody."

"Well, wait a minute," Treadwell said, confused. "What?"

"Where is the show?" I asked.

"At the Melkweg," said the punk. "We're a UK band. Come on, Yanks. We'll look for yous."

"I'll take them," I said. "But where is this place?"

"The Melkweg? It's over there, down a block on that one-way."

The punk pointed toward a corner of the square, where a one-way street entered the Leidseplein.

"Got it," I said. "We'll try to be there."

"OK, gents. See you then, alright."

We visited the Middle Ages Torture Museum. By the time we arrived at the Anne Frank House, the entrance line was far too long for our attention spans. Instead we retreated to our hotel and got ready for the Melkweg.

"I got us another one," said Timmons, as he held up a joint.

"When did you have time to do that?" I asked.

"I popped in a coffee shop near the hotel yesterday when I went down to pay us up for tonight."

"Well, at least you were thinking of us," said Treadwell. "Let's get going. We can smoke up over there."

Music poured from the entrance. We pulled aside thick black curtains, then entered. Except for dim stage lighting, the space was pitch black. This was a no-seating venue, though some people were sitting on the floor, and others were lying down. You had to move carefully so as not to trip over anyone. We paused to let our eyes adjust to the smoke and darkness.

"*Damn!*" exclaimed Treadwell, bending to grab his shin.

I looked down, only to see a girl crawling between him and me, barking.

"I want some of that shit," said Timmons.

We got some of that shit.

31

June 21st, 1987

Dad,

So much to share.
How are you holding up?
~~*I didn't realize how long someone could be gone from the Bunker before anyone noticed they were not on leave. Turns out five duty days.*~~ *I won't bore you with the details, but suffice it to say that I've been learning a great deal.*

~~*There is an office competition each week for the most pages of fiction read during duty hours. The top dog so far this year once completed three novels in a single week.*~~ *We have plenty of time for personal development.*

~~*No one gives a rat's ass about the mission in the Bunker, but by god they all buy enough bullshit to remind them someday*~~

of how much they hated it. People take
advantage of sightseeing and souvenir
collecting to remember their time spent in
country.

*Last weekend, I had to scrape my
roommate off the floor from an LSD-
induced meltdown. He seems OK now.* We
have plenty of R & R opportunities outside
the Bunker.

*Half the people assigned to the Bunker
have forgotten or don't give a shit about
what is real, while the other half miss the
point entirely by being medicated just
enough to prevent them from going into
a paranoid rage or wrist-cutting depression.* I've come to realize the importance of
education.

Roy

32

On summer vacations, Mom always found unusual layovers along the way to give us "a taste of the real world." One summer we stopped at a pig farm.

"You know we cut their incisors at six weeks," the farmhand told us.

"Really? *Why?*" I asked.

"Stops 'em from fighting and hurting others as they grow."

"From fighting?"

"They fight, alright. And when they fight, they can cut the meat, become infected, lose weight, and die, so we do it to keep them alive."

"Do you use painkillers?"

"No. We turn 'em over, hold 'em down, then cut."

I stared, eyes wide and jaw open.

"Then we throw slop on the ground and put 'em on it."

"Doesn't it hurt?"

"Doesn't hurt 'em. They might squeal, but only until they get the food."

"Do they bleed?"

"Only if they're cut by accident, but the slop distracts 'em."

"Wow."

"It's over quickly. Once they have slop, they forget all about it."

"Cut them to save them," I said to myself.

"Exactly, young man."

It was in that pig farmer's interest to ensure that no pig harmed any other pig. The farmer had to maintain order, and one component of that order was making sure that no pig retained the sharp incisors they would otherwise use for their own protection. The pigs were set up to settle down into what would be a new routine for life.

This assimilation of pigs worked no differently for the inmates. Each arrived at the corral after first being run through the chute of newbie indoctrination. It would be important that no animal was missed during incisor cut, and that the pen in which the animals lived would be the only world they knew. None of them could be allowed to escape, and all of them could see only what the others saw.

Sunshine welcomed us most summer days. Unlike prior years, as some recounted, the daylight rained down on us like it would last forever. I spent the occasional afternoon out of the Bunker, sitting on my patio and planning my evenings with Rachel. Except for Treadwell, no one in the Bunker knew. Few people cared how others spent their time. After all, talking about it would only serve to implicate the guilty with their frequent and obvious absences. Instead, Bunker debates centered on weightier subjects.

"Have you been back there to take a look?" I asked.

Back there meant the wire-service terminals located in the watch area—the AP, UPI, and Reuters. The Intel community had to know what the civilian community knew at any given time.

All three printed nonstop stories from their reporters around the world. As had become part of my daily routine,

I pored over world events that would never make American news.

"You think a national paper won't print something if they know something?" asked Chief.

"I know they won't," I said. "I even concede that they can't print everything. There isn't enough paper. All they can do is decide what is *news* and what is news*worthy*."

"They print what is news," said Hlavacka.

"Someone is making a decision about what they want you to see," I said.

"If it's important, if it's news, the *Times* prints it," added Hlavacka.

"Go look," I said. "The wires are running nonstop. I've looked. I read them. Not even one percent of what is reported worldwide makes it into American papers. It's impossible."

"How much can any one person read, anyhow?" asked Woody.

"It's absurd," I said. "I mean, one paper I read talked about subsidizing books for school dropouts. Someone wanted *more* books available to help teach the same illiterates who didn't show up to school in the first place. Then guess what, the illiterates the program was designed to help never showed up! I'm not sure what's worse—the futility of trying to help someone who won't first help themselves, or the waste of print space to explain a waste of time."

"Well, it's a story," said Chief.

"*Everything* is a story," I said. "I'm asking what is *worthy* of the limited space and attention. What is *important*? Beirut is tearing itself to shreds. Who would know that? Instead, we need free goddamn books for illiterates."

"What do you suggest they print?" asked Hlavacka.

"How about Beirut?" I asked. "How about anything of substance on the Red Army Faction bombings and shootings? Americans are oblivious. This is on our doorstep over here."

"I once read something about that," said Chief.

"Unlike the Russians, we don't have one paper," I said. "But collectively, American papers all print the same mental mush. It's American *Pravda*."

"Chisolm, you should check what you're saying," said Hlavacka. "You're starting to sound communist."

"They print what needs to be printed, what we need to know," said Chief.

"Need? *Need?*" I asked. "You're all half-wits. And I'm no communist. The American newspaper industry, taken together, is the communist. They'll print what the party line tells them to print. Not one fleeting thought more. They just call it news."

"Keep talking like that and the OSI is going to show up," said Chief.

"They haven't shown up during the stupendous waste of our time here, but they'll show up for Airman Chisolm stating the obvious?" I asked rhetorically.

"People hear things," said Hlavacka. "Walls have ears, Chisolm."

"Well, you can't avoid the obvious and you can't avoid logic," I said. "They can arrest me for that. American *Pravda* is distracting us, is all I'm saying."

"You go with that," said Hlavacka.

"Yeah, I'm going with that."

An inmate had to make it clear where they stood, for reasons of survival. Every inmate knew this to be true, even if it was never spoken. This served to harden positions about who was in or out, or who was *it*. Inmate arrivals and departures continued, evenly disbursed, throughout the year. This contributed greatly to maintenance of the Bunker way of life, since adequate spacing proved useful for the Bunker's vise grip on the balls of ambition. Even if a newbie caught on a little late, it invariably worked. Inmates always ended up buying it, except in the case of our newest inmate, Technical Sergeant Southwark.

"I can shit, shower, and shave in five minutes," Southwark claimed.

Southwark arrived pressed and polished. His sideburns were squared and in line with the inner edge of his ears, while his mustache width was within a hair of either side of his mouth. Even his gig line was straight and narrow.

"My horse dick takes more than five minutes to wash," said Hlavacka.

Those present broke out in hysterics.

"Stop jerking off and it won't take you so long," replied Chief.

Southwark's high and tight was shaved clear to the skin at the sides and back. The top of his head was squared to a tabletop.

"That is one wicked cut," I said. "But five minutes to do all that? Can you even get clean, man?"

"Regulation four-dash-three, Airman Chisolm," said Southwark. "Show some respect for the rank."

Four-dash-three being Southwark's four stripes to my three stripes.

"I'm hearing you talk about washing your asshole and someone else talking about washing a horse's dick, and you say *I'm* the one who isn't showing respect?"

"Even if you *could* do all that in five minutes, *why*?" asked Hlavacka.

"Because you never know when you're going to have no time."

"No time for *what*?" asked Chief. "We're programmers. We're not loading bombs or fucking around with airplane engines."

"How about just get up a little earlier and take more time?" I asked.

"This is the military," said Southwark.

"This isn't a flight line," said Legal. "And really, you should take more time washing your ass. Last thing we need down here is your man-ass smell when we're on lockdown."

"What were you doing before, anyhow?" asked Hlavacka. He began to throw his yo-yo.

"Engine mechanic, C-130s."

"How on earth did you get from that to this?" asked Chief.

"I've been trying for a few years," said Southwark. "Tired of being covered with oil and grease. I wanted an office job before I get old."

"Yeah, but *how*?" asked Chief. "The career fields aren't even remotely related."

"You've lived your entire Air Force life governed by strict rules and regulations, and you wind up here?" asked Legal.

"Legal, does that qualify as the real Air Force?" I asked.

"Were you forward deployed anywhere or see any combat?" asked Legal. "You don't have the rank or enough time to have been in Vietnam."

"Weather squadron, pretty much."

"That is aircraft, all the same," said Legal. "Hmmm. You are real Air Force, on a technicality. But listen up. Just because you had to follow regulations to take a piss doesn't mean that things work like that here."

"How's that?" asked Southwark.

"You worry me," said Legal. "Tsk-tsk."

"What do you mean?"

"You're *ate up*, that's what. We need *smart* in here, not *ate up*."

"I passed the tests to get in the career field, didn't I?"

"I don't know, *did* you?" asked Hlavacka. "You said you've been trying for years to get in. What do you mean by that?"

"The military aptitude test didn't qualify me when I joined. They said I'm a mechanical type, so they put me in aircraft engines."

"*What?*" asked Chief.

"It took me four years to cross-train into programming," said Southwark. "You can only take the programming entrance exam once every two years. I just barely missed it the second time, so I requested a waiver."

"And they *gave* you the waiver?" asked Hlavacka despondently.

"You don't have to be so down on me," said Southwark.

"Will wonders never cease?" asked Chief.

"Is this your first assignment as a programmer?" asked Legal.

"Yes, here," said Southwark. "I made it."

"That you are here, this is true," said Legal. "That you made it remains to be seen."

33

"Your hair, Airman Chisolm," said Southwark.

"What about it?" I asked.

I had just entered the programmer office after Intel-acceptance testing for my new and improved version of AardVark.

"You need to get it in regs."

"*That's* what you're worried about?" I asked. "I just delivered on a promise to Intel."

"Waxing it down fools no one. It's dangling everywhere."

"I'm just trying to look pretty for you, sir."

"Who is this guy?" asked Southwark.

"I'm the guy doing what Intel needs. Some call it the mission."

"Has anyone back there mentioned anything to you?" asked Southwark.

"Yes they have," I said. "Many times. They wonder why we need all this dead weight in here."

"You are *out* of line, Airman Chisolm."

"Settle down, girls," said Legal. "Chisolm's hair does look purty."

"He needs to get it under control," said Southwark.

"Maybe you could look in a mirror there, Chisolm," said Legal. "Purty or not."

"Yeah, I'll get right on that," I said.

Another newbie arrived at the bunker around the same time as Southwark. Curly was husky and tattooed, an Ohio welder in his former life. He was assigned to the OPS floor.

"Cheapest way to keep it cut," said Curly, as the conversation in the dorm went one evening. His bowl cut matched that of Moe of Three Stooges fame. However, he wouldn't tolerate being called Moe; he loved Curly.

Curly had joined the Air Force to learn something that would keep him out of the cold. If computer operations didn't work out, he was going to audition for the WWF when his enlistment ended. Though more backbreaking than welding, wrestling was at least an inside job.

I'd occasionally run into Curly on my rounds when he worked day shift. He was not one for words. Computer operations didn't require it, which was well and good. The constant shift changes from days to swings to mids toyed with the minds of the computer operators. Their roles were best performed by rote. Fewer mistakes would be possible this way, and the last thing we needed was any kind of mistake.

As luck had it, Curly landed on C flight, though really B flight would have been just as good. Flights were simply teams assigned to a given shift. The A flight supervisor kept a small notebook in which he documented every infraction that anyone on his shift had ever committed. He also noted all required and legitimate actions, even down to timing latrine breaks. On A flight, mum was the word.

The opposite held true for B and C flights. Sure, the tapes were mounted, the backups were completed, the print jobs were folded, and their asses were clean. But as far as individual control went for computer operators, it depended on which shift you were working. When C flight did mids, they took advantage of the nighttime hours by catching up on sleep. They'd have killed anyone who said it, but it was true. They even had a cot set up behind one of the mainframe computers. C flight hot bunked it as time allowed. Several cots were stowed throughout the Bunker as part of our war footing. C flight ingeniously put those cots to efficient use. Same thing B flight did, which A flight could never imagine doing. Besides, the sum of work done on mids could be handled by any one of the four inmates assigned to each flight.

Programmer duty hours were officially known as daytime Monday to Friday. But since we supported Intel 24/7, we were required to show up at a moment's notice if Ivan got testy or to resolve any mission-essential problems. On one late July evening and with Woody unreachable, the C flight supervisor called me. After coming in and fixing the problem, I found Curly snoring on a cot. The two other operators were slouched asleep in adjacent chairs. The supervisor was deep into a sci-fi novel, running the nightly backups between chapters. This is how OPS fought this war.

I savored the late twilight of these summer days at our northern latitude. I threaded together my time with pinpoint accuracy. While SAC had afforded me neither diversion nor discretion, that was old school. Here I could maintain every ounce of commitment, all without the encumbrance of conformity. This Cold War didn't seem so bad.

"It's gonna be a *great* weekend," said Schmink aloud in the programmer office, intending to solicit information from me.

Schmink had made buck sergeant in July. He'd declined a move to an opening in the Q, choosing instead to remain in his shared dorm room. Making buck sergeant was perfunctory and in no way aided by the amount of fiction he consumed weekly. He made it the old-fashioned way—by keeping his head down.

"Oh *yeah*?" I questioned. "What's going on with you?"

"Me?" asked Schmink. "No, *you*."

"What *me*?" I asked. "Why do you continue to live your life by watching me like I'm some TV show?"

"I'm sure you've got something grand planned," Woody said.

"He gets his work done, he's done," said Hancock. "That's the deal here. He's sticking to the deal. I'm sticking to the deal. That's the deal."

"Even if I did have something planned, you've got no more than a thirty-second attention span for me to tell you," I said.

"I've seen that cherry arm candy, Chisolm," said Legal.

Hancock glanced at me. "Arm candy, huh?"

"I'm not waiting for the world to end," I said.

"Copy that," said Hancock. "Just swaddle Intel like a baby and get on with living."

"Bullshit," said Hlavacka. "Where you goin'?"

"What do *you* have planned?" I deflected.

Hlavacka let out his Muttley laugh. Schmink stared at me, awaiting the requested information. I wanted someone else to pick up that bone and run with it.

"He's going somewhere," said Schmink, intent on divining an answer.

Left to their own devices, the inmates colored inside the lines.

"You're right," I said. "I'll go somewhere. We *all* go somewhere, don't we?"

"I'm going to Ramstein until Thursday," said Hancock.

"For two days?" asked Schmink.

"I'm working on my OTS package."

"Want to be an officer?" asked Legal. "How's that going for you?"

"It isn't. But I'm working on it."

"You just got here, and you might get *out* of here?" I asked.

"It's an annual submission," said Hancock. "I'm working on my package for next year."

"That's one way to get out of here," said Woody.

"The drive to Ramstein has been insane the last two times I went," said Hancock. "What's up with all the convoys on the autobahn?"

"ReForGer," said Legal.

ReForGer was the Army's annual Return of Forces to Germany war game.

"Those tanks are huge," said Hancock. "The trucks moving them take up more than a lane."

"Well, yeah, M1 Abrams," said Legal.

"They can hit a bird in the eye at two miles," said Woody.

"How would you even know?" asked Chief.

"They do the math," said Woody.

"Yeah, they *say* they can hit a bird at about two miles," said Chief. "But you could miss it by a hundred feet and the thing would be blown to hell. Just need a big enough explosion."

"True," said Woody. "But they can measure how well they target."

"Dead on arrival," said Chief. "Just like us."

"Don't worry," said Legal. "Something or other gets all of us sooner or later."

"I'm shooting for later," said Hancock. "That's why I'm trying to get out of here."

"Good luck with that," said Chief.

34

"What do Germans think of Americans?"

It was a Friday night at my apartment. Rachel and I were sitting on the couch.

"Oh, this is strong," she said. "What is it?"

"It's called an old-fashioned—whiskey, bitters, dab of sugar, cherry, and orange mashed up," I said. "You like?"

"Where did you learn this?"

"I read about it in some magazine. I wanted to try it."

"I like it," Rachel said, sitting on one leg and smiling ear to ear.

"Me too," I said, swishing my drink. "So, what do they think?"

"Amees," said Rachel.

"Amees?"

"We call you 'Amees.' Short, or slang, for *Americans.*"

"Oh, like us calling you 'Krauts.'"

"I guess. That's an old word, though."

"But what do Germans *think* of us?"

"Well, many think you're occupiers."

"And *you*?"

"You're definitely occupiers, or invaders."

"*Invaders*? You're the ones who tried to blow up the world. Twice!"

"*Ja, ja. Komm schön.*"

Rachel spoke German to me when she disliked something I said.

"We weren't the invaders," I said.

"But you are occupying, no?"

"Well, what do you expect?" I asked. "After two world wars, what were we *supposed* to do? We learned our lesson."

"What lesson?"

"You couldn't keep your hands in your pockets. We sure as hell weren't going to leave only to have to come back a third time."

"Those were the Nazis. We learned."

"I think we all learned. That's why we're still here. Who knows where an attack will come from next? Which reminds me, I've got to get a haircut."

"You get a haircut, you get yourself killed, Roy. I told you."

"I'm not going to get killed over a haircut."

"You don't read the news like we do."

"I get plenty of news, Rachel."

"*Do* you? Do you know about the NATO school bombing in December 1984?"

"That doesn't prove anything."

"*We* know about it. That's just two years before you got here. And what about the Siemens manager killed last year in July? He looked like a businessman. The RAF wants to kill businessmen. The RAF also wants to kill military, especially Amees."

"You've got a lot of hate over here," I said.

"I don't hate, Roy. Just don't look military. That gets you killed."

"How about another drink?" I asked.

"I'll try another one."

I went to the kitchen to make new drinks.

"You sound as if you really like me, Rachel. How can you like me if I'm an invader?"

"There are a lot of good Amees. Besides, I love you, Roy."

I put down the drink glasses. Rachel wiped some tears from her eyes and walked over to the kitchen. She hugged me from behind. I turned around to hold her and look in her eyes.

"*Really?*" I asked.

"Really, and I don't say that easily."

"I fell in love with you the moment I saw you, Rachel. And I don't just say *that*, either."

"You don't just say that for sex?" Rachel asked, smiling coyly at me.

I bear-hugged Rachel as I lifted her off the ground.

"OK, maybe just a *little* because of the sex," I said.

Rachel hiked up her skirt. She had on my favorite pair of gloss-black Mary Jane pumps and thigh-high stockings. No panties.

"You want to invade this, occupier?"

"P-Day invasion!"

"Yes, occupier. Invasion," said Rachel. "When is Tready home?"

"Not until Sunday. He's in Frankfurt for the weekend."

"Perfect timing for us."

"Hang on," I said. "Let me get us new drinks. You dance for me, beautiful woman?"

"I will."

I pressed a cassette into the player and cued up "She Sells Sanctuary," Rachel's favorite song. She took off her shoes and climbed on the table, and with the high ceiling offering ample room, she danced her sultry moves.

Rachel and I drank and fucked until the wee hours, when she cooked breakfast, and then we spooned to sleep. Early

Saturday afternoon we woke, freshened up, shopped for food at a market, and then continued on to Rachel's place.

"My family didn't want me to be with an American," she said.

It was evening. We were sitting at her table over a dinner we had cooked together.

"Didn't or don't?" I asked.

"*Didn't*, at least back then."

"Now they don't care?"

"They care, but it's different for me now."

"How so?"

"Family is strong. People don't leave here. They talk. They know me."

"Lots of people know people."

"But I'm the one who dated an Amee."

"You *work* for Americans."

"You don't understand the Old World," Rachel said, looking away from me. "I'll never be *normal* here."

"It can't be that bad," I said, trying to counter the gravity of Rachel's claim.

I refilled our drinks. Wine tonight.

"It's like a scarlet letter, Roy."

"Yeez," I said. "You're serious about this?"

"I've been trying to tell you for a while."

"I'm listening," I said, pointedly looking into her eyes.

"No judging?" asked Rachel.

I took a gulp of my wine. Rachel hadn't touched her glass since dinner.

"I won't judge you, or anyone," I said.

"He was persuasive. He wanted me to have the American Dream."

"This was the guy your family didn't want you to be with?"

"Yes."

"OK."

"I love without condition, Roy," Rachel whispered. She swallowed her next words twice before continuing. "I was about to give up everything for him."

Rachel placed her hands flat on the table. I reached out and held them.

"I wanted honesty," she said. "I didn't want *any* man, I wanted a *real* man, one who says what he means."

"OK," I said, looking askew at her. "This doesn't sound too much to ask."

She was holding back tears.

"'We should have a family,' he'd say."

"Alright," I said.

"Six months before he was due to leave, and not unexpectedly . . ."

Rachel closed her eyes, leaned her head back, and raised her shoulders. Her tears began. I got up to hug her. She stood and tucked in her arms, her hands under her chin.

"Everything changed," she said, wiping her eyes.

I held her and felt her breathing calm. I pulled my chair directly in front of her and clasped her hands. We sat back down.

"What *happened*?" I whispered.

"He panicked."

"Hmmm," I said, trying to figure out the right response.

"He was no man," said Rachel, "but he was right about one thing."

Rachel looked at me, her eyes conveying strength from an anger that can only come from having been wronged.

"What was that?" I asked.

"He said that I'd never find him," said Rachel, her eyes welling up again. She looked out the window. "But I'd never want to find him."

An hour's worth of silence went by in ten seconds. Rachel looked back at me. Her chin trembled.

"I never saw him again."

I took a deep breath. Rachel sought reassurance in my eyes. I nodded and tucked her hair behind her ears.

"I would have had a daughter," she said.

We leaned into each other with our foreheads touching.

"I'm so sorry."

With her eyes closed, Rachel sighed and said, "My babies will always know their father."

I took her by the hand, washed her face with a warm wash-cloth, undressed her and undressed me, and then we climbed into bed and spooned.

"However, whoever, whatever got us here, I won't do that to you," I whispered.

We faded into sleep.

Bam bam bam. Rachel's front door rattled Sunday morn-ing at 05:45. We both jumped out of bed. I put on my T-shirt and shorts, then ran to look out the front window. She slid on a housecoat and followed me.

"Is that Treadwell's car?" Rachel asked.

"Hell if it isn't," I said. "Let's see what he wants."

I opened the front door. Treadwell was in uniform. On Sunday morning. At 05:45.

"Goddamn it, Chisolm," said Treadwell. "Get your act together."

"What's going on?" I asked.

"We're recalled. Let's go. I'll explain on the way."

I scrambled to get dressed, then headed for the door and bear-hugged Rachel on the way out. She had toasted a bagel in the meantime, and she shoved it in my mouth.

"Technically," she said, "I made you breakfast so you aren't leaving hungry."

"I love you. Always. All ways," I mumbled to her, running out the door.

Rachel giggled and mumbled the same sounds in return.

I had no time to warm up my own car. I jumped in with Treadwell and rolled down the passenger window to lock eyes on Rachel. Treadwell put it in gear, and we sped away.

35

"What's this all about?" I asked.

"They're at it again," said Treadwell. "We get to the apartment and you've got five minutes. I'm waiting in the car for you."

"Southwark must love this," I said.

"We need to get to the Brook and make that shuttle bus."

"Why not go straight to the Bunker?"

"No civilian vehicles allowed. They don't want to rattle the locals with all the off-hours traffic."

In less than five minutes, I had dressed and returned to Treadwell's waiting car. I took my razor and dry-shaved as he drove. I could smell Rachel's scent on me. We arrived at the Brook with two buses waiting and already filled with riders. Treadwell and I were the last to board the second bus. It lurched forward before I sat down.

Upon arrival at the Bunker, we pulled all the way up to the entrance. Everyone double-timed it into their respective duty stations.

"Where the hell you been?" asked Chief. "We've been calling your place."

"Am I supposed to wait around for the phone to ring?" I asked.

"Dick."

"Limp dick."

"They need you back there for something," said Legal.

"Where's Hancock?" I asked.

"OFO," said Chief. "He's not critical at this juncture anyhow."

"That guy has planted roots at Ramstein," said Legal.

"Woody, have you tried to help them back there yet?" I asked.

"Can't. It's too specific," said Woody. "The captain in DiAPERS needs a read on what they're seeing."

"Alright. Let me verify something first."

I hung up my jacket, stopped briefly by the server room to check that all AardVark routines were up and running, then headed straight to the Intel section.

"What are we looking at?" I asked the AardVark NCO.

"We're looking at *you* right now, Chisolm," said the NCO. "You smell like alcohol, brother. Don't get too close to anyone."

"Well, how was I to know you guys would do a recall?"

"Thank Ivan, not me. They lit up bigger than daylight an hour ago."

"Understood," I said.

"There he is," said the watch captain. "Over here, Airman Chisolm."

"Yes sir," I said.

"Take a look at this, will you? Does it look right?" The captain cocked his head and squinted at me, no doubt smelling the alcohol on my breath.

"Give me a minute, please, sir."

The concern was one of equipment count and location. The minute I requested was to get my head screwed on straight. I still had a buzz, though this was snapping me out of it.

"Those look accurate as of my most recent data import."

"When was that, Airman Chisolm?" asked the colonel from up on his high perch.

"Thursday last week, sir. That was the latest courier run."

"That can't be right," said the captain.

"That's the latest data I received, sir."

"I don't doubt that, Airman Chisolm," said the captain. "My doubt is how we got the information in the first place. Look. We've got a new swath of Ivan's equipment showing up where it never was before."

"I'm seeing that, sir," I said. "That's what I received, sir."

"Captain, get Spangdahlem up in the air now. Major, I need you to contact 4-EQ about what we see. Airman Chisolm, I need you to do a capture of this."

"It's recording, sir. I verified that our capture is running before I came out here."

"Stay within earshot, Airman Chisolm," said the watch captain.

"Roger that, sir. I'm not going anywhere."

I hustled back to the OPS floor to monitor the activity. I stared at the computer monitor, soaking in the therapeutic sound of white noise.

"That's it, Chisolm," said Hlavacka, slapping my back.

"I'm up," I said, snapping to.

"They're winding down back there. Intel says it was just a blip."

Some of the Russian blips were brief, just like ours—designed with enough frequency to test the enemy's response.

"You've got to line up your groove nights with Ivan's schedule," said Hlavacka, kicking my chair. He was standing over me with his arms crossed, smiling.

"I've been sitting here for an hour?" I asked, looking at the clock.

"*Sleeping*," said Hlavacka. "You've been asleep."

"This is annoying," I said.

Ivan's war game schedule was well known, so we knew when to prepare for lockdown. Blips, on the other hand, came up out of nowhere and ended almost as quickly.

"I'm glad you're always ready to die, Chisolm," said Hlavacka.

"Who's still here?" I asked.

"Everyone's on their way out. Let's get out of here."

I walked over and kicked the cot behind the server where Treadwell was sleeping. "Up," I said. "Let's go. We're done."

I joined the sluggish retreat leaving to get on buses for our return journey.

October ushered in shorter days and an early cold snap. At this time of year, the sinuous Bunker road, cut so narrowly through the tall pine forest, allowed for little direct sunlight to touch it.

My life became one of reason and of diversion. I wouldn't say diversion in the sense of being diverted from any expectation placed upon me. Rather, I found diversion in the absence of America. And you'd be nuts to think I wouldn't. Inmate departures confirmed the premise that once you were gone, you were gone. You checked in, did your time, then checked out. Or rather you checked in, checked out, then waited to go home.

This ain't on me. You edged me out of where I once stood.

"Who's eagle eye over there?" I asked Wagner.

On the OPS floor one late-October afternoon, a new person stood across the room, talking with Hlavacka. I could not hear their conversation, but the guy kept eyeballing me. I snapped my head quickly toward him a few times and he just stared at me.

"Legal's replacement, I think."

I approached the conspirators.

"Hi. I'm Roy Chisolm."

"Hello, Airman Chisolm," said the new guy, as he reached for a handshake. "Sergeant Burns."

Burns had a short, pear-shaped torso on toothpick legs and an oil-shined bald head.

"Just in, huh?" I asked. "You were staring. I thought something was wrong."

"You look like a civilian," said Burns, laughing. "But you're in a uniform."

"Don't let that trick you," I said.

"Which part, you being a civilian or being in uniform?"

"Either one," said Hlavacka. "It's heads or tails with him."

"I do what counts," I said. "What will you be doing?"

"Systems. I'm taking Legal's place."

"Legal's place?" I asked. "He isn't scheduled to leave until when, next spring or so?"

"He's got to get trained," said Hlavacka.

"Still, that's over half a year of training."

"Hey, don't blame me," said Burns.

"No kidding," I said. "Where are you coming from?"

My worry now was if Burns came from a real Air Force uptight-asshole-generating squadron.

"Direct from tech school. I cross-trained from air traffic operations. Scott via Keesler."

Goddamn it, another Southwark cross-trained ate-up asshole.

"Well, welcome to the Bunker, Sergeant Burns. You're going to love this place."

"Thank you, Airman Chisolm."

Wagner had wandered over to within earshot of us.

"Have you met Sergeant Wagner?" I asked Burns.

"In passing."

Wagner and Burns nodded at each other.

"Wagner, what's your number?" I asked as we moved to the other side of the OPS floor.

"Eighty-three."

"You keep making all the programmers look bad," I said. "You're going to run out of library at this rate."

"I picked up a new batch last week."

"Good for you. By the way, it's fourteen hundred."

"I know what time it is, you dick."

"Adios, Sergeant Wagner."

"Hasta luego, Mr. Airman Chisolm."

I left the OPS floor to go find Woody. "Congratulations again, Sergeant Burns," I said in passing.

"OK, Airman Chisolm. Thank you."

"Sergeant Hlavacka, sir, have a wonderful day," I said.

"You can cut the act, Chisolm."

"No act, sir. Proper order, sir."

"Go fuck yourself, Chisolm."

36

On November 5, Legal entered the OPS floor with two men. He gestured for silence, handing me a business card: *"Act normal and make no mention of what you see."*

One of the men wore jeans and a flannel shirt. He carried a six-pronged antenna. The other man wore slacks and a pressed shirt. Strapped around his shoulder was a briefcase-sized radio with numerous knobs and dials. This same man had on headphones connected to the equipment. The men inched their way along the outer walls of the server room, holding the antenna at various angles and continuously repositioning the knobs and dials.

I handed the card to Curly. We shrugged.

"Hey, you going with us to drop off Jensen?" asked Curly.

Curly was replacing Jensen on the OPS floor C flight.

"Depends on the plan," I said.

"What do you mean *plan*?" asked Curly. "Someone's getting fucked."

I paused, realizing that our "normal" behavior might not have been what our spooks had in mind. I was right. I looked toward them and they grimaced, but they kept moving along at their task. Legal paid no mind.

"Jensen flies next Friday," continued Curly. "Thinking about Frankfurt on Thursday for an overnight."

"Who all is in on this?"

"Treadwell and me, for sure."

"That figures he'd be in on this," I said. "Oh, what the hell. I'm in."

Jensen's enlistment ended when his Bunker tour ended. He would be a civilian once out-processed stateside and didn't care about anything except leaving country. Curly would need to be back at the Bunker for shift change by 15:00 the next day. He would have no relief. Treadwell and I, we'd earned a respite.

"Does anyone think ahead?" I asked as we arrived in Frankfurt and began searching for a room.

"We don't all have the time you've got, Chisolm," said Curly.

"This is your plan," I said. "Besides, how long does it take to call a hotel?"

A convention had come to town, thus narrowing our options. Treadwell stopped at four random hotels along a main thoroughfare, and Curly checked each for availability. On our fifth stop, we had luck.

"Who's paying for what?" asked Jensen.

"We each cover ourselves and split Jensen's costs," I said. "That's only fair."

"So long as he doesn't go nuts," said Curly.

"Jensen, you going to go nuts?" Treadwell asked.

"You think I'm going to stop now?" asked Jensen.

"I'm capping what I spend," said Curly. "I got three hundred deutsche marks. For everything."

"That's only about one hundred fifty dollars, you cheapskate," I said. "Even I have more than that, and you all outrank me."

"How are you always broke?" asked Treadwell.

"Exactly," I said. "You're supposed to be driving this. How the hell do you show up with only three hundred?"

"Just don't go crazy, Jensen," said Curly.

"I've heard all about the crazy," said Treadwell.

"Ain't no one knows nothing about me," said Jensen.

"That's a triple negative," I said.

"What say we head out to Sachsenhausen after we get some food?" Jensen suggested.

"Sounds good," said Curly. "What do you know about it?"

"Frankfurt's nightlife district," said Jensen. "I know other places to go too."

"OK, where?" Treadwell asked.

"To get laid. *Hello?!*" said Jensen. "They have a good red-light district."

The room went quiet as Jensen tapped his fingers on the desk, panning the room.

"And pay for it?" Curly asked. "I'm not paying for it. I can cover your part of the hotel and some drinks. I also have to pay my part of the hotel and my own drinks."

"Curly, you need to plan better," I said.

"I'm in," said Treadwell.

"I'll look but I ain't touching," I said. "Who would take sloppy seconds, anyhow?"

None of them answered. Instead they fidgeted as if they didn't hear the question.

"Fine, I'm in," Curly said.

"How well do you know it?" Treadwell asked.

"Trust me," said Jensen. "I know it."

"And *how* do you know it?" Treadwell pressed.

"How do you *think* I know it, dumbass?"

We weren't dumbasses. Prostitution was legal in many parts of Europe. It was legal even in little Ostenhof, and many villages and towns had their operations.

"Why the hell drive all the way to Frankfurt to pay for it?" I asked.

"It's like no-limits gambling," said Jensen. "Only here, it's no-limits nasty."

"Bingo," I said. "So the stories are true. You *are* sick."

"What secrets you got, Jensen?" asked Curly.

"I don't know what you're talking about," said Jensen. "I don't have any secrets. Everyone knows I'll pay for no-holes-barred."

"Holds," I said. "It's *holds*."

"Holes," said Jensen. *"Holes."*

After eating bratwursts and fries at a nearby snack stand, and per Jensen's directions, Treadwell drove us to the red-light district. We parked and began plying the area on foot.

"OK," I said, "so what is the story I heard about you and some soup fetish?"

Jensen grinned.

"I haven't heard that one," said Curly.

"What do you want me to say?" asked Jensen. "These bitches are nasty."

"You say *these bitches*, but it sounds more like *you're* the nasty one," said Treadwell.

"Freedom of expression, baby."

"Define this so-called expression of yours, please?" I asked.

"I paid one bitch to eat some tomato soup."

"You *paid* to feed *her*?" I asked. "That's called a date, Jensen."

I looked at Treadwell. Curly was staring off into space.

"I don't get it."

"Then I gave her an enema."

"What in God's name?!" I said.

"Dayyum," said Curly.

"She blew that shit all over the place," said Jensen, hunched over in hysterics.

"Jesus Christ, you are sick, man," added Treadwell.

"No *wonder* you have to come here," I said.

"You come, you do your time, you leave," said Jensen. "After the Bunker, you deserve anything you can get. Besides, back home, no one is the wiser."

"That *is* what it is," I whispered to myself. "They haven't got a clue, do they?"

"What's that, Chisolm?" asked Curly.

"Disregard," I said. "You *do* deserve what your heart desires."

"Now Chisolm's going soft on us," said Treadwell.

"Quite the contrary," I said. "I'm seeing it for what it is."

"Why not cut to the chase?" asked Jensen. "If you're gonna fuck 'em, then get to it."

"Get to it," I said, looking at Jensen.

I couldn't fault Jensen. Left to his own devices, this is where his conclusions took him. He sought freedom from the Bunker on his terms. He was honest about it. He had to be. The number one rule about the classified world was honesty. Jensen holding a top-secret clearance? No problem. Sergeant Crowley had it right—out of sight, out of mind. The inmates *were* out of their minds. And could it have been otherwise? Certainly no one back home had their sights on us. Only Ivan did.

Jensen knew street names and parking locations. He knew the scope of services offered by street and building, and even the services offered on given floors within a building.

"I know this one," he said.

We entered an almost-century-old building and trekked up a flight of stairs. The year 1889 was carved into the corner-stone. The foyer, stairwell, and hallways were lit by red bulbs. By the looks of it, the building had once been a hotel. Most of the room doors were open.

Unlike in Amsterdam, where the girls sat behind plate glass windows and passersby viewed their options from the street, these girls could be viewed up close, as each sat on a barstool positioned in front of their doors. Of course the terms of engagement would be handled properly, one on one. Upon agreement, client and provider entered the room for services rendered.

"Let's get out of here," said Jensen after reviewing the girls in one hallway.

We followed him out of the building and crossed the street. The next building we entered was seedier and more dimly lit. The smell of musty carpets permeated the place. These girls were older—well traveled, one might say. On the third floor, the top floor, the hallway was lit only to the level of a black light.

"This is the nasty bunch," said Jensen in a hushed tone, looking back at us. "This is good."

Jensen was on a grade-school zoo trip—cages, animals, feeding the animals, getting the animals to do tricks. The hallways smelled of cigarette smoke, stale sex, and unvarnished filthiness. But this was Jensen's choice. We had to oblige. I was holding up the back of our pack when Jensen made a deal with one of the women. He turned to us.

"One fifty."

Jensen didn't negotiate long or fervently with the woman, but he was firm on the number. She spoke quietly, in broken English. She stood about five-feet-nine in heels. The cottage cheese in her legs cropped out between her panties and stockings. Jensen looked and felt. She turned around, then twisted her torso from side to side, proud to show off her big, jiggly tits. I'd never seen eyelashes so long. Not even on Schmink. Her uniform—panties, bra, garter belt, and stockings—showcased her body as well as it could for her age. But crow's feet don't lie. This bitch was old. The soft lighting blunted any further buyer's remorse.

"One fifty?" asked Curly "For that old bag?"

"Keep your voice down," said Treadwell.

"Pay up," I said. "It stinks in here. And you don't want to step in anything."

Treadwell collected fifty deutsche marks from each of the three of us.

"We'll see you out front," said Treadwell, handing the money to Jensen.

I was the first out. Curly and Treadwell emerged a few minutes later.

"Why are you two lagging?" I asked.

"Checking out the wares, dude," Treadwell said.

"Checking out the wares?" I asked, looking at Curly. "How can you even afford it?"

"Maybe that's why he's always broke," said Treadwell.

"That actually makes sense," I said.

"Is that what it is?" asked Treadwell. "Are you broke all the time because you're out fucking whores?"

"No," said Curly, short on conviction. "Maybe sometimes I get out. That might mean fucking whores. Then again it might *not* mean fucking whores. Jesus, you're sure worried about me fucking."

"Nailed it," said Treadwell. "He's out fucking whores."

"Who cares?" I asked. "We're fucked, pants up or pants down."

Jensen took twenty minutes. Rain clouds moved in, and a slight drizzle started. The three of us stood in the doorway until Jensen returned.

"What do you get for twenty minutes?" I asked.

"A suck and a fuck, no anal, nothing weird. That's extra."

"That's all you get?" asked Curly. "Too bad you don't get anal."

"I think anal would fall into the *weird* category," said Treadwell.

"Ain't bad for the price," said Jensen. "Especially when you choose the pussy."

"I'd keep my money and go with a dorm ho before I'd pay for that old bag," Curly said. "And I ain't doing a dorm ho."

We had our dorm ho's, our half dozen enlisted females occupying the second floor of the dorm. A few were assigned to the Intel squadron, the others to the transportation unit or my squadron at the Brook. Entering any engagement with them would be a dicey proposition. One, because they were fugly, except for Ginger. Two, because when things inevitably went tits up, you'd be forever confronted with them where you lived. And three, because the inmates knew who was fucking whom.

We meandered down a few blocks.

"Five bucky sucky fucky," said Treadwell.

"A lot more than five bucks," said Jensen. "And I'm ready for more."

"Seriously?" Treadwell asked. "You just had a go-round, or couldn't you get it up?"

"Ah, he couldn't get it up," said Curly.

"I got it up, asshole. I just want to go again."

"Who's paying for that?" asked Curly. "He just got laid. No need to be greedy."

"I'll cover you," said Treadwell. "But only one more. And don't be thinking it's an unlimited deal, either."

"I'm in," I said.

"Go where you want," said Curly. "I'm not paying."

"Over here, this place," Jensen directed.

We entered a two-story building with the scent of candles burning. The girls appeared college age. Though red lights illuminated the place, the interior was bright. The hardwood floors didn't allow any stink to build up. Good. Customers shuffled in the halls. Jensen made a proposition within minutes. Between two of us contributors, we offered another one hundred and fifty deutsche marks. Before Jensen could negotiate a final price, Treadwell pushed him into the room and threw the money in behind him.

"Last one, man," Treadwell said. "See you downstairs."

"So why aren't you getting laid?" I asked Curly as we exited the building. "And where the hell is Treadwell?"

Curly and I had made it out with Treadwell nowhere to be found.

The drizzling rain had subsided for the moment. Curly and I sat on a bench in front of the building and watched traffic roll by.

"I'm like you, man. I don't pay for pussy."

"You seeing anyone?" I asked.

"We're not all lucky like you, Chisolm."

"You can pay, man," I said. "I don't judge."

"I ain't paying."

"I don't blame you," I said.

The thing that bothered me was Curly holding out on contributing his share of Jensen's departure night. Hell, Curly was the planner. That was deceitful and selfish—neither one an appropriate trait for someone who was holding a clearance.

Jensen and Treadwell exited the building at the same time.

"What did you do, a threesome?" I asked.

"I saw something that looked good," said Treadwell.

"Alright. Alright," I said.

The wind picked up and the rain now poured. The storm drains couldn't mitigate the flood. We hopscotched into a few bars to dry off between rounds of drinks. At about midnight, the rain stopped. Everyone but me was well lubricated. I convinced the crew to call it a night, then led the four of us to Treadwell's car. I took his keys, everyone piled in, and we headed toward the hotel.

The winds and water had left debris in the roadway. Enormous puddles had formed in some areas, while in others even concrete curbs were dislodged. Water exploded from underneath the car as I drove over some of the deeper puddles. I calculated that we had enough weight in the car to keep it straight, and I drove accordingly. I dodged everything I had time enough to see.

As I rounded an arc in a boulevard, hurrying to beat a changing light, I saw part of a curb lying smack in the middle of my lane. I made a quick decision. The exhaust pipe was under either the driver side or the passenger side. I guessed the passenger side and barreled over the concrete piece. The exhaust system got hammered somewhere under my seat, and the sound of the engine immediately changed volume. I pulled into a nearby gas station and stopped under the canopy. The exhaust system from the driver's seat to the rear end had been ripped from the car. Curly ran down the street to retrieve the muffler. Fortunately, it fit in the trunk. The car screamed all the way to the hotel. I'd made an educated guess and came up wrong.

I offered to pay for the damage or even help fix it. Treadwell declined both offers. It could have happened to anyone, really. Besides, his car was a traditional piece of crap. If you were junior enlisted like us and had a car, your car would be an old piece of crap. That's all we could afford.

The next morning we dropped off Jensen at Rhein-Main and departed for the Brook, screaming exhaust and all. Coasting down to the end of Autobahn 26, into the Immelbrücken valley, my angst returned. After dropping off Curly, Treadwell and I made it to our apartment, then crashed for the day. Treadwell had the muffler welded back onto his car the following week.

It would be a rare day of sunshine or clear skies for some time. A low-pressure trough hung over our latitude for weeks. Real downpours of rain would not start, and the drizzling wouldn't stop. This relentless, unnerving gray, gray, gray and absence of city lights and billboards; the inability to buy something any time I wanted, to see a movie in English upon release, to have a breakfast at 7:00 p.m. or a Big Mac at noon—anything and everything had gone missing or was unobtainable by any other means. I hated this place.

Inmates added and subtracted from the numbers on the front of this Cold War. It didn't matter what any one inmate achieved, because there was always someone who would do what others couldn't or wouldn't. We just needed the numbers. That's what mattered. We were uniform in the only way that mattered: by the numbers. If one of us was gone, it was only in numbers that our circumstances varied. We would plus up. It mattered only that we had the right count.

Curly just knew he would hear from Jensen at some point. But Jensen vanished. No inmate ever heard from him again.

37

The familiarity of scuff-marked Bunker corridors had become etched in my mind. On this day, my stride to leave this place was even more hurried. As I approached the exit, sunlight poured in. I wasn't running from anyone or anything. I was on my way to pick up books for college classes.

"Well, *hello*, Roy," said Mr. Chamberlain, as if seeing a loved one again after some long absence.

Mr. Chamberlain's office was on the Brook, tucked away on the second floor of a remote wing in the HQ building. You might have found your way here if you were lost, or for the less-likely reason that you'd come here intentionally. A sweet scent of burning pipe tobacco wafted out of his office, with an ever-so-slight tinge of marijuana mixed in.

"Hey, Mr. Chamberlain, how's it going?" I asked.

The Department of Defense hired education counselors for overseas locations to help those assigned sift through their college and course options. The colleges themselves had no counselors, so the military obliged by filling those holes. Mr. Chamberlain filled one of them. To get my tuition fully paid, I had to get a sign-off from him for each class. He'd signed my enrollment form earlier that week, so I didn't need to see him. But I had to pass his office, since it was in the same hall as the college representative from whom I would pick up my textbooks. Mr. Chamberlain's hours were limited to two afternoons per week. The rest of the time he spent at various other posts and bases, performing the same role. I'd landed here on one of his office days.

"Roy! Good to see you, my friend. Good. To. See. *You*, sir."

Mr. Chamberlain extended both his hands to greet me, grabbing my right hand in a vise grip. Not many inmates were in for formal education, so when someone showed up, Mr. Chamberlain rushed to welcome them. He needed to see me. He needed to see everyone.

"Yes. Yes, Mr. Chamberlain, good to see you too, sir."

"And what's new with you, Roy? Are you telling your colleagues to come see me?"

Mr. Chamberlain wanted every inmate to get an education.

"I am, Mr. Chamberlain. I tell everyone who will listen."

"Good. Good. That's what I want to hear, Roy."

Mr. Chamberlain always wore the same tweed jacket with patched elbows. His disheveled hair, handlebar mustache, and corduroy pants had resisted years of fashion evolution. Half the time his button-down shirt was misaligned by one hole. Two psychedelic rugs hung from one wall, while Led Zeppelin and Jefferson Airplane posters were pinned to another.

"I'm going to make it, Mr. Chamberlain. I've selected my remaining classes."

"Roy, you are my hope. No one has a plan like you do."

"It's your plan too, Mr. Chamberlain."

"You give me too much credit, Roy. You are going to make it." Mr. Chamberlain slapped my back.

"If I don't make it, it's because I'm dead. I won't give up."

"Well, you're not going to die on me, are you?" Mr.

Chamberlain asked, in what appeared to be all seriousness. I may have freaked him out.

"So long as no one gets trigger happy, right?"

"Ooh, *ohh*. That. Yes," Mr. Chamberlain said, laughing. "Wait, *what?*" He buttoned up his face and stood up straight with concern. "What are the odds of that, do you think?"

"No, no," I said. "I wasn't being serious, sir."

Mr. Chamberlain squinted and looked down his nose at me. "The world could do better without all this saber-rattling. Don't you agree, Roy?"

"If it wasn't us, or Ivan, it would just be someone else."

Mr. Chamberlain looked to the ceiling in analysis of my proposition.

"You may be right about that, as much as the world could do better."

"I'm on the side of trying to do better, Mr. Chamberlain."

Mr. Chamberlain regained his jovial, passive composure.

"Of course you are, Roy. So. Good. To. See. *You!*"

The inmates were on the front line. Mr. Chamberlain brought the daisies for our rifles.

"I'll be back in six weeks for the new term."

"Or sooner, if you need anything." Mr. Chamberlain again reached for a two-handed vise-grip handshake.

"Yes sir. Or sooner if I need anything."

"And tell your colleagues to come see me."

"Every time, sir. I do. Have a good day, sir."

"So good to see you, Roy."

I did all I could to engage Mr. Chamberlain. He was alone on an island otherwise. He told me so. This Cold War was also his war. I agreed with him. But I couldn't fill my schedule with more classes, nor time with Mr. Chamberlain. My schedule already pinched my time with Rachel. Cold War be damned, I was getting laid.

38

"Can I tell you something?" I asked, looking at Rachel.

Rachel looked back at me as we lay in her bed. I'd skipped class that evening. It was Rachel's birthday.

"Sure," she said, examining my face.

"This is not what I expected it to be," I said.

"How so?" Rachel asked.

"I thought this was a fling."

"A *fling*? After all this?"

"No!" I said, stopping Rachel's sideways-thought momentum. "I mean I *thought* this was going to be a fling. When we started."

Rachel turned completely sideways with her undivided attention on me.

"I never thought that, not for a minute."

"I'm being honest. I'm telling you who I am," I said. "I was wrong. I didn't know it at the time."

Rachel relaxed. "When did you know it?"

"I think maybe I always knew it. I just didn't *expect* it. I mean, how does anyone know when the right one comes along?"

"I didn't doubt you."

"But does anyone *know* right up front?" I asked. *"Really* know?"

"I get it."

"I mean, one day my time will be up here. How does this work out? Us?"

"How *does* it work out?" Rachel asked.

"You've been here before," I said. "I haven't."

"What do you mean?"

"You made promises. He left. You're still here."

Rachel closed her eyes.

"Are you different?" she asked.

I paused, intent on being pointed. "I am different."

"You all promise that you'll be back and visit and write and call."

"Ouch," I said. "That isn't everyone."

"What are you saying?" asked Rachel. "Even *you* tell me that people leave the Bunker and are never heard from again."

"Yeah, maybe some of them aren't helping our cause."

"You Amees say you are friends forever, but then you vanish."

"Blame it on the Wild West."

"What do you mean?" asked Rachel.

"A theory Wagner and I shared one day."

"Ah, Wagner. Your philosopher friend in the Bunker?"

"Yeah, that guy."

"What about the Wild West?"

"It's the system—or in this case, our way of life—that makes us how we are."

"What is this system?"

"Your culture. My culture. Anyone's culture. *That's* the system."

"Well, duh, Roy."

"But it can't be that obvious. You know *that* Amees

are superficial, but you don't understand *why*. It's not so obvious."

"Maybe."

"It's the system. In my case, it's the Wild West that explains *why* we are superficial."

"Tell me."

"In the Wild West, you had to make friends quickly. You needed protection from anything or anyone that might kill you or steal from you. Plus you needed water and food and other stuff. So what did you do? You did what you *had* to do, and that was to make friends, and the sooner the better. That's what everyone had to do for the best chance of survival."

"Even if that's true, it doesn't explain why Amees always disappear."

"Everyone is moving around and going places and finding land and following the sun and whatever. They move on and they move often. You hear stories of distant riches and open lands and opportunities. The Wild West was a place that made us the way we are. Americans still feel this way. It wasn't that long ago. Americans still hear whispers of distant riches and opportunities. They're *just* on the other side of the mountain or over a state line or across the country. So they leave. They vanish."

"Wow, *you're* the philosopher, I think."

"I'm just trying to figure it all out."

"Are you going to disappear?" asked Rachel.

"I'm not going to make any promise I can't keep," I said. "Not because I want to disappear. I want to know how this good thing goes."

"I'd never ask you to do anything you don't want to do."

I stared resolutely into Rachel's eyes.

"I'm not like them." My breathing slowed but deepened. "That's not me."

"We can say anything for now," said Rachel.

"We've got two ways to go, as I see it," I said.

Rachel sighed.

"I don't want to hate myself for you not coming with me," I said. "But I don't want you to end up hating me for having taken you from the place where your family has existed for centuries."

I rolled onto my back and looked at the ceiling, reaching for Rachel's hand.

"All I know, Rachel, is that we have to be right, one way or another."

39

November 29th, 1987

Roy,

I can't believe you've been gone almost a year.

I know you won't be home for Christmas, but I'll set your place all the same. I talked with the neighbors about your assignment. They are impressed with you serving our country.

I've never been able to find you on a map, but that's got to be important work you're doing. Good thing you got some R & R. Glad to hear that you are learning a lot. Your mother always said you'd figure it all out.

Remember the two horses? The vet didn't give them half a chance. I wrapped their up-keep into my routine. They survived. No one has shown up to claim or adopt them. That's

OK. They're always happy to see me. Truth be told, I'm always happy to see them.

I'm saying my prayers for you.

Dad

40

"Waste of time," said Schmink.

Two weeks into the new school term, I was reading one of my college textbooks.

"That came out of nowhere," I said.

"What are you trying to prove, anyway?"

"Mr. Chamberlain needs a friend," I said. "You should consider visiting him."

"How much more you got?" asked Chief.

"If I stay on schedule," I said, "I'll be done just before end of tour."

"Can't be done," Chief said. "I've yet to see or hear of anyone making it."

"Then I'll be the first," I said. "But it is a lot of classes."

"You'll kill yourself trying," said Schmink. "Your commutes are at night. Too much black ice."

"That stuff is deadly," said Chief.

"It'll get you," said Schmink.

"Stay on schedule, Chisolm," said Hancock. "You can't afford not to. Trust me."

"Who the hell do you think you are, anyhow, Chisolm?" asked Schmink.

"I'll do it or I'll die trying. I've got promises to keep."

"To who?" asked Chief.

"People," I said. "My mom, for one."

"Oh, a momma's boy," said Southwark, chiming in upon entering the office.

"Shut up," I said. "What are *you* going to take away from this place? A cuckoo clock?"

"Yeah, smart guy," said Chief.

"Nothing but a bunch of downers in here," said Hancock. "Make something of yourselves, why don't you?"

"Realists," said Chief. "Realists in here."

"Optimist here," I said.

"There you go again with your optimism," said Chief. "Give it time. I was once optimistic."

"What went wrong?" asked Burns, folding a Systems report at his desk.

"Nothing went *wrong*," said Chief. "I got married."

"What's getting married have to do with this joint?" asked Southwark.

"Similar kind of thing," said Chief. "You sign up for something thinking it will be the best thing in the world. Time goes by. It grinds you down into a stump. No one's fault but your own. You signed on the dotted line."

"Jesus, that's pathetic," said Burns. "You needed a tour in the Philippines."

"Doesn't matter where you go," said Chief. "It'll grind you down."

"Doesn't seem to have affected your dart game," I said. "If anything, you're getting better, no?"

"Want real happiness, Chisolm?" asked Chief. "Set your sights on a smaller target, a more manageable target."

"So true happiness is hitting an ever-shrinking bull's-eye?" I asked.

"You could say that," said Chief. "Everyone can win. Make it small enough, then keep throwing everything you have at it. You're bound to hit it sooner or later."

"Interesting take," said Burns.

"Frightening take," I said. "I can only hope to achieve your level of nirvana. I'm going to consider your guidance, most humble sage of Borlingau."

"Goddamn smart-ass," said Southwark. "It's going to bite you one of these days, Chisolm."

This war was not one of weapons, nor of explosives, nor of fury and fists and guns and knives and bravery, but of and about fear. For it to work, no one could opt out. A war like this required a shadow of fear cast deep and long over all of us. We are all involved here, sweetie. Miss Ohen, my third-grade Catholic-school teacher—she too was on the front lines. She campaigned for compliance, to instill in us children the idea of fitting in and finding our place in society. Miss Ohen met a Vietnam War vet and fell in love, and on one of our last school days back in 1975, she married. She never returned to our school again.

In grade school, in our rows of desks, in our disciplined routines on any given day, I fought this Cold War then as I do now. I am not now on the front lines in a far-off place. The front lines are the white picket fences. The front lines are a backyard. The front lines are a shopping mall, a movie theater, and an ice cream shop.

Everywhere we are, this is war. Wherever one stands, it is war. The side you are on only depends upon how you see it, and how "they" see it.

You sent me to fight the Cold War, to stand watch over *your* fear, to incubate *your* fear through my patience to remain steadfast in the pursuit of pursuing nothing but annihilation, that I might ever be the end-all of freedom.

I lost it night after night, trying to hold myself together over each day, making as if I had a clear mind and conscience. *They* drank. *They* medicated. *They* screwed. They could not scratch one sixteenth of an inch below the surface of this derived reality.

Still, I maintained my bearing.

I bawled my eyes out that I had lost hold on reality. I wanted to pursue no more than one sixteenth of an inch in any form or fashion, but I'd torn something too deep to hold me back from seeing something I neither sought nor asked for. Yet I saw. More and more, I saw.

You cut my incisors early on, fed me the slop, then expected me to survive this Cold War. You held me down way back when. You gave me no choice. You didn't tell me what you were doing. I would never have known otherwise. But you did know what you were doing to me. *You* had a choice. *You* had an obligation to never begin the mistrial of painting derived portrayals of a reality far removed from the truth of this life. Perhaps you only perpetuated what you knew of your own derivations. I concede this. I fell deeper than one sixteenth of an inch into the peace of a good night, an *honest* night. You did not let me down, you let me go.

"Can you give me a hand with one of my reports?" I asked Schmink.

I needed someone to help me try and break the software.

"Yeah, I'll get right on it," said Schmink.

"Seriously. I need someone to test it who knows nothing. I mean about the report."

"I'm not helping you do anything."

"C'mon, man. It's for the mission."

"Find someone else. I've got stuff to do."

"You don't have anything to do."

"He's tired from coming in on mids," Hlavacka said.

"What?" I asked. "Why would you be here on mids?"

Schmink readjusted himself in his chair, let out a sigh, then continued reading.

"Come on, Mr. Schmink, pretend you're still in the real Air Force," I said.

"Get over it, Chisolm."

"How about sometime next week? That's not asking too much."

"Why are you here on mids, Schmink?" asked Hlavacka.

Schmink huffed.

"I'll give you an hour," said Schmink.

"For the mission," I said, pounding a fist on my desk. Doing so dislodged something, as my desk now wobbled.

"What the hell was that?" I muttered to myself.

The thud got Chief's attention.

"What's that?" asked Chief.

"Nothing," I said. "I need to put something under a leg or two to square my desk again."

I stuffed a sticky-note pad under each of the two front legs. When I did, a folder fell to the floor from between the wall and the back of my desk. I retrieved the folder.

"Hey, what's this?" I asked.

"What have you got there?" Legal asked, peering around his partition.

"Not sure," I said. "By the looks of it, change requests."

"Let me see," said Legal.

I took out a few pages and then handed the folder to him.

"Damn, this one's more than two years old," I said.

"Wow, that was assigned to your predecessor, Chisolm," said Legal, noting the name at the top of the form.

Hlavacka pounded his fist on his desk with laughter. Legal continued his forensics.

"Schmink, here's one with your name on it," said Legal. "And here's another one, from last year. Good job, sir."

Schmink put down his book and sat up.

"Let me see that," said Schmink.

"Good job?" I asked. "In what universe?"

"It's a rite of passage," said Hlavacka.

"These aren't supposed to be found until after you leave, Schmink," said Chief. "You failed, idiot."

"How was I supposed to know he'd be poking around?" asked Schmink.

"Poking around?" I asked. "That's what you call fixing my desk?"

"Should let things lie where they are, Chisolm," said Hlavacka.

Woody entered the office.

"Woody, I may have bumped your ship," I said. "I had to reseat our desk."

"I'll take a look," said Woody. "What's all the fun?"

"I just found a folder behind our desk," I said.

"Folder for what?" asked Woody.

"Not *for* what, *of* what," I said. "Change requests. Lots of them."

"Seriously?" asked Woody.

"Seriously," I said. "No wonder there isn't shit done around here. No one keeps track of or knows what needs *to* be done."

"Didn't you write a program for that, Chisolm?" asked Hlavacka.

"I wrote it alright," I said. "You're one of the geniuses who said that program wasn't needed."

A round of laughter filled the office.

"There's a little happiness for you, Chief," I said.

"Ah, joy, Chisolm," said Chief. "If it weren't for life's small victories."

No inmate would entertain the idea of scavenging for "lost" change requests, as those could reasonably be expected to incur more work. Everyone held tight on to their desk. Chance discoveries of hidden requests were possible—according to rite—but normally long after an inmate left country. My accidental revelation might have proven problematic, though any purposeful search would have been an exercise in futility. This sort of futility would never be tolerated in the Bunker.

Every other Wednesday, Hancock and Legal took turns leading our project-status meetings. Hancock accepted what the inmates claimed. He had no choice. He was rarely in the Bunker. Legal didn't particularly give a damn one way or another about user requirements. He was Systems. No user issues ever came his way. Our Wednesday meetings were the one stable, static event in the Bunker. In early December on just such a Wednesday, I showed up for the status meeting.

"They grow while I'm at work. I'll cut 'em while I'm at work," Southwark said, taking off his shoes and socks.

"That's goddamn nasty, you dirty bastard," said Burns. "And in the wrong way."

"You stink, Southwark," said Hlavacka. "Put your shoes back on, for God's sake. I gotta breathe."

"In a minute," said Southwark. "In a minute."

"Your nails are plinking all over the floor," I said. "We've got to live in here."

"Who's this we, Chisolm?" asked Southwark. "I'm here all day. And I'm within 35-10."

AFR 35-10 was the Air Force regulation covering dress and appearance conformity. Southwark's grooming time usually coincided with our status-update meetings.

"That's your measure of success?" I asked. "Why not go for

six minutes getting ready in the morning? Add your toenails to it."

During status-update meetings, it was imperative to be convincing. One also had to forecast project-completion dates. However, since there was no requirement to show one's work, there was no way to judge whether real progress was ever made. If an inmate sounded convincing, their words were taken at face value. To sound convincing, an inmate just had to be present for the Wednesday meeting.

"Meeting postponed until tomorrow," said Legal.

"What's that all about?" asked Woody.

"So, I came in for nothing?" I asked.

"Be here tomorrow, same time," said Legal.

"De La Cruz's replacement is at the Brook," Chief said.

"What?" Schmink asked. "You knew this and didn't say anything?"

"Who is it?" I asked.

"Frazione," said Chief. "Hasn't been here long. He's in De La Cruz's old office."

"What've you heard?" asked Woody.

"We might be getting reorganized," said Chief.

"How do you know this?" asked Schmink.

"I passed his office yesterday," said Chief. "I peeked in. He had an org chart on his whiteboard."

"That doesn't mean anything," said Schmink.

"Keep dreaming," said Chief. "All our names were on it, and not in the structure we've got now."

"Where's Hancock?" I asked. "He's supposed to be here today."

"I told you about that guy," said Legal. "Hancock's planting roots at Ramstein."

"What do you mean by that?" I asked.

"For one thing, he's dead set on being an officer," said

Legal. "For another, he's married to another active duty. She's at Ramstein."

"Well, no wonder," I said. "You think he might have made that known?"

"I heard it," said Woody.

"How am I the last to find out?" I asked.

"Be here sometimes, Chisolm," said Chief.

"I'm here all I need to be," I said. "And then some."

Burns scowled at me, then slowly shook his head no.

"I've got my short-timer calendar," Schmink said. "Who cares?" He continued his reading.

"There goes the neighborhood," said Hlavacka.

"Changes be comin', bitches," said Sosa.

"Has anyone actually met the guy?" I asked.

"He stopped in twice last week," said Legal.

"You assholes couldn't tell me?" I asked, looking at Chief.

"If you were ever here, dick, you'd have known," Chief replied.

"Showed up oh-dark-thirty, both times," Hlavacka said. "Stayed briefly. Cut out. Showed up at the end of both days. Only looked around."

"A goddamn clock watcher," I said.

"Legal, what's your take on this bullshit?" asked Chief.

"It's about to get real, boys," said Legal.

"Well, drop your socks and pick up your pencils," said Sosa.

Damned if I need to worry about any reorganization. Frazione is going to love me.

41

I arrived punctually on Thursday at 09:25, in time for the scheduled 09:30 staff meeting. I heard no discussion as I approached the office door. Rather than hanging up my coat first, I strode inside.

"Let's begin," said the senior master sergeant, glancing at me.

The room was crammed with people like never before. The senior stood at the other end of the room. He had creases like mine. His gig line was pristine like mine. His hair was cut top to bottom with guide comb length one. *That's Frazione. I'm screwed.*

I sat on the corner of the desk closest to the office door. Frazione looked down at a clipboard in his hand.

"I'm going to call your names, people. Reply when called." He rattled off the names of twelve programmers assigned to the Bunker. All were present.

"People," said Frazione, "we will get things right in this office. You're in the Air Force. There are rules we follow."

Southwark's posture stiffened, that bastard.

"I've been watching your little operation for some time,"

said Frazione, looking at me. "We've got some changes coming, and I don't need all of you to support me to make them work."

I panned the room and saw no hint of anyone prepared to chime in.

Frazione continued. "Effective on the new year, the Apps section will undergo a few changes in reporting structure."

For another twenty minutes, my intestines descended deeper as Frazione got into his monologue of office changes.

"And get a haircut, Airman Chisolm," said Frazione, as he departed our office for the Brook. "For Christ's sake, you're not a civilian."

The Systems guys were untouched. Hancock took over an all-new team, Distributed Data System, and would lead three inmates. DDS would move to an office elsewhere in the Bunker. I wasn't going with them. Instead, my new shop, the Report Services Section, was just my old shop in the same office with a new name. RSS would be led by Southwark and include me, Schmink, Chief, and a new guy with one stripe.

The new guy made his way to the Bunker with Frazione. The burly, freckle-faced newbie looked an ounce away from being overweight. His uniform was ironed but not creased. His tight curly hair was a judgment call away from being out of regulation. Everything about him was borderline.

"What'd you say you go by?" asked Chief.

"JED," said the newbie. "It's my initials."

"Where you coming from?" asked Hlavacka.

"Straight from Keesler," said JED.

"What are they thinking, sending a newbie here straight from tech school?" asked Legal.

"Maybe they wanted someone who isn't jaded," I said.

"Give it time," said Chief.

"I'll be at the Brook and Ramstein at least half the time anyhow," said Hancock.

"How the hell do you wrangle that?" asked Hlavacka.

"Control oneself or be controlled thy self," said Hancock.

"Take your goddamn control and shove it somewhere it don't shine," said Chief.

"It doesn't shine in here," I said. "So he's already done what you said to do."

"Chief, why hate?" asked Hancock. "Do something about it."

"This is the truth," added Legal. "And you, Southwark. What's your take on all this?"

Southwark, the snake, had been silent all morning.

"This is how it needs to be," he said.

"Ain't no wiggle room," said Chief, walking out of the office. "I'll be on the OPS floor if you need me."

"I'll be back later," said Woody. "I'm going to scout the new office."

"One thing's for sure," I said.

"What's that?" asked Legal.

"I'm not going to be anyone's dick sucker."

"Unfortunately, you're under a microscope," said Hancock.

"He's been under a microscope for a while," said Southwark. "Just no one's controlled him as of yet."

"What do you mean *no one*?" asked Hancock. "He's been working for me. He's done everything needed and then some, unlike you."

"I'm here, aren't I?" asked Southwark.

"*Here?*" asked Hancock. "The most anyone could say about you, Southwark, is that you're *assigned* here."

"Truth," said Legal.

Southwark didn't reply to Legal. Moral authority always rests with those who have seen combat. Even an idiot like Southwark knew this.

"Do you want to become what they've become?" asked Hancock, looking at me.

"Hey, now," said Schmink. "That's an asshole thing to say. I'm doing just fine."

"See what I mean?" asked Hancock.

"I know what you mean," I said.

"You can only go so far as you can go, right, Schmink?" asked Hancock.

"What's that supposed to mean?" asked Schmink.

"It means you end up where you end up," said Hancock. "But do *you* choose where you end up, or does someone *else* choose where you end up?"

"What say does anyone have in where they end up?" asked Schmink. "You, me, anyone—hell, even Chisolm?"

"It all depends upon what *you* say it depends upon," said Hancock.

Schmink disregarded Hancock, pulled his latest novel out of his drawer, and continued his fiction.

"I know where I stand," I said.

"Good luck in the new shop, Chisolm," said Hancock, looking at Southwark.

"He don't need luck," said Southwark. "He needs a boot up his ass."

I palmed my chest.

"That's a stupid habit, Chisolm," said Southwark. "It will get you nowhere."

"It's a habit that will get me where I need to go," I said. "Everyone is right about one thing in here."

"What's that?" asked Legal.

"This place isn't real."

"Time to *get* real," said Southwark.

"*Now* we're going to play real Air Force?" I asked. "By your definition, I can safely say that *playing* your game and *doing* the mission are not the same thing. I'll be doing the mission."

"*I'm* doing the mission," said Southwark.

"You're concerned about anything *but* the mission," I said.

"They've got targets and watch duty back there, and your only concern is my haircut? And when I show up. When I show up, I make things happen. *Important* things. When you show up, you don't do shit. But by god, your nails are within regs. I suppose I *could* play your game, but why?"

"Because that's the way this works," said Southwark. "By the way, Merry Christmas. Invest in an alarm clock for the new year."

I left for the OPS floor.

"I'm fucked," I said as I walked up to Wagner's exile. "I need a good one."

"Oh yeah?" asked Wagner. "What's up?" He put down his latest novel and reached for his container of fortune cookies. "Catch," he said, throwing a cookie my way.

I cracked it open.

"Hmmm."

"What do you got?" he asked.

"'When you see it, you will know it.'"

"'Hmmm' is right."

"Yeah, hmmm," I said. "It's a dud. This is one of those that can mean *this* or *that*. It's never right and it's never wrong."

"You might have a keeper there," said Wagner.

"Would *you* keep it? More importantly, *why* would you keep it?"

"There is no downside to this one."

"It's like the sun rising each day," I said. "It's neither right nor wrong."

"Not really. This one is different. It's *always* right, *never* wrong."

"You got a real-world example of what the hell you're even talking about?" I asked.

"Let me think."

"Take your time."

Wagner popped a cookie in his mouth and chewed for a

minute. "Here's food for thought. Priests and scientists alike share equal claim to knowledge of the universe."

"Yeah, well, what's that got to do with this?"

"Maybe that's the *it* your fortune describes?"

"That is a fairly specific *it*."

"But the fortune is open enough for interpretation that *this* it might be *the* it."

"What if it is? I mean, *this* it?" I asked.

"Neither priests nor scientists can prove or disprove the *why* of our origin. One either espouses a belief, which is neither provable nor unprovable, or one states what is observed, which is limited by what one sees. Neither is at odds with the other. Neither is inconsistent with the other."

"Complete agreement, Buddha."

"We live within one universe, yet our position within it defines our existence differently. But this isn't the strange part about it."

"Continue, enlightened one," I said, clasping my hands in prayer and doing a bow.

"Some on each side claim that the other side is dead wrong. But neither side is inconsistent with the other. In fact, they can coexist. In a way, they complement each other."

"I don't think that's what I'm asking," I said. "But I do agree with you, Wagner."

"On one side are the believers. On the other side are the observers. But neither side can show or explain how this all *started*, let alone how it will end, or what is on the other side. By *this* I mean *us*, the *universe*."

"Come back to the question," I said.

"What question?"

"The fortune. What is it trying to say?"

"I'm getting there. I mean, I am there. I'm telling you."

I sat down at a terminal, then nodded at Wagner and gestured for him to continue. When he got going like this, it was better to let him go. Kind of like Mr. Chamberlain. He just needed a friend to listen to him.

"Where was I?" Wagner asked, scratching his head. "Right. Presuming, of course, that *started* is even a possibility. If you think about it, how could anything start from nothing? There must always have been something for anything else to begin. I mean, you can't get something from nothing, can you?"

"They're trying to get something from me, alright," I said. "And that's a nice hypothetical theoretical, but I'm asking you to answer the *it* related to the real world. Today. Now. *Me.*"

"Oh, you want *that* sort of real-world example?" asked Wagner. "Well, then yes, you may be fucked."

"The *why* still isn't answered," I said. "God*damn* it. Now I'm starting to think like you. At SAC, *show* time meant accounting for results. We had to prove ourselves in order to keep the planet from being annihilated. In here, *show* time simply means *showtime.* Show up on time and be in your seats. It's all acting, yet nothing is choreographed. It's all staged, but there is never a show to see. That's all. Show up. And get a goddamn haircut."

"They want you to play ball. They want you to want twenty." *Twenty,* for those seeking it, being the number of years you had to remain on active duty to qualify for a pension.

"I'm not buying twenty."

"Maybe the mission *is* to play ball?"

"You cannot believe that," I said. "I know you don't."

"I don't," said Wagner. "But it also depends upon what *they* think is the mission."

"I was let go and now they want me back. I suppose I could play ball. But I'm pretty sure if they thought about it, they really don't *want* me to play ball. And I don't need saluting drills and a fast ability to distract from what I'm not doing to not worry about the mission or annihilation or fist fucking or cunt licking or drawing conclusions about stories I've read in books that paint pictures of places that aren't real, to be read by people who aren't in the real Air Force. God*damn*, this place is fucked up."

"Feel any better?" asked Wagner.

"This isn't helping, and that fortune only confounded it."

"It'll come to you."

"I'll be back later, sir."

"I bid you farewell and Godspeed, Mr. Chisolm."

42

"What are you doing with that?" I asked Schmink, upon my return to the office.

"What?" asked Schmink, shrugging.

"What do you mean *what*?" I asked. "Woody's *ship* what."

Hlavacka pushed back in his chair to see what was going on. JED hadn't a clue what this was all about and left the office. Legal kept at a new handheld golf game. Southwark observed, tapping his fingers on his desk.

"I'm just having a little fun," continued Schmink, reaching a pencil inside the bottle and teasing off a piece of the ship.

"What. The fuck. Are you doing?" I whispered inches from Schmink's ear.

Schmink continued to work on the ship.

"Get your goddamn hands off that bottle," I said, standing up.

"Get lost, dick," said Schmink.

I clenched the top of Schmink's chair, then leaned over, my mouth just inches again from his ear. "Get. Your. Goddamn hands off the bottle."

Schmink rested the bottle on Woody's and my desk, then held up his hands as if under arrest. I eased his chair back.

"Don't touch my chair, dick," said Schmink.

I didn't take one tenth of a second for my next thought. I headlocked Schmink, then pulled him out of his chair and wrestled him to the ground. His feet kicked and banged into his own desk. Southwark and Hlavacka jumped at me and grabbed my arms.

"Chisolm, *stand down!*" said Legal.

I didn't let go, despite having Hlavacka's fingers dug into me.

"You're *insane*, Chisolm," said Southwark.

"If you touch that again, I'll break your neck," I said into Schmink's ear.

"Let go, Chisolm," said Legal.

I let go.

Schmink twisted away from me in an alligator roll and got up. I jumped up to meet his face. Hlavacka moved between us. I looked around his head to stare down Schmink.

"You're a crazy asshole," said Schmink, defiantly pointing at me.

Books and papers were strewn about.

"Jesus Christ, Chisolm," said Hlavacka. "A little overkill?"

I straightened my gig line.

"Protects his own desk like it's Fort Knox," I said. "He had it coming. Who is he to lay his hands on someone else's property?"

"You're going to explain this to the Shirt," said Southwark.

"Explain what?" asked Legal.

"Chisolm going batshit crazy," said Southwark.

"*Then* what, Southy?" asked Legal. "Then he's thrown out of here? And you take over DiAPERS? *You?* I don't think so."

"There's your free lesson in respect, asshole," I said, looking at Schmink.

Schmink gave me a bug-eyed *I don't give a damn* stare.

"Chisolm, give it a break," Legal said.

I stood down and returned Woody's ship to his drawer.

JED returned to the office with a soda, aghast at what he saw.

"Don't worry about this, JED," said Legal. "It isn't as bad as it looks."

43

"How is your game today?" asked Hlavacka.

Chief had just arrived for the day.

"Near perfect," said Chief.

"BOHICA," said Legal.

"I'm not bending over," I said.

"Oh, you'll bend over, alright," said Hlavacka. "Get ready to squeal."

"If you all did your jobs," I said, "we wouldn't be in this mess. Where did Frazione come from, anyhow?"

If someone had come in through the pipeline, they were proven *and* competent. The pipeline ensured it because this was the means used to groom success and weed out incompetents. Short of this, every inmate still proved themselves, even if only as an imbecile. If someone were a proven imbecile, at least it had been proven. This was important. After all, how could one be unproven *and* be let loose on our war network? That would have been insane.

"He cross-trained from some admin career field," said Chief.

"Then how did we end up in this mess?" I asked. "He should have been a pushover."

"Chisolm," said Legal, "how soon you forget that when you arrived, you were airman of the goddamn century."

"Still am," I said. "Mission first."

"It took us forever to get you to settle down," said Hlavacka.

"You're confusing me not playing your game, me being on the outside, with 'settling down,'" I said.

"Uh-huh," said Chief.

"I have never wavered from my commitment to them," I added, pointing toward the Intel area.

"That is the truth," said Legal.

"How did no one giving a damn become a thing in here?" I asked. "I mean, how long has this been the standard operating procedure in this place?"

"Always been," said Legal. "Besides, this ain't a war."

There was no pressing work for me at the moment. I decided to take a hike and go see Woody's new office. He wasn't there. I headed back to Intel by way of the Battle Cab.

"You up there, Woody?" I shouted, looking up at the command room.

Woody stood up and put his hands and face to the glass window.

"I'll be right up, sir," I said.

"Grab a seat," said Woody, pointing to a chair across from him as I entered.

"No one would believe this bullshit," I said.

"Sure as heck isn't what I had in mind."

"What are you doing up here?"

"Thinking."

"I figured that. About?"

"Getting out," said Woody.

"Really?" I asked.

"But where would I go?"

"You need a plan," I said. "You got a plan?"

"That's a good question," said Woody, knocking his fists on his knees.

"All I know is this whole thing is a sham," I said, looking into the Battle Cab.

Woody looked at me, scrutinizing my sincerity. "You're pretty much right."

"Maybe it's the same phoniness everywhere," I said.

"Well, I can make anywhere work," said Woody, staring at one of the safety lights.

"You've been on the run a long time," I said. "How do you know when to stop? How does *anyone* know?"

"I suppose you can run until you die," Woody said, "and you might never know. Isn't it always better 'over there'?"

"I think you just need to know why you're doing what you're doing," I said.

"*Why?*" asked Woody.

"Yes," I said. "That appears to be the question."

44

I woke on December 28, a year to the day in country. The Bunker had gone to minimum manning for the week between holidays. I slipped on some clothes, then went for a walk in the chilly morning air. Few cars passed my village on any given day. Fewer still could be heard this morning. Low, dense clouds hovered. Silence enveloped me. Several chimneys smoked. I walked along a path at the edge of the forest. Where the path entered the forest, I stopped and turned to look back at the village.

I remained there in the cold until two villagers passed and entered the forest. I palmed my chest and returned to my apartment, where I sequestered myself until the afternoon. I lay in bed for two hours. By then I could see the sun up in a bright sky, yet I was underwater at depth without oxygen. *How long can I hold my breath? Can I make it to the surface before I sink further? Maybe my lungs will give out and the answer is out of my control.*

Rachel visited her family for Christmas, then she and I spent New Year's Eve at her place. It was my only respite of the holiday season.

On the first duty day of the year, I woke up in a strait-jacket. Now assigned to Southwark, I'd learned that one of the requirements was to arrive at the Bunker by 07:30. My body had long since regulated itself into a seven-hour sleep pattern. Of course, the pattern was predicated upon waking after the sun came up. The night before I'd tossed and turned, unsure whether my alarm would sound. I hadn't used it in months. Just in case, I'd also wound up my travel clock.

"What are your future plans?" Treadwell asked.

Treadwell and I carpooled. We used his car. We were environmentalists, plus the heater in his car worked.

"You mean about staying in?" I asked.

"I mean about your *immediate* problem," said Treadwell.

"Good question," I said. "You're sitting pretty."

"You've gotta watch it."

"I keep hearing that."

"Southwark wants to break you."

"*Why?* I'm all about the mission, dude."

"There's your problem," said Treadwell. "Their mission is you fitting in."

"What do they know about the mission?" I asked under my breath.

"Your idea and their idea don't match."

"Obviously," I said, conceding on the merits. "What's your new office all about? And how didn't I get over there?"

"We'll be babysitting. It's all legacy stuff. It doesn't even make sense that they moved me to Hancock's shop."

"Why is that?"

"I'm short, man."

"When do you think you'll be gone?"

"If I burn thirty days of leave, I'll be out of here by late February."

My heart sank. *Stiff upper lip,* Mom used to say.

"Slim odds of me finding a replacement," I said. "I can't

afford this place on my own. The exchange rate sucks. In all likelihood, I'm going back in the dorm."

"Not good."

"Right?!"

I entered my old "new" office. Schmink, Chief, and JED were present, seated, and quietly reading. Legal and Hlavacka had yet to arrive. Southwark glared at me from his seat. I sat down and glanced at my watch. It was 07:40. *I'm ahead of the game.*

"Seven thirty a.m. civilian time, so you understand it, Airman Chisolm, is when I said to be here," Southwark said, pulling out a cigarette and walking to light up in the hallway.

"Breathe that shit out there," I said. "You know I carpool with Treadwell."

The hallway was one of the few official places where you could smoke. In reality, if few people were around or cared, a smoker might light up in the office. I cared. Southwark had to exit the office proper to pollute.

"The duty day begins at oh-seven-thirty. Remember that."

"As I said, I came in with Treadwell. We—"

"Sit down, Airman Chisolm," said Southwark.

I watched the second hand move on the wall clock. The fluorescent lights hummed.

"What is our mission, sir?" I asked as I took my seat.

"Don't be a smart-ass. Showing up on time is our mission."

"The mission is back there," I said, pointing toward Intel.

"It's right here, Airman Chisolm," said Southwark, pointing at the floor.

"We're facing down annihilation every hour of every day, which means I will be here when needed at any hour of any day to support Intel, which means that I am already here, even when I'm not here, because no matter where I am, I'm going to be here when I need to be here."

"You need to follow my example."

"Does that include getting rid of the library in this office?"

Still not so much as a peep or a glance from the three others present.

"You just need to be here on time, Airman Chisolm. And you need a haircut."

"So you want me to look sharp, be sharp, shit sharp, and sharpen pencils. But why are we here?" I asked. "In *here*? What *mission*? What *work*?"

Southwark returned to his desk, looked at the clock, then lit up another cigarette as he returned to the hallway.

"I don't need to be in your shop," I said.

"I'm not letting you out of it, Chisolm. You'll be sucking my dick before I let you go anywhere else."

"We could die in minutes, yet you want me to worry about the minute I arrive on station?" I asked. "Who's crazy in this picture?"

Southwark's face slackened.

"I recommend you get a haircut, Airman Chisolm. It'll be good for morale."

"I see world peace in our future," I said.

"And take up smoking," said Southwark. "Consider it a matter of health."

"So let me understand. You want me to get in on time to ensure that I am here, regardless of how or if Intel is supported, but await a direct hit while looking pretty?"

"I'll have you in for an Article 15, Chisolm. And if that doesn't do it, I'll have you dishonorably discharged for insubordination!"

An Article 15 was nonjudicial punishment, as opposed to a full-blown court-martial, which took time and effort. With an Article 15, a commander had discretion to mete out punishment of extra duty or forfeiture of pay to members who weren't buying it—I mean, conforming.

I would not allow myself to be deposed from my place in

this war at the hands of anyone who hadn't actually killed me. I hadn't threaded the string of commitments in my life that had led me to this place, only to be threatened with fear and force that I should wear some scarlet letter of not conforming, when this nonconformance was the outline drawn as one of conformance.

"Alright," I said. "I'll go get that haircut right now, if only to get out of the smoke you're blowing up everyone's ass."

"Get it cut on your own time."

"My hair grows on duty hours. I'll cut it on duty hours."

"I thought you said you carpooled in with Treadwell?"

"Of course, I did," I said. "I'm taking the second bus back to the Brook. I'll be leaving in fifteen minutes."

"How are you going to get back up here?"

"Good question," I said. "But I am getting a haircut."

"Goddamn it, Chisolm. Then go. But find a way back up here. Son of a bitch."

"We don't need the Russians to annihilate us," I said. "We're doing just fine by ourselves."

I took the second morning bus back to the Brook.

Helmut acted the part of a barber on the Brook. I say "acted" because he had the shears and wore the uniform of a barber, though he had few skills of the trade. The story went that Helmut had suffered a mild stroke some years earlier. Because of that, he stood a bit hunched over while cutting hair. He also tilted to his left side. One might have mistaken Helmut for the offspring of Quasimodo and Peter Lorre. Huffing and puffing all over your neck, he'd do his work. Once the cutting began, half the time the shears wouldn't contact hair. None of this bothered me too much.

Two weeks into my arrival in country, I'd gone to Helmut. As I closed my eyes in therapy at the thought of home, the shears went full throttle. When the cutting stopped, Helmut had finished me. I came out balder in some spots and still bushy in others.

I went back to Helmut four weeks after that first pruning. It would have been two weeks, but I needed the extra time for the shaved-off patches to grow back. I made certain that I conveyed my intentions clearly. I spoke American to him—all English, but louder and slower, so he couldn't misunderstand me. He huffed and pursed his lips, then nodded in agreement.

"Ja, Ja."

He did it again. After that, I figured the closest I'd ever come again to seeing a haircut from that guy would be on an inmate. True, I had gotten a few haircuts here and there when I was at Ramstein. But eventually I stopped getting them altogether. I learned to use a dollop of hair gel to "conform" my hair in place. Of course, I had to be careful not to bump my head against anything. It also helped that I wore headgear one full size too big. Occasionally the gel surrendered its grip and my hair escaped. But I heeded Rachel's good advice about the RAF, conformity of my hair be damned.

I arrived with no illusions this third time. *It's artistry. That's all it is.* Helmut butchered me again.

Since I was on the Brook, I stopped in the education office to pick up my books for the next term, connecting briefly with Mr. Chamberlain. Following that, I hitched a ride to my apartment.

Over the next few days, I drove myself to the Bunker. I needed the time to think. On Friday morning, I needed to see Wagner.

"If bullets aren't flying, they resort to the irrelevant," I said.

Wagner joined me at the operations desk.

"Those mousers have a better chance of survival than we do in here," I said.

"Different death for them, is all," said Wagner.

"You know how people see their entire lives flash in front of them before dying?"

"How would anyone know that for sure?" asked Wagner. "Even if it happens before they die, they're dead."

"Well, someone's obviously been there and back for us to even hear about it, right?"

"So then are they dead or not?" asked Wagner. "How would anyone know what the dead see when they're dead? You can't. You're dead."

"Whatever you want to call it," I said, "I think I just had that this morning."

"That's only if you're dying, though, right?" asked Wagner.

"Yeah, well I saw my life flash before me and dwindle to nothingness in a fraction of a second, but it actually took about ten minutes."

"Understand that what Southwark sees is from one hundred feet up. You and I are talking about something at a hundred thousand feet. He won't see what you see, but you can see what he sees."

"What is he seeing?" I asked.

"He's a lifer. He sees you as a possible roadblock to his retirement."

"Why would I even end up in his shop if I'm an obstacle?"

"Rumor has it that Hancock outmaneuvered him for DDS. You were not moving because of AardVark. And DiAPERS."

"How did I not hear any of this?"

"All I *do* out here is *hear*," said Wagner. "Everyone comes out here for privacy. But I'm always here. I don't necessarily want to hear, but I hear."

"How can you possibly hear with all the noise in here?" I asked.

"Everything echoes between the two aux CPU boxes, right to my chair. It's a quirk. I discovered it after I set up my office."

"Office?" I asked. "Exile. So, now you tell me that you hear everything?"

"Pretty much whatever anyone says out here."

"I think I'd hate that," I said.

"It isn't like I want to hear. I don't. But if everyone knew I *could* hear, they'd force me to move. I can keep my mouth shut. I don't want to move."

"At least you are proven reliable," I said. "What's your count?"

"One-oh-six."

"I'll be damned. And they worry about my haircut."

"That's their worry."

"How's this going to end, you think?"

"Define *this*."

"Here. Me. This predicament," I said. "I'm going to need some guidance."

"Hold please."

Wagner retrieved a fortune cookie and threw it to me.

"What are we told?" asked Wagner.

I cracked it open. "'Only half the world can say you are upside down.'"

"I like it, but it wouldn't make my top nine."

"I think the whole world might think this joint is upside down."

"Roger that," said Wagner.

"Who will ever know that we've been here?" I asked.

"No one's got the slightest."

"I want to go home."

I spent the weekend at Rachel's apartment, where she tried in vain to repair what she could of my hair.

45

January 17th, 1988

Dad,

   I hope you are well.
   ~~They are trying to break me.~~
   ~~No one knows what they're doing. No~~
~~one cares about being annihilated.~~
   *You've asked me several times about
my job.* ~~I spend a good amount of time~~
~~avoiding assholes who think buying cuckoo~~
~~clocks or getting wasted on their drink or~~
~~drug of choice is our mission. The rest of~~
~~the time,~~ *I write programs and reports;* ~~the~~
~~output of which may very well go into a~~
~~black hole, for all I know. Sure as shit the~~
~~data can't be verified as accurate.~~
   ~~We're in a goddamn war, but there is~~
~~no fight. Winning is how well we hunker~~
~~down for the count inside this bitch. From~~
~~what I can see, we don't need to launch~~

~~anything.~~ We don't get much sun and it's very cold here.

~~People leave the Bunker, never to be heard from again. This isn't SAC HQ. This isn't the real Air Force. This isn't America.~~ I miss home.

~~We don't need the Russians to kill us. We're killing ourselves.~~ I'm holding my own.

Roy

46

"I hope your wills are in order," said Legal.

"There go the doors," said Schmink.

This was our turn to test the Russians.

"Library?" asked Legal.

"Check," said Hlavacka.

"C-rats?"

"Check."

"Bunks?"

"Check."

Our C-rats would last one week. The bunks were our cots with wool covers, set up in sleeping quarters on the lowest-level deck in the Bunker.

"L-rats?"

"Double check."

"Get ready to kiss your ass goodbye, boys," said Legal. "It's showtime."

"We're going to need medevac on standby for Ginger," said Sosa.

"Chisolm, you still dating that lanky German?" asked Chief.

"Rachel? Yes."

"Deploy B-rats," said Chief.

"B-rats?" asked Legal.

"Blue ball rats. For Chisolm."

"Don't worry about me," I said. "I'm taken care of, coming and going."

"Lucky bastard," said Hlavacka.

"Destiny, brother," I said.

"Don't bend over," said Chief. "Or at least cover your ass around Chisolm."

"I don't think it's me you need to worry about," I said, widening my eyes as I looked at Chief.

The commotion stopped for a second, then picked up again.

"Don't look at me," said Sosa.

No one looked at Sosa.

"I'm not the one who gets blue balls," said Schmink.

"Because you climb on that donkey back there?" I asked.

"Asshole," said Schmink.

"Drink up, Schmink. You're sixth on Ginger duty tomorrow," Hlavacka said.

The programmers broke out in hysterics.

"Hlavacka, please deploy L-rat containment device Tango," Legal advised.

"Tango device deployed."

"One swig each, no bogarting."

Our war games would be one of the rare moments when all inmates played military, even if it included tequila, whiskey, vodka, and rum rations.

"One swig. Pass left. Commence firing," Hlavacka said, seconding orders from Legal.

"You think it's a little early for a drink?" I asked.

"Your stomach doesn't know what time it is," Schmink said. "Pass it here."

"I said to the left," directed Legal. "Proper order, sir."

"Sir, yes sir," said Schmink.

"How do you think this will end?" I asked rhetorically.

"The usual," said Hlavacka. "Everyone dies."

"If anything like '83, we just might end up dead," said Chief. "Otherwise, with two weeks of leave for me."

"What *exactly* happened in '83?" I asked, having heard only snippets of the story.

"Able Archer," said Legal. "Closest we came to Cuba '62, and we were only playing a game."

"I haven't heard much about it," I said.

"No one has," said Hlavacka. "At least not civilians. You think they want to panic everyone?"

"How bad was it?" I asked.

"We were close," said Hlavacka. "*Real* close."

"Think about our buildup," said Legal. "Then combine that with the exercise. Hell, everyone knows how suspicious and paranoid the Russians are."

"What do they expect when we play with fire?" I asked.

"Exactly," said Legal. "Hell, you're part of this buildup, Chisolm."

"This ain't on me," I said.

"In a way, it *is* on you," said Legal. "It's on all of us."

"How do you figure?" I asked.

"Able Archer was believed to be cover for a preemptive nuclear strike. I understand it took one sane, midlevel Russian officer to save everyone's ass. He recognized Able Archer for what it was, a game."

"Logic would dictate that when either of us holds a war game, we are within inches of the real thing," I said.

"Logic would dictate, yes," said Legal.

"Makes you wonder," said Chief.

"Wonder what?" asked Hlavacka.

"There was no WintEx last year," said Chief. "They canceled it, but I haven't heard a reason why. Has anyone?"

"Good question," said Legal. "You know, they never did tell us."

"Something is going on," said Hlavacka.

"You were lucky last year, Chisolm," said Chief. "Enjoy your first official one."

"Canceled on our side only," said Hlavacka. "Ivan had two of his own last year."

"What is the usual game plan?" I asked. "We're not so involved in here, or are we?"

"Some more than others," said Legal. "Meaning, *you* more. You'll get the hang of it. Just keep DiAPERS going."

"I get all that, but where does the game take us?" I asked. "How is this played out?"

"You can observe from the top floor of the Battle Cab," said Chief.

"It's all scripted," said Legal. "Red team and Blue team go to war. We scramble equipment. Things happen, but only up to the point of shooting. Hopefully."

"Then?"

"Same outcome every time. During the first two days we get civil unrest. Agitation grows from the Red team. They get belligerent."

"Then?" I asked.

"We prove that we have the balls to launch an all-out nuclear strike."

"How do we prove that?" I asked.

"We know that Ivan is watching us at all times," said Legal. "Just like Ivan knows that we are always watching him. Seems stupid, or insane, but staring without blinking keeps either of us from falling off the knife's edge."

"How does that prove that we've got the balls for this?" I asked.

"We observe the Russians in their exercises. They watch us in our exercises," said Legal. "And because we know that Ivan is watching, we *must* launch—at least *exercise* launch. Anything short of that is weakness. We can't convey weakness. Ivan sure as hell doesn't convey weakness. If we launch, we win. But in any *real* win, we would lose. Does that make sense?"

"In a convoluted way, yes," I said. "This seems to be a universal truth."

"If we don't launch first, we lose. Then again, if we launch first, we'll still lose because the Russians will retaliate. Basically, it's a win *and* a loss. But we would win on the technicality of being first, so we win by first annihilating everyone, everywhere."

"This war is winnable," I said. "But with no one and nothing left afterward to make that judgment, it would be unprovable."

"Right," said Legal.

"So, short of actual rocket launches," I said, "we need to do something to prove our will to fight and win. Our way of life depends upon our willingness to kill everyone. If we aren't willing to kill everyone, we lose?"

"Correct," said Legal. "Our war games must end with the same outcome every time—absolute decimation. We just need to *prove* that we're going to do it if Ivan rears his ugly head. There is no need for an actual launch. That would be stupid."

"So basically, if we're annihilated, it's my fault?" I asked.

"Correct," said Legal. "Survival is all up to you, Chisolm."

I did twelve-hour shifts for one week. Woody worked the opposite shift helping me support DiAPERS and the reports I had written. The war ended on the seventh day. Everyone was incinerated.

"You were right," I said to Wagner, standing outside his exile on the final game day.

"I'm usually right," he said.

"I mean about *will*. Survival amounts to a game of *will*."

"Yes, everything boils down to will. Or annihilation."

"How utterly simple," I said.

"Back home, everyone lives under it every day, and they don't so much as speak a word of it, what with the worry about making it to dinner on time."

"If you knew you could die in under thirty minutes, what would you wait for?" I asked.

"Nothing, obviously."

"Yes, you'd wait for nothing," I said. "Nothing means everything."

47

"Schmink, I need five bullets," said Southwark. "And don't bullshit me."

After the war game ended, the inmates returned to their most pervasive Bunker spectacle—jockeying to stay out of position. But unlike speculating, card playing, R & R, and every other distraction, this would be undertaken with keen focus.

"I got it. I got it," said Schmink.

Southwark returned to his seat. "I don't want to have to do a lot of writing, either."

"Schmink is writing his own review?" I asked. "What the hell is he going to say?"

"Shut up. I've got plenty."

"You mean the change requests you buried?" I asked. "That's all you can go with."

"You're going to need more than just being here," said Chief.

"Thank you," I replied.

"I don't need your help, Chief," said Southwark.

"Just don't use my work for your bullets," I said. "In fact, I should probably review what he says, just to make sure."

"You ain't reading shit, Chisolm," said Schmink. "I'll make sure of that."

Getting a stellar annual review had proved easy. From the merits of an inmate's work alone? Forget it. Except under Hancock, one would be hard-pressed to find gradation between inmates based upon work completed. If you were *in*, and your productivity wasn't passable by objective measure, you could still vie for top marks on your annual review. But if you were *out*, no matter how exemplary your undertakings, you could expect a tougher slog to reach those top marks.

A week later, the results were in.

"All fives and two fours, boys," said Schmink.

"For *what*?" I asked.

"He's playing ball, Chisolm," said Southwark.

This outcome raised not so much as an eyebrow. When the new RSS office was formed, Schmink's only project followed him, though I never saw him working the hours necessary to complete it.

Chief got up and stood about a foot away and to the side of Schmink.

"Alright," Chief said. "You've had eons to get this project done. What's the *real* status?"

Schmink looked up at Chief and blinked his eyes rapidly, then pulled out a folder with papers inside.

"I've got the shell of four routines written," Schmink said, folding his arms and looking away. "Two more any day now."

"Look at me when I talk to you," said Chief.

"I'm not looking at your dick, asshole. I said I'll be done any day now."

"'Any day now' is the same status for months," said Chief. "What gives?"

"Nothing gives. I'm working on it."

"Don't try to bullshit a bullshitter," said Chief. "This better not fall on me."

"Yeah, well, it'll get done soon."

"How long is that?" asked Southwark. "You've been saying *days*. I'll look like an idiot if I tell that to Intel one more time."

Establishment of a given software delivery date was never driven by the programmers, but rather by the Intel teams. The importance of managing a delivery date always had two sides, the way the inmates saw it—what was desired by Intel and what could be obfuscated, aggressively renegotiated, and postponed ad infinitum by the inmates. At least until Intel needed a project to produce results that our collective lives might depend upon or, as was the case here, for support in negotiating an international treaty.

By this measure, Schmink's superb performance in dodging his side of the delivery date was medal worthy.

"I just need a little more time. That's all."

Southwark clenched his fist and hit his desk.

"Chisolm, why don't you go with me to talk to the major?" asked Chief.

"*Me?* That's Schmink's baby," I said. "Besides, why are you even worried, Chief? He works for Southwark."

"For reporting, yes, he's under Southwark," said Chief. "But I'm still the lead for this project. That didn't change."

The object of this game was simple. Stay away from anything requiring complex or lengthy analysis. The snag was that an inmate ended up becoming dispensable. So, to compensate, the more dispensable you became, the more important it was for you to ally yourself with the group. This spectacle was one of my favorite pastimes—watching people shirk responsibility, then kiss ass to remain on the inside. There was only one rule: you had to play to win.

Because of Schmink's dereliction, Southwark and Chief were forced to dance their way to a two-month reprieve.

"It's day one of February, Schmink," said Southwark. "I got you your two months to finish it."

From early on, I learned the meaning and cost of commitment. I also learned the value and expense of one's word. I harbored no illusions that holding tight to commitments and words could sometimes corner you to do something you might not wish to do. One had to be cautious, depending upon where you wanted to stand. Then again, how often do you really have a choice in the matter?

A few years after Sergeant Clegg moved away, so did my family. Dad's career took us to Chicago. There were fields everywhere around my new neighborhood. This was where Frank, Dean, and I lived an American life. We had meaning. We knew no limits to discovering all we could. We bivouacked in backyards, pissed off bridges, commandeered water-pressure fire extinguishers for our firefights, and even collected refundable glass Coke bottles for hamburger money. We found no boundaries.

We had countless ways to pass time. One of them was to jump the fence into a nearby summer camp and use the facilities out of season. To test our sea legs one day, the three of us pulled canoes down from a stack stored near a small lake. Frank took one, while Dean and I shared another. The canoes were not in great shape to begin with, and as Dean and I launched from shore, ours began taking on water. It wasn't a whole lot, so we kept on rowing.

"Captain, we're sinking," I said.

"She's blown a hole there, matey," said Dean.

"I am not getting wet, damn it. *Row!*"

"I'm rowing, goddamn it!"

"She's going under!"

"Dive, dive, dive!"

"Man overboard!"

We'd almost made it back to shore when a rust spot broke open and she went under. We bailed out.

We survived by means of our own design. In all things,

we knew, our freedom would last only so far as we made the choice. Most, I knew, had no choice.

Mr. Argent lived in a new housing development, which was a gold mine for us. The housing development was going up next to our neighborhood. The residents must have hated us archaeologists coming into their area, but we had discoveries to make.

"This one looks perfect," Frank said. "Still no doors and windows."

We'd arrived at a house about halfway complete.

"We got an hour before dark," said Dean. "I gotta be home then or my old man will kick my ass."

"Your dad is a hard-ass," I said.

"I mean seriously, he will kick me *in the ass*. Just watch the time, man."

Upon entry, Frank found a ladder for us to make our way to the second floor. Ladders were always the first thing Frank scouted for at construction sites. He was our ladder man. As required, we took the liberty to uncover finds as we worked our way through the place.

"My aunt had plastic on her furniture," said Frank.

"What for?" I asked.

"To make it last."

"Must have been uncomfortable as shit," said Dean.

"It is, or at least it was. She had one couch all her life."

"How do you even know that, man?" I asked.

"As far as I could tell, anyhow," said Frank. "Old-fashioned as shit but looked new."

"Why the hell would she cover it in plastic?" asked Dean.

"I told you," said Frank. "To make it last. And if she let you sit on it, you had to stay still. Only then, your skin stuck to it."

"How stupid, man," said Dean.

"Who got it after her?" I asked.

"Trash dump."

"What the hell?" asked Dean.

"No one wanted it?" I asked.

"Dad said she took care of it for us to have one day," said Frank. "Hell, I wanted to use it for a trampoline."

"Fucking waste, man," said Dean.

"Big fucking waste, man," said Frank.

"How stupid," I said. "She protected it for you, and you threw it away?"

We climbed to the second floor, all the while hunting for anything of interest. I picked up a sawed-off end of a two-by-four and ejected it out one of the windows.

We bullshitted another minute.

"Shhh. Footsteps," Frank whispered.

Thinking it could be the cops, we froze for a second.

"Who hit my house?" asked a voice downstairs.

"Take a look," I whispered to Frank.

Frank edged slowly to the opening and looked down, then he walked around with an Oompa Loompa gait.

"Sorry, sir," said Frank. "We didn't mean to hit your house."

"You kids get down here."

Frank yanked up the ladder.

"I said you kids! Get down here."

"You're not very polite, sir," said Dean. "Ask us *please*, and we might."

We could trace the sound of the man's footsteps all around the first floor.

"Me me me me me! La la la la la!" sang Frank. He then began singing in a funky foreign language. His parents had immigrated from somewhere in Europe, which gave him an air of sophistication.

"Well done, kind sir," said Dean of Frank's singing.

"Weow, weow, weow." I added the compulsory police siren.

"That's it. That's *it*, you delinquents. I'm calling the cops."

Once we figured out how to pull someone's chain, we did it

enough to annoy them, but we'd stop short of boring ourselves. That usually didn't take long. Our interests evolved constantly.

The man left the building and we watched him enter his house. Then Frank dropped the ladder and we ran for it. Running past the man's mailbox, under threat of being captured by the enemy, time slowed. I read the name on the mailbox: Leonard Argent.

On the inside, Mr. Argent believed he had protection. But nothing was further from the truth. From the outside, any onslaught could be levied.

When I've run a gauntlet, I usually come out the other side, and I'm not always sure how I made it. That happened to me one early February morning en route to the Bunker.

It was three weeks after WintEx, and I had spent the night at Ramstein, temporary billeting after a late-evening class. On the occasions when I did this, my typical morning commute was sixty minutes from Ramstein to the Bunker. For some reason this day, I'd zoned out thinking the drive had taken me thirty minutes. It took ninety minutes.

I entered the office.

"Can I ask everyone to leave?" Southwark asked.

"Time to play hangman," said Burns.

I remained standing until the inmates left, with Hlavacka closing the door behind him as I slid into my chair.

"Why are you late, Airman Chisolm?"

"My gig line is perfect."

"What? I'm not talking about your gig line."

"But it's perfect," I said. "Just look at it."

"I'll be the judge of that. I'm the one who has to look at it."

"And so, you see it is perfect."

"You make no sense, Airman Chisolm."

"I'm in line where I need to be in line."

Even in apparent chaos and anarchy, I found order and meaning. I palmed my chest.

"Why are you late?"

"I'm trying to protect us."

"That's no answer."

"It is *the* answer."

"I want you in here tomorrow in full dress."

"What did—"

"That's all. You can continue your work now."

"Can we—"

"I said that's all."

48

"What's your guess?" I asked, milling about the OPS floor.

"No clue," said Sosa. "Maybe a promotion."

"You think?"

"Could even be that Article 15 he's been hanging over your head. He's probably talking to the orderly room. Why else would he kick everyone out?"

"None of this is real," I said.

"They've given you enough rope to hang yourself."

"These assholes do nothing."

"Except they play ball," said Sosa.

"I'm not touching their ball," I said.

"They might like it if you did."

"You know what I mean, goddamn it. Can you straighten up for just this once?"

"Look, they know how fast you can write programs. They *need* you."

"What time is it?" I asked, cutting off further conversation.

The wall clock stood a few feet away. The manufacturer imprint read Chicago Lighthouse for the Blind.

A tool designed to do one thing, made by people who can't use it to do that very one thing.

"This whole joint is nothing more than blind obedience," I said, thinking aloud.

"It's a wake-up call," added Sosa.

"Look what it's done to Wagner over there."

"Yeah," yelled Sosa. "Hey, Wagner, what time is it?"

"Time for you to do more masturbation drills, you dick," shouted Wagner from his exile.

"Don't forget to log another one in ten," said Sosa.

"He doesn't need that," I said. "Aren't you the type who's supposed to have feelings?"

"Let me go check the door." Sosa disappeared in the direction of the office, then returned to the OPS floor. "Open!" He gestured with his head for me to follow him. "What are you going to do?" he asked.

"I get that question a lot," I said. "Or maybe it's just in my head a lot."

We entered the office. Others trickled back in over the next half hour.

"Why don't you lay off the guy?" Sosa interjected, breaking the silence. "You're in a catch-22."

"I'm not in anything," said Southwark.

"Southy's from the real Air Force," said Sosa. "Uptight in the worst way."

"The only one in here from the real anything is Legal," I said. "And I've personally only known two people from the real anything."

"And who's that?" asked Sosa.

"Well, one of them was a neighbor of mine when I was a kid," I said. "A Vietnam vet."

"I remember you mentioning that," said Legal. "What's the story?"

"I don't think he did well over there."

"Why so?"

"Soon after he got back, he built a fortified perimeter around his backyard. Conducted watch detail for an entire summer, waiting for Charlie to show up. I did supply runs for him."

"You did *what*?" asked Legal, turning his chair to look me square in the eye.

I hesitated.

"He didn't ask me to do it," I said. "I just tried to help him."

"What exactly did you do?"

"I kept him supplied with water. Sometimes I brought him a sandwich. I'd squirrel away food and anything I could for him. I was five years old. That's all I *could* do."

"You know anything about him?" asked Legal. "What he did over there?"

"Not exactly, but he left me a note one day."

"What did it say?"

"Hang on," I said. "I kept it. I've got it right here."

In my desk drawer there was a box holding my military awards, important pictures, and a few personal effects. I glanced back to see Legal sitting stoically.

"What's up with the canteen?" asked Southwark, laughing. "Like *you* know combat, Chisolm. Ha!"

"It's something important to me, is all."

I held my canteen with a firm grip of memory.

"Chisolm is G.I. Joe," said Schmink. "Who'd have thunk?"

A round of laughter filled the office.

"I've kept the note all this time, inside my canteen, from Sergeant Clegg."

"So read it," directed Legal, in a serious tone.

Room chatter stopped.

"'Bravo Company, 1st Battalion, 26th Marine Regiment—17

March 1968—whoever finds this, to my last round, I never gave up. Staff Sergeant Clegg.'"

"What did you just say, Roy?" asked Legal.

I gulped.

"'Bravo Company, 1st Battalion, 26th Marine Regiment—17 March 1968—'"

"Stop," said Legal.

I awaited his next directive.

"That platoon was in Khe Sanh during the Tet Offensive," said Legal. "They had the hell kicked out of them day and night for over two months."

I awaited Legal's next order.

"Why did he give you that note?" asked Legal.

"I'm not sure. On the last day I saw him, before his family moved away, he left it attached to my canteen at our resupply point in my backyard. Within a day, he was gone for good."

"And you supplied him that summer?" asked Legal.

"I mean, with what I could—water, sandwiches."

"You know why Khe Sanh survived?" asked Legal.

I waited for Legal's enlightenment. He looked at the floor for a slow minute, opening and closing his fists a few times. The others attempted hushed discussion of lighter topics.

"There you go, Chisolm, playing G.I. Joe," said Southwark.

"They survived because of supply runs," said Legal, snapping out of his trance.

Discussion once again ceased.

"They couldn't land with all the flak flying," Legal continued, "so they flew in low and pushed supplies out the back on parachutes. Those Marines never gave up. The supply drops were made under heavy fire to keep the Marines alive."

Legal pushed back in his chair, stood up, and approached Southwark.

"Stand up," commanded Legal.

Southwark hesitated, then stood. He backed as far as possible against his desk, to the point of tilting backward. Legal moved in the same motion toward Southwark.

"What's going on with Chisolm?" Legal whispered, clenching his teeth. His jawbone protruded from the side of his face each time he clamped hard.

"You see what's going on around here," said Southwark. "He doesn't listen for shit."

"And you *do* listen for shit?"

Southwark struggled to clear his throat. "You gotta play by the rules, man, right?" he asked.

"What rules? *Your* rules?"

"Come on, Legal. This isn't—"

"Here's how this plays out, because you *do* listen for shit, right?"

"You're not in my chain—"

Legal made a gun finger and slowly poked it up under Southwark's jaw. "Shhh. I just asked you something, you maggot fuck."

Southwark breathed haltingly.

"You do anything to Chisolm, and I slip all seven inches of Betsy into your back. Then I knock out your teeth so the only thing you'll be left fucking after that is my dick in your mouth. There's your *real* Air Force, you son of a bitch."

Betsy was the bowie knife that Legal kept strapped to his right boot.

Southwark's eyes bugged out. He kept his mouth shut. Legal poked his gun finger deeper, tilting Southwark's head back another two inches.

"I don't give a fuck what chain you're in," said Legal. "You fix this or I fix you, fuckface."

49

"Airman Chisolm reporting," I said, entering the office, rendering a salute at attention. This was the next morning, and I was on time.

Legal got up and peered at me, looked at Southwark, then back at me. He sat down again without a word.

"Get lost, Chisolm," said Southwark.

"I'm here and I'm dressed and pressed," I said.

"You can give it a rest now, Roy," said Legal.

"You really *are* in the military," said Woody.

"Yeah, like in the reserves," said Chief. "Still no haircut."

"And you can give it a rest too, Chief," added Legal. "Unless you got something to take up with me."

Chief got up to leave.

"Well, *do* you?" asked Legal.

"Not at this time," said Chief. "If you need me, you know where to find me, boys."

"Good, then," said Legal. "We're all one big happy family."

I looked at Hlavacka, who gave me a nod, and I left for the Intel floor. In the Bunker, it was only a question of timing as to when one might need to prove something. I could prove my bearing from here to kingdom come. The needs of the moment required the inmates seeing that I could play ball, as well as all the other things.

The following week during our staff meeting, Frazione conveyed that few replacements would be in any time soon. Unfortunately, this loosened up dorm space. In preparation for departure, Treadwell moved into temporary lodgings on the first of March—the unintended consequence of which was that I was forced out of the apartment. By mid-March, I had returned our government furniture and moved back to the dorm. The same day I moved in, Treadwell took a train to Frankfurt, where he spent two nights before flying home on Saint Patrick's Day. I never heard from him again.

Since several holes were still unfilled, I landed a room in the dorm to myself. Sometimes a seemingly insignificant victory can be a sufficient win—in this case, I at least had a personal retreat. I would be a ghost in the dorm, as I'd now spend most of my time at Rachel's place.

A pastime for dorm insiders was coining new words, such as *quitcherbitchin*. New words were used to delineate the insiders from the outsiders. If you were an outsider, even if you spoke an insider word, you were an outsider, because everyone knew where you stood. The outsiders pretty much stuck with normal English anyhow. But if an insider used normal English, the insider just looked stupid, or was very likely drunk. New words were just another part of who bought it first, and with the most commitment. But no matter the words used, they were just another means to define those on the inside and those on the outside.

In the dorm, the scales of victory over confinement in the Bunker were, of course, measurable and stratified according to the number of novels read, who beat AC in a wrestling match, or even the precedence and proper order for banging Ginger.

These delineations had to be made. Inmates needed to know where they stood.

Sosa was due to leave soon, with orders in hand to someplace warm. His residence was located on the first floor, where it had always been. Though his rank granted him access to the Q, he'd elected to remain on the Brook in his own one-bunk room. Sosa pretty much kept to himself, never venturing to the third floor. Best I could tell, he didn't particularly care one way or another whether he fit in, but he was widely known to be on some super-hyperpersonality-averaging drugs.

The last weekend in March began as weekends always had—binge drinking, stereo wars, open doors, and gyrations into the night. However, for the sake of variety, one of the third-floor residents hatched a plan. It was his weekend to hold the master keys to the dorm in the event of emergency. This wasn't unusual. What was unusual was entrusting such responsibility to proven derelicts. Why he came up with this "plan," I didn't ask. I wasn't part of it. I had no interest in hearing it. And I wouldn't have if not for the third floor momentarily falling silent as I walked to the latrine. I couldn't help but overhear the plans being laid by the perpetrator, because his door was wide open when I passed.

The chief planner would unlock Sosa's door and thrust it open, a second accomplice would rush in to turn on the lights, and a third agent would snap a Polaroid picture. Of what, no one was sure. But Sosa was too secretive. He had to be up to something—jerking off most likely, the three of them reasoned.

What were the odds of such success? I mean, how would anyone know someone else's schedule for jerking off, if they didn't themselves know the jerkoff—and his schedule—to begin with? I didn't believe this was a viable plan, let alone anything anyone would act on. I returned to my room. By Monday, those odds were known.

At the moment of flash, Sosa had been under Curly, taking it doggy style. Sosa ended his charade and boasted soon
afterward that his assignment to the Bunker had given him
freedom he'd never known. Curly never admitted to anything
but being drunk and not remembering it. You could do almost
anything on an assignment to the Bunker. No one back home
would ever know a goddamn thing.

The Polaroid made its way to the Shirt. Damn those spies
and their callous disregard for our need to keep holes filled.
Without a photograph, it was plausible deniability. Only an
idiot would have created such evidence in the face of our staffing needs. Such idiots would never be cut loose from filled bil-
lets. But a proven homosexual? For this there would be zero
tolerance, holes be damned.

At an inquiry about Sosa's background, and to weed out
anyone else closeted, a new discovery surfaced. Turned out
Sosa's late-night calls to the Bunker for "software problems"
were really a ruse for him and Curly to meet up for mutual
blow-job and jerk-off sessions behind the servers.

Sosa had reenlisted six months prior but found himself
booted for the convenience of the government. The "convenience" method was a catchall to use on anyone if no other
military law was broken. It was also one of the easiest ways to
do the least amount of harm to someone who may have pre-
viously played ball. Sosa wanted to remain on active duty and
loved the military, but there was nothing he could pull out of
his ass to satisfy the service. He never returned to the Bunker.

First-term airmen often received the benefit of the doubt
for transgressions, whether by correctional custody or Article
15. But in Curly's case there was no attempt to re-blue him.
He too was immediately relieved of duty and never returned
to the Bunker. To the Air Force, the problem wasn't a pen-
chant for ass, but rather the choice of ass. Had Sosa or Curly
gone with a whore, no problem. Choose sloppy seconds from

Ginger? You're one of the boys! But introduce another dick into the equation and it was heresy.

"They should've just put a chair behind their door," Burns said.

Though Burns was due to relieve Legal at some point, he usually took up residence in the DDS office. Legal passed along information when they both routinely met on the OPS floor. Otherwise, Burns maintained office-visitation rights. He was in the RSS office this morning.

"They should've just not been sucking dick," Southwark replied.

"You know what's funny is that they managed such a good picture," Burns said.

"Has anyone *not* seen the Polaroid?" I asked.

"I've got a copy right here," Southwark said.

"Holy fuck, someone made copies?"

"Now that you mention it, how *did* you get a copy?" Burns asked, looking at Southwark.

Southwark retreated to his newspaper.

"I'm fifteen minutes late and you want to bust me," I said. "Yet you assholes make copies of evidence used to oust two people and nothing happens to you?"

"It ain't like people don't know," said Burns, shrugging. "Everyone knows by now."

I looked at Southwark. He kept his nose in the newspaper.

"Ain't that the shit," I said. "No one is busted for Ginger in the Battle Cab, but mutual blow-job sessions behind the servers are a no-no."

"You know what's seriously fucked up is two dudes caught going at it," said Schmink.

"We've established this point of fact, Schmink," said Hlavacka.

"The Nepa Hut had shit like that," Burns said, with his two-packs-a-day laugh.

"Nepa Hut?" asked Hlavacka.

"In the Philippines, a strip club where I used to go when I was stationed there," Burns said.

"So, you're into dudes too?" asked Schmink.

"No, you idiot," said Burns. "I said it was a strip club. *Women.* But with weird shit all the same. Like this Pinoy slut who could squat and pick up a stack of silver dollars with her pussy."

"Are you serious?" I asked.

Those present looked at me and laughed at my apparent lack of world knowledge.

"Yeah, and once she grabbed a bunch, the MC asked for change back."

"*And?*" I asked.

"She could squeeze out change on command," said Burns. "That bitch had the tightest cunt."

Despite the very real fear that Air Force HQ might permanently cut slots, there was no other choice. Sosa and Curly had to go. In the Bunker, you had to know what hole you fit into. Or at least barricade your door. Get it wrong, you were gone.

50

April 10th, 1988

Roy,

I haven't heard from you in a while. Your last letter left me a little concerned.

I've written for the past three months. I wasn't sure that you've been getting my letters, so I contacted the USO. They told me to keep writing. As best they can tell, my letters ought to be getting through.

I understand that you write computer programs and such. I also get that it must get quite cold over there. You must be neck deep at work.

Just let me know how you're doing.

I say my prayers for you.

Dad

51

Dad kept writing. I kept reading. I stopped writing. I saved every one of Dad's letters. How could I say—in the most respectful of terms, of course—that I did not choose to pursue the accoutrements of American life. I did not seek to control sole ownership of even one dollar in a trust fund, not that this would have been offered, let alone existed. No, I sought to understand *why*.

I didn't want to find what I found. I'd tried to reach for a hold on to what once was. I resented the system that taught the inmates to do what they did. The reduction to derived reality, further narrowed to a tunnel vision squeezed into place by two hundred tons of pressure per square inch.

These lunatics were pursuing pursuits entirely unrelated to survival, their freedom of expression distracted to weigh whether an inmate should or should not defend as freedom some image of a hot blonde bitch being fist-fucked. Freedom of thought constrained to what was discussable the morning after an evening of dramatic portrayals of life lived vicariously through their situation comedy of choice, itself invented by the perverted greed of someone else looking to make millions off a distracted mind. No sir. Not me.

I peeled back the cleverly manufactured beliefs of freedom, like peeling an onion two inches from my eyes. I cried from it. I hadn't dreamt up this sort of "freedom." I hadn't coerced myself into believing that as long as I could afford to buy the right gift for Christmas, I would make someone so very, very happy that they would likely feel complete and loved for all the thought I'd placed into giving them such a piece of distraction, which I never would have wanted in the first place, just to be distracted into buying in the first place, so just let me go off to solve how I can get by until maybe a few days before my next paycheck, because I am so fucking broke from trying to live as I am expected to live.

But I held my own.

Everyone told me that I would need to find a means to survive the Bunker. Well, I found my means, and quite by accident. In one of those early months in country, while searching for my apartment, I took a wrong turn at one point and ended up on a dead-end road on the crest of a hill. The hill overlooked a village in the valley where I had just viewed an apartment. At that moment, it was sunny and clear and the views were as far as the eye could see, well over the tops of hills farther in the distance.

This became my retreat. This became my means of survival. This became my hill. My hill served as my courtroom, where I deliberated this, that, and the other thing.

The contrails of planes in air routes above went westbound. I traced the planes as they flew. I could see winds rustle a patch of giant firs off in the distance. Jet engine noise made its way down to me. I followed the arc of each plane until the sound could not be heard and the jet could not be seen. Those arcs were others going somewhere, and always west. I needed the west, and those arcs, and this means of holding on to the sanity, which came from knowing that I too would one day follow westbound.

"Schmink, status?" Southwark asked.

"Almost, man."

Schmink was due to depart the Bunker in ninety days—no doubt believing, if not hoping, that he could simply fade away.

"You're going to have to show us something," said Southwark. "You've had this thing long enough. Intel is breathing down my neck."

"What's this *us*?" I asked. "*You* need to see. *We* don't need to see."

"I need answers," Southwark said, lighting up a cigarette.

"Why the rush?" asked Schmink. "Why today?"

"You're trying to skate out of this," said Southwark. "I see right through your bullshit."

"Sure as shit it's not being dumped in *my* lap," said Chief. "Word is that Intel has something big going on back there."

"He can't possibly be close to finishing it," I said. "He never works."

"Don't lie, Schmink," said Southwark. "Where are you with it?"

Schmink opened a desk drawer, pulled out a thin stack of papers, and slapped it down.

"Now explain what I'm supposed to be looking at," Southwark said.

Schmink glanced over at me and then Chief, cautiously pushed the papers to Southwark, then stood up to leave the office.

"Where do you think you're going?" asked Southwark. "What am I looking at?"

"What do you mean what are you looking at?" I asked. "*You're* his boss. Here, let me look."

Southwark didn't block me, but instead sat back while I leaned over and quickly scanned the pages.

"Holy hell," I said. "There's nothing in here."

Chief came over to look, riffling through the pages. "He's right. This only says what each program is *supposed* to do."

"That imbecile hasn't done anything," I said.

"Hey, that looks like my work," said Chief.

"*Work?*" I asked. "*What* work? That's a fairy tale."

"Go screw yourself, Chisolm," said Chief. He pointed at Schmink. "It's a lot more than this bastard has ever done."

"So, this was actually your project before Schmink got ahold of it?" I asked.

"It's supposed to connect to one of the systems I babysit," said Chief.

Schmink's "work" amounted to Chief's advice for the project: a single file containing several paragraphs explaining what Schmink thought the users wanted the reports to do. No design work had been done, let alone any actual programming.

"Schmink, you asshole," said Southwark. "*Damn* it all to hell."

It was one thing to follow orders, stay focused, and uphold the clusterfuck, but accomplishing no actual work still required *some* accountability.

"I can get it done, man," Schmink said.

"You don't know a rat's ass about what this will take," I said.

Schmink didn't debate me. Southwark lit up another cigarette, then smoked the whole thing before commenting. His shoulders drooped. He took a deep breath.

"Airman Chisolm, we're going to need your help."

"Oh, no," I said. "He's your boy and this is your baby."

"Chief, what do you know about this?" asked Southwark.

"What the hell *should* I know? He's not assigned to me."

Hlavacka stirred and began throwing his yo-yo. "You're not going to be able to do it without him," he said.

"*Who* him?" I asked. "I run DiAPERS, and AardVark, for God's sake. That's their bread and butter back there."

Southwark got up and stood in the hall, looking back in the office.

"Need your help, Airman Chisolm."

"You're out of your mind," I said.

"Schmink, put down your goddamn books and get ready to work," Southwark said.

"Yes sir," Schmink said. He straightened up and put his current queue of books in a drawer.

"Schmink's half-ass seriousness is quite cute," I said.

Schmink made no retort.

"You got no choice there, Southy," said Hlavacka.

Southwark strained his neck, finished his latest cigarette, swallowed hard, then returned to his seat.

"I'll make you a deal," I said. "But you idiots have to do it my way."

Southwark punched Schmink's shoulder.

"Alright, Chisolm," he said. "What?"

"I need a couple days to look at the damage. I don't even know what it's supposed to do."

"How hard can it be?" asked Southwark.

"You want to sort it out yourself?" I asked. "Your boy's had it forever, and all you've got to show for it is sunshine up your ass."

"*Christ*, I need a smoke," said Southwark.

I palmed my chest. They all saw me do it. Not one of them had a word to say.

"Schmink, you bonehead," Southwark added.

"What are you going to do?" asked Hlavacka.

"Who is *you*?" I asked.

"Southy."

"Chisolm . . . ," said Southwark, with a noisy exhale.

"You want my help, or don't you?" I asked.

"*Yeah*," said Southwark.

"Give me a day or so to figure it out, then we march," I said. "My way. Agreed?"

"Ain't got a choice, Southy," said Hlavacka.

I pressed Southwark for an answer. "I'll give you marching orders once I know. Agreed?"

"Agreed. *Fuck*. Schmink, you pick up another book between now and when you leave this joint, and I'll kill you."

Schmink remained silent. Chief observed, surely blessed that he hadn't been selected to lead this cluster. Hlavacka put his yo-yo to rest.

I left for the OPS floor.

"You never told me why you came in," said Wagner.

"That's a two-parter," I said. "You don't have the time for it."

"You know I do."

"Well, my mom wanted me to pursue my dreams. So I did. I joined the military. But she didn't dream of this as a choice."

"Always choices."

"I don't regret it," I said.

"What's the other part?"

"A promise I once made as a kid."

"What was the promise?"

"A promise to one Sergeant Ricky Clegg that when I was old enough, I'd join the fight."

"Ah, yes. Your Vietnam vet neighbor."

"Might seem weird, I know, but I'm actually starting to believe that maybe we aren't at war, after all."

"We aren't?" asked Wagner. "We have fifty ICBMs staring at us. I think this is war."

"Maybe this is how peace looks."

"How do you come up with that?"

"Someone needs to start shooting so we can see who dies to prove who's won. If there isn't any shooting, isn't that peace?"

"Defend your position."

"I mean, if you say that war is in our DNA, then it doesn't matter how many guns, bombs, missiles, knives, ships, tanks, or anything else we've got; so long as no one goes berserk and makes the first move, we're at peace *and* at war."

"For Christ's sake, Chisolm, *you've* been down here too long."

"Seriously, right?" I asked rhetorically.

"But you do make sense."

"I mean, what else do we do while waiting for the shooting to start? Nothing."

"Shhh," chided Wagner. "Keep it down or *you'll* end up getting promoted."

"Hardly," I said. "I'm taking on Schmink's project. Besides, you're already verifying the clock. How insane would that be to have me verify your verification?"

"You've got a point," said Wagner.

"What number?" I asked.

"One twenty-two."

"Still climbing."

"My pace is way off," said Wagner. "This place is grating on me."

"You are turning gray," I said. "I didn't want to state the obvious."

"I come in, it's raining. I leave, it's raining. And this god-damn printer never stops."

"It's getting to you," I said.

"Hell, it gets to everyone sooner or later. It's getting to that new troop already."

"JED?" I asked. "What do you mean?"

"Seen him lately?" asked Wagner.

"He's blimped up," I said. "And he hides a lot. That I do know."

"The hiding in *here* is what worries me."

"Why so?"

"He sits on the cot and just stares at the wall. I checked in on him a few times but stopped that bullshit."

"What happened?"

"He mumbled something about us, or him, not being afforded the courtesy to kill someone."

"I think half these zombies in here might snap and do just that," I said. "Just watch your six."

"This joint's going to fix him up, alright," said Wagner.

"Does he have a choice?"

52

I picked up my car keys, then put on my coat.

"Where the hell are you going?" asked Chief. "Ain't you got a project to do?"

"The Brook," I said. "Picking up books for my next term. Back tomorrow."

"How much left?" asked Hlavacka.

"Next year, right at tour end."

"You think you'll make it, huh?" asked Hlavacka.

"Too well planned," I said. "How am I *not* going to make it?"

"Smoke and mirrors," said Chief. "All designed to give you hope."

"If it weren't for *just one more* bullshit session in here, every last one of you bastards could be getting an education."

"Always a dreamer," said Hlavacka.

"Realist," I said. "What do you plan on doing once you're cut loose?"

"A real job," said Hlavacka.

"Like what?" I asked.

"You think you're better than us, Chisolm," said Schmink. "You aren't."

"I never said that I'm better," I said. "But I do know one thing."

"What's that?" asked Hlavacka.

"You've got a choice, boys."

"I'll take it as it comes," said Schmink.

"That too is a choice," I said. "Just bear in mind, when you say yes to something at any one moment, you say no to everything else."

"See?" asked Southwark. "That's the cocky son of a bitch I was going to break."

Southwark had been unwilling as of late to engage me.

"He's making sense," said Hlavacka. "And if you yourself weren't such a holier-than-thou dick half the time, maybe Legal wouldn't have almost killed you."

"Drink up, boys," I said, departing for the Brook.

As I stood in the hallway outside Mr. Chamberlain's office, a sweet tobacco aroma wafted past me. He waved me inside.

"You're really burning the candle at both ends to do this, Roy."

"I'm going to make it, Mr. Chamberlain. You're keeping me on target."

"Three courses this term?"

"Yes. And if—I mean *when* I complete the schedule you mapped out, I'll have eight weeks to spare."

"Roy, you. Are. Good." Mr. Chamberlain tapped his hand on his desk with each word. "Is your Bootstrap application in?"

The Bootstrap program allowed for full-time study, completely free from reporting for duty, for up to one year.

"I've got it in and I'm awaiting word."

"Have they hinted at anything?"

"Commander said I could have two terms," I said.

"Four whole months? Boy oh boy, you are good, Roy."

"I will stop back in a few weeks with an update, Mr. Chamberlain."

I got up to leave. Mr. Chamberlain followed, giving me his two-handed shake.

"So good to see you, Roy. Boy, you are something."

"Thank you, Mr. Chamberlain. I couldn't do this without you."

"Tell your colleagues to come down here."

"I do sir, often."

"I'm waiting for them. You can't go out in the world without an education."

"Certainly not, Mr. Chamberlain."

He was still shaking my hand. He wouldn't let go.

"Thank you, sir. I'll be back with an update."

"Good. To. See. You. Roy."

"Thank you. Goodbye again, Mr. Chamberlain."

"Goodbye, Roy."

He let go of my hand.

Earning an education was a life requisite that Mom instilled in me. It went without saying that every waking hour of my life was a part of my education. However, Mom knew a formal education would give me the means to get where I wanted to go. "You just need commitment, Roy," she always reminded me, "and it'll see you through to forever."

Back when I was ten, I conducted a door-to-door greeting-card sales campaign. I got the idea from an advertisement on the back of a *Boys' Life* magazine. The company from which I consigned the cards would pay me in cash or products, whichever I chose. In my imagination, the products appeared double the value of the cash alone, and I wanted to earn my way to a telescope. Desperation overcame me once the mountain of greeting cards arrived at my house. During that ice-cold Chicago winter, I pressed my sales nightly after school. That telescope at the other end was an incentive.

Dean was conducting a similar sales effort. He was in it for an air rifle. We each worked on one side of every street in the area. We sold all our greeting cards in just over a month, only to find out that the company I'd worked my ass off for had run out of telescopes. Dean's rifle never materialized, either.

The bastards at that company probably never had any items in stock. They got the kids to buy it up front, and then when it was all over, *Sorry, boys, we're plum out.* They got the kids to the end through pure distraction. I received an apology letter with a check. I took the check and picked up a second-hand telescope on my own from a local hobby shop. But I did it. And I *had* to do it. I wanted to see forever.

53

"How was your week, babe?" asked Rachel.

"The usual," I said. "Trying not to get myself killed."

Rachel and I were lying on our backs naked on her kitchen table, legs over the edge, feet on chairs, looking up at the ceiling.

"This isn't easy," said Rachel.

"It'll come to us," I said.

"Yes," Rachel said, looking up.

As much as we tried to avoid it, the *What are we going to do?* conversation would occasionally rear its head.

"You're not like anyone I've known," said Rachel, turning back to me.

"Maybe I am and you just don't know yet."

"You're not," Rachel insisted. "I know."

"I'm just trying to figure it all out before I die," I said.

"Too many shiny objects."

"I give you all the free time I have, which isn't much, I admit. I wish it was more. And you don't give up."

"Why would I give up?"

"You do what you say you will do. I notice this."

"I love you, Roy. You know how love is."

"You don't try to squeeze me to death."

"Love is like quicksilver."

"How's that?"

"If you find it, you must hold it gently in an open hand. Otherwise the more you squeeze it, the more it slips through your fingers."

"That's a good one," I said.

"Only the ones who love *really* live."

We pulled each other into a hug.

"Why are you so good to me?" I whispered.

"We Germans have a saying: *Wer rastet, der rostet.*"

"Which means?"

"He who rests grows rusty."

"Another good one," I said.

"You keep looking for answers. You never rest."

"There are many questions. Like, How do *you* not grow rusty?"

"Because I'm with you," said Rachel.

"And before me?"

Rachel's entire body sighed as she let out a deep breath. We returned to lying on our backs.

"My family has been in the nearby villages since the 1700s. Before you, I lived like everyone here lives."

"That's a long time."

"You ask every day why you are here. Why we are *all* here."

"Does that bother you?"

"No, no," said Rachel. "I want to live. It makes *me* ask too. But it is hard to get out of something that you've been in forever."

We spooned.

"I think of leaving my village, my family, my country someday," said Rachel. "Then I think I will never be back, and that scares me."

"If it weren't for the world getting in our way," I said.

"I would follow you anywhere."

I pulled Rachel tighter. She squeezed my arms with the feel of love, crying a cry of being in love, curling back into me.

"Anywhere," I said, "is wherever we are."

54

"I think we need to get some time in over the weekend," Southwark said.

This was the first Friday of August.

"Let's meet Sunday at oh-eight-hundred," he added.

"What are you *talking* about?" I asked. "We're going to be ready for delivery without any overtime."

For the prior month, I'd hammered out the overall design and programming for most of Schmink's project. The system comprised nine programs, five of which I would write, with two each for Schmink and Southwark.

"Schmink and I aren't going to make it without more time."

"What's that got to do with me coming in?"

"We need your help," said Southwark.

"You two know the parameters I send your programs. I've given you the design steps."

"Intel needs this in their hands by nineteen August. What if we don't make it?"

"Keep your boy from banging that warhorse back there and we should be fine."

"I don't know," said Southwark.

"Who's driving this?" I asked. "That gives me an entire week to test, plus another week in case of any revisions, plus time to demo this thing."

"You think we're on track?" asked Southwark.

"I just looked at both of your parts two days ago," I said. "Stick with what I told you to do and we'll be fine."

"I think we're good," said Schmink.

"No thanks to you," I said.

"Intel trusts you, Chisolm," said Southwark.

"Like I said, we aren't going to fuck this up because I'm not fucking this up. For once, you deadbeats have a real job."

"Thank you for your guidance, *Airman* Chisolm," said Schmink.

"Aren't you sick of sloppy seconds?" I asked, thwapping the back of Schmink's head.

"Mind your own business, Chisolm," he said.

"I want to. But look where that got me."

"Stop," said Southwark. "He's not screwing anyone or reading anything or fucking off. He's here. We'll be here."

"Problem solved," I said. "I will not be here this weekend."

Southwark and Schmink completed their work. The reports went live on August 22. Southwark never again questioned my time, my schedule, or my whereabouts. Or my haircut.

"I need one," I said to Wagner, sitting at an OPS floor console.

"Stand by," he said, retrieving a cookie and throwing it to me.

"I'm spent."

"I heard you hit it out of the park."

"Who says?" I asked.

"One of the Intel guys."

"It's some kind of important," I said.

"Must be. They've been printing reports out the ass all week."

"What do you think?"

"Not sure. But something, dude. What's your fortune?"

I cracked open my cookie.

"'Happily ever after exists.'"

"Keeper?" asked Wagner.

"Keeper."

I placed the fortune in my wallet, along with my other two keepers.

"Matches my eternal optimism," I said. "I like this one."

"I thought it was your realism?"

"Maybe equal parts both."

"Strange thing lately," said Wagner. "I don't feel the weight of it like I used to."

"Ah, so you trust them with the button back there?"

"So long as we've got double Ds on station, I trust them *more*."

"What double Ds?"

"I've been piecing together a new hypothesis."

"And?" I asked.

"If they expect to get laid this evening, they'll be hesitant to launch today."

"How does that even correlate?"

"Think about it," said Wagner. "Sex is an insatiable act. They'll be back to square one the next day, because they'll want to get laid again the next night, and the next night, and so forth."

"Your theory is that the thing between us and war is *Ginger*?"

"Kind of. Yes."

"No."

"Maybe not directly, I guess," said Wagner. "But kind of. Survival—procreation—is in our DNA. Just like war."

"Yeah, but they're not making babies, they're just fucking her. Where's the survival?"

"The *will* to survive. For all of us to survive, to make more people, you've got to get laid. The urge to fuck is in our DNA. It's our survival instinct as a species, creating our descendants. Fucking is basically our means to peace."

"That's Nobel Prize genius."

"I mean, are we *that* insane to wipe out everyone simply because we don't like those guys?"

"I don't like those guys."

"No one likes those guys," said Wagner. "But you don't like Schmink, either, and you haven't killed him."

"Well, one small problem—what if the Russians move a division into New York?"

"OK, then maybe."

"You see what I'm saying?" I asked.

"But why would they? Besides, the place is rat infested and overpopulated."

"I hear the pizza's good."

"I wouldn't know."

"Focus, man," I said. "You're basically saying that Ginger is the reason for the survival of our species?"

"In a roundabout way, yes," said Wagner. "She is."

"I'll be damned if that doesn't make sense."

"She can't get orders out of here or we're all fucked," said Wagner.

"If she *doesn't* get orders out of here, some are *still* fucked."

We both keeled over laughing.

"Hasta luego, Mr. Wagner."

"Good day to you, sir, Mr. Chisolm."

I left for the programmer office.

An assignment to the Bunker included the constitutionally guaranteed freedom of expression. If it wasn't a pissing fetish, maybe it was fisting a princess to orgasm. Now don't judge me for what I'm saying is "normal" or "deviant"; this was all justified and warranted, I assure you.

Jensen, Treadwell, Sosa—all the inmates—held the secrets of what we did in the Bunker. And out of the Bunker. But come on, could you fault them for their diversions? In their defense, you may recall we had no shopping malls, no drive-throughs in sight, certainly no picket fences, no sound-bite news distractions that you had back home, nor any other diversions from the norm you kept from us. For that matter, you cocksuckers, you should have been quite enamored by the fact that we were even *in* this fucking Cold War on your behalf.

"Southwark," Legal said. "Phone call."

"Who is it?"

"Timmons."

"Got it."

Southwark took his call.

"What?" Southwark asked. "*What?*" he asked again, then promptly hung up. "I've got to go to the Brook."

It was noon.

"For what?" asked Legal.

"Apparently I've got orders."

"What the . . . ?" said Legal.

Southwark jumped out of his chair, put on his coat, and departed the Bunker without so much as a goodbye.

55

September 26th, 1988

Dad,

I miss home. I miss a lot of things. Mostly, I just hope you are well.

~~I often find myself wondering if you discovered what I have found in life, and yet you stuck with the asinine program all the same.~~ You were always a great example of how to be a man.

~~I can understand why we moved to different cities, following your career. You did whatever they told you to do, no doubt because some assholes dangled carrots and sticks over your head.~~ I am proud that you are my father.

~~Not a day goes by when I don't want out of what you were in. If it weren't for the Bunker, I might have never figured out this bullshit, and I would forever be fucked.~~

I hope that I have become the man you raised me to be.

~~On a tucked-away, dead-end road near the Bunker, I can sometimes be found parked on a hill. It is there where I have found a gravity of calm stronger than any fear. It is also there where~~ *I say my prayers.*

Roy

56

"Why so glum, Southy?" asked Hlavacka.

"You know damn well why," said Southwark.

It was one week after Southwark had gone to the Brook to pick up his orders.

"It isn't *all* bad," said Chief. "You're getting out of here."

"Right back to where I started," Southwark said, slamming his hand on his desk. "Damn it."

Southwark's orders pulled him back into his former career field.

"No choice in the matter?" I asked.

"They can do what they want with us," said Legal. "He signed on the dotted line."

"I honestly can't see how," said Southwark. "Why did they let me cross-train into programming if that's the case?"

"That is a good point," said Legal. "And if that's true, there's another part to this puzzle."

"How could their holes be more important than our holes?" I asked.

"How gay is that, Chisolm?" asked Hlavacka.

"It's just a question," I said.

"Because planes can't fly without enough mechanics," said Legal. "But why would they have let you out to begin with?"

"How much time did they give you?" asked Chief.

"Sixty days to report."

"That's like a few weeks left in here," said Legal.

"Already on it," said Southwark. "Wife's flying in three weeks."

"When are you flying?" asked Hlavacka.

"Shooting for five weeks from now."

"Schmink's as good as gone too," said Legal. "When's his last day?"

"I believe end of next week," said Southwark. "But he'll only be turning in his tickets. He ain't going to be *back* back."

"Well, isn't that pretty," I said, as I got up to leave the office. "I'll be out in OPS."

Schmink's departure began a wave of cuckoo clock purchases, since all the old-timers were due to leave within months. Few replacements made their way to the Bunker that year. No one understood what was going on, but the holes created by departures were making everyone nervous.

Sosa was long gone. Schmink was a ghost. It made no difference that Southwark was about to depart. Their names remained on the sign-out board. Chief requested and was approved for a move to the DDS section. In return, Woody moved back to my shop. JED and I were the last remaining members of the original RSS section.

On September 16, I drove Southwark to Frankfurt's civilian airport. With such short notice, he couldn't get a seat on the MAC flight for that week. I volunteered to drive him. First, it was a Friday, and I had a weekend class in Heidelberg the next day. Second, I wasn't a dick.

"You know I don't dislike you," said Southwark as we drove.

"I don't take it that you do."

"If you just wouldn't act like you're better than us."

"I'm not an actor."

"That's what I mean. *See?* Right there."

"*What* right there?"

"*That.* You talk down to us."

"Not at all," I said.

"Sure as shit comes across that way."

"I'm easier to understand than finding west on a clear day at dusk."

"It's hard to find west when you're in a place without windows or daylight."

"Fair point," I said. "But remember this too. It's all up to you whether you believe that you're less than anyone or anything else."

Southwark went quiet.

"All I'm trying to do is what's right," I said. "It isn't what time I show up or leave or read or smoke, eat, sleep, shave, shine, fuck, *whatever.* If every one of them was in on it like I am, then things could have been different. But they're not. You *know* that. I'm doing my part to win this war. That's why I came in. That's why I'm here. You figure that out, you figure me out."

We remained silent until we arrived at the international terminal twenty minutes later. Southwark retrieved his bags from the trunk.

"I forgot to drop off a set of keys at TLQ," said Southwark. "Can you do that for me?"

"I'll do that."

We shook hands.

"Listen, you take care of yourself," Southwark said.

"I'll keep an eye out for a postcard."

Southwark lugged his bags onward.

The following week, on Monday, I stopped by the Brook to drop off the keys.

"What's going on over there?" I asked the clerk.

"Over there" was the local Army personnel office sharing a wall with the Temporary Lodging Quarters office.

"Not sure," the clerk said. "She's been in there a while."

A woman on the other side hollered. German, from the accent. She'd apparently lost her boyfriend, one Private Binscon, the father of her child. Private Binscon—according to the terrified woman—said he was "going to the field" for seven days as part of some undetermined war game. She waited ten days for him. Turns out, her Private Binscon had done no such thing. In fact, the Army personnel clerks were downright confused at the woman's insistence about a war game for they had no knowledge. Instead, the clerks could confirm that Private Binscon left on orders back to the United States. The howls turned to a panicked scream.

The woman directed her attention toward an acquaintance of Private Binscon. At least I surmised that was who he was, since the woman made mention of sexual relations—at the same time, in the same room—with both this acquaintance, a Private Tre'Ajon, and her Private Binscon. Regrettably for the woman, the whereabouts of departed soldiers could not be disclosed—due to Army policy and regulation, of course. Making matters worse, Private Tre'Ajon could not offer or suggest any other means of tracking down her Private Binscon. Try as he might, Private Tre'Ajon could not console the woman one bit.

I left TLQ, passing the Army personnel office. The woman had a toddler hanging on her legs as she stooped over a desk, screaming at Private Tre'Ajon. He looked at me briefly, rolling his eyes. Tears streamed down the woman's face as she glanced back at me. She attempted to regain her composure, using the back of her hand to wipe tears from her face, sobbing to the point of breathlessness.

No wonder they hate us. What would you keep a commitment for, if not even for blood? I knew her, in a way. Surely she will be on easy street, crawling back into the welcoming arms of the Old Country. How easy—indeed, too easy—to get in and get accounted for, and then to hell with the responsibility at all costs.

57

You, *you* could sit tight over there. You could wake up each day and not have to see what we had to see—the second hand overwhelming the volume of fiction read under the paralysis of possible annihilation should someone flip the exercise of will, just for the sake of ending the catatonic wait-state of nothingnowhereness.

Dad can't find me. I don't get to see what you get to see, but I want you to see what I have to see just one day, that we are ready on a moment's notice to fire at will. We, yeah. You and me. "We."

It was staff meeting day in the Bunker, early October. I arrived half an hour ahead of time.

"Hey, Burnsie," I said. "You're back. Where you been, buddy?"

I didn't care where Burns had been. This was a polite hello.

"Who gives a flyin' fuck?" Burns asked. "Where the hell have *you* been?"

I'd noted Burns's aged vehicle in the parking lot when I arrived. Since Burns was already in, I knew he'd have gone on a manhunt to track me down. He had to. He would soon replace

Legal. Burns would then be our senior-ranking programmer, a role also serving as official Intel liaison. However, because of my close working relationship with Intel, they often just came to me. So I was Burns's go-to person for intel on Intel.

"Can you back up three feet, please?" I asked.

"For what?" asked Burns.

"Or stop eating garlic. One or the other."

"I don't smell nothing."

"That's a double negative."

"Look, where you been, buddy?"

"I've been looking all over for you, man," I said.

"Bullshit. I've been looking all over for *you*."

"*What?*" I asked rhetorically. "No, not that again, sir."

"You're crazy," said Burns.

"I'm just asking where've you been."

"Ramstein optometry."

"For the third time in two weeks?" Hlavacka chimed in.

"You need a new story," I said.

Burns avoided further eye contact while moving to sit at his desk.

"Who's in charge here?" he asked.

"You're talking to him," I said.

"I am," said Burns. "Can you just try and be here? Please. In case anyone needs us."

"What's this *us*?"

"I'm not always gonna be around. You need to be here in case anyone needs something."

The lying annoyed me.

"So where have you been this morning?" Burns asked me again.

"Optometrist," I said.

"Damn it," said Burns. "I know all about you making us look stupid in here."

"That's on you, Burnsie."

"Goddamn it, Chisolm," said Burns. "Are we having a meeting today or not?"

"Of course we are."

"Chisolm, you swell son of a gun, you," said Hlavacka.

Frazione showed up soon after.

"I'm in and out of here today, people," said Frazione. "Let's get started. You all know Sergeant Watkins, our budgets and personnel liaison from the orderly room."

Senior Master Sergeant Watkins followed Frazione into the office and stood behind him.

"Welcome, Sergeant Watkins," said Burns.

"Thank you," said Watkins.

"I'm going to get straight to it," Frazione stated. "Effective immediately, Sergeant Watkins will be taking over lead duties here."

The news had already come through the grapevine. Watkins served as the unit budget administrator. In this role he also did double duty as assignments coordinator. Because of Watkins's blatant disregard for the mounting number of holes in the Bunker, he was promoted. His superior ineptitude allowed for many positions to go unreconciled. For superior substandard performance in the face of high expectations, Watkins also received an achievement medal.

"You might think it's a can of worms, but they give top-flight support to USAFE's best," said Frazione.

"What is your background, Sergeant Watkins?" Chief asked.

"Munitions, but obviously moved into budgets and staffing."

"He's going to be the new Applications Programming lead, or what we're calling the ApPLe," Frazione said. "I'll be swapping into his old job."

"Munitions and budgets?" I asked. "How do you get into programming from that?"

"I'm from Computer Operations, actually. Cross-trained about eighteen months ago and came straight here, but the commander slotted me into a budgets and staffing vacancy."

"Programming skills aren't required for the role that Sergeant Watkins will play," Frazione said.

"Bullshit!" Chief said, under a very harsh sneeze.

"Where will you be sitting?" Burns asked.

"I'm maintaining my office on the Brook," Watkins said.

"And I'll be on the Brook," Frazione said.

Frazione's sights were set on real leadership someday. Pentagon, maybe. He couldn't move up very well if he was buried underground in a can of worms. As for Watkins, they gave us no benefit of the doubt. His leadership of the inmates amounted to a proven imbecile being placed in charge of people who were capable of denial and diversion on a grand scale.

With Frazione's move, we might get the holes filled. Watkins would rely upon the inmates to keep him abreast of the goings-on. He had no choice. This, of course, the inmates translated to mean telling Watkins what he wanted to hear, even if it was couched in terms of loading bombs. Our weekly staff meetings changed to once a month.

"How'd it go, man?" I asked AC, on a sojourn to the OPS floor.

This was a Monday and a day shift for AC's flight. He and Chief had just returned from a one-week trip to Spain. AC was three months from end of tour, and he was damn well going to see something of Europe.

"Incredible."

AC's humiliation and wrestling days were over, as he'd turned out to be a natural dart player. He was also the only one who could sometimes beat Chief.

"Oh yeah?" I inquired, with a raised brow.

"The pussy was *good* down there," AC said, as if he'd gotten a most desired present on Christmas morning.

"Good for you, brother."

"Tell you something else," AC whispered, checking to ensure there were no passersby.

"Yeah?" I asked, leaning in and whispering to play along. "What's that?"

"We tried some acid."

"Intentionally?"

"One of those 'targets of opportunity,'" said AC.

I sighed out of concern. "I worry about you, AC. First rule of secrets is to not speak of them. To *anyone.*"

AC's enthusiasm ebbed. "I'm cool, man," he said, trying to regain my cheer. "It's out of my system."

Timmons would soon depart Europe for an assignment back in the US. As a matter of simplification and improved control, the role of drug testing was subsumed by our higher HQ at Ramstein. When crossing borders in Europe, active-duty personnel required leave papers and a US military ID. The leave papers required annotation of countries to be visited. The drug czars at Ramstein would "randomly" drug test anyone taking international leave.

The randomness was, in effect, self-determined. But Chief outsmarted them. He acquired an American passport for crossing borders. He did put in for leave—after all, he'd be gone a full week. But Ramstein never selected him. He had since made it all the way to staff sergeant, so he used his room at the Q as his leave address. And he kept his mouth shut.

AC had no passport. And the drugs were not out of his system. However, AC was fortunate—if *fortunate* meant "staying in." His status as a first-term airman, combined with Watkins's personnel-staffing fiasco, resulted in an Article 15—one month of extra duty, loss of one month's pay, and drug rehab. Yes, AC medicated himself, much like other inmates. However, AC made one mistake. The inmates couldn't *choose* what to take. They were *told* what to take.

58

"You got your basic gin," Legal said. "You got your Jack D."

Legal would soon be gone. He inventoried the dwindled remains of a once-substantial L-rat collection.

"That's strange," continued Legal. "These are *all* lower than where I marked them."

"I heard they're postponing our next WintEx," said Woody.

"Who'd you hear that from?" asked Chief.

"Intel."

"Which one of you assholes has been requisitioning moonshine?" asked Legal.

"The end of an era," Hlavacka said.

"You could have contributed," Legal said.

"Everyone could have contributed," I said. "I brought in two bottles last time. Hell, they were empty within three days."

"It can't be all bad," said JED.

"Like hell," said Chief. "The bar is damn near bone dry."

"I mean with the exercise being postponed."

"That's weird in and of itself," said Hlavacka.

"Maybe it's a ruse," said Woody, "to trick those commie bastards."

"Still have time to run it," said Legal. "They could change their minds in the next month."

"I'll be long gone," said Hlavacka.

"We'll write you from the other side, boys," said Legal.

Legal and Hlavacka would vanish before year-end.

I didn't think for a minute that the inmates lied about wanting to write. I wasn't even skeptical. I believed every one of them had a clear intention to do it. But *could* they? I just didn't buy it. After all, who in their right mind would dillydally writing a letter when all that would do is reignite every waking moment of grief of depression of terror and, of course, ass fucking, represented by and packed into a cuckoo clock now hanging in your living room?

In late fall, I received a postcard from Hlavacka—the first time anyone who'd departed and told me they'd write, wrote. The front had a drawing of a nineteenth-century clipper sailing into the sunset. On the back it read, "You're not made for this. Get out. Good luck."

I wrote to Hlavacka at the address he left me and awaited a reply. Nothing. A month later, I sent another ping down the line. I received no word. Hlavacka messed up. He didn't follow proper order—to fall off the face of the earth. Instead, I'd received those nine words. Hlavacka was alive. He'd proved it. But I would no longer be known, as far as he could tell.

"I'm going to school," I said.

I was on the OPS floor, picking up a print job.

"Your Bootstrap?" asked Wagner as he mounted a tape.

"Yup."

"What dates?"

"January into April. The two full-time terms I need."

"I'll have one month left when you get back."

"I wouldn't miss your departure," I said. "Hell, I was here for your demotion."

Following the conclusive results of an exhaustive

investigation into Sosa and Curly having had encounters on the OPS floor—dozens of used condoms found under a sub-floor tile behind the mainframe—the senior operations NCO fought, but ultimately lost, his own battle against a promotion to the Brook. The B flight NCO took over as acting senior operations NCO, while Wagner was demoted back to B flight shift leader. The TADPoLe position had been retired.

"You may very well make it, sir," said Wagner.

"Oh, I intend to."

"How's Rachel?"

"As good as ever. Seeing her tonight."

"You give it much thought?" asked Wagner. "I mean after leaving here."

"Lot of ways it can go."

"She worth it to you?"

"That isn't the question."

"What is?" asked Wagner.

"How can I expect her to go six thousand miles away with me, when her family's been here since the dawn of time?"

"Hmmm."

"What I'm trying to avoid is overthinking it and drilling out every angle of her reason for existence, only to be left with someone who hates me for doing so."

"Probably best not drill, eh?" proposed Wagner. "Maybe wait on that revelation thing."

"My thinking exactly."

"The universe does dictate terms, sooner or later."

"No time for a cookie," I said. "I'll catch up with you tomorrow."

"Auf Wiedersehen, Mr. Chisolm."

"A fine day to you, Mr. Wagner."

Most inmates lived by an inherent search for restitution within the confines of our straight and narrow. The nonspec-ificity of this restitution meant that their search didn't have a real aim. It couldn't. The target that the inmates aimed at was unknown. For the record, they did deduce that "something" should be pinned down as remuneration for an assignment to the Bunker. Absent the cardiovascularpsychosocial effect of America riding shotgun in their minds, the inmates were shooting blanks at nonexistent targets, in a hunt to kill for said remuneration.

"Can you sit still for five minutes, Chisolm?" Chief asked.

"Living life," I said. "Things to do."

"Smugness."

"You're mistaking *driven* for *smug*," I said.

"Holier than thou," said Chief.

"I've never said that I'm better than anyone else."

"You *think* it," said Chief.

"I just know where I'm going," I said.

"And where is that?"

"Home," I said. "Don't we all go home?"

"Someday," said Legal. "Maybe."

"Yes," I said. "Someday."

"Or you die," said Chief.

"I'm in survival mode, just like you," I said.

"Just a matter of time," said Legal.

"I heeded the words of our former TADPoLe back there," I said.

"And what were those?" asked Chief.

"'Why do we go where we go? Is what we are leaving worse than where we are going?'"

"When we're hit, we're gone," said Chief. "At least we have a chance anywhere else."

"*If* we're hit," I said. "Aren't we here for the *if*, not the *when*?"

"Yeah," began Chief, blowing a bubble with his gum and popping it. "As I said, smug."

59

The last day of fall coincided with Woody's final duty day. We decided to celebrate his departure with lunch in the Bunker chow hall.

"I'm not going to write," said Woody.

"So, you're really going through with it?" I looked out the window just as a mouser dashed under an adjacent building.

"It's phony for anyone to say they will if they won't," said Woody.

"No one can say that you don't keep your word."

"Even though I won't, I would if I said I would."

"I've always taken you at your word," I said with a nod.

The mouser ran by once again.

"It's a funny thing, the Bunker," I said, still looking outside.

"How's that?" asked Woody.

"We all talk about getting out. Then one day, you just walk out."

"If that is what you call funny, then this is pure comedy," said Woody. "And you're right. It is all about getting out."

I walked over and picked up a dessert and coffee, then returned to our table.

"I think we know where we stand," I said.

"Let me get a coffee."

When Woody returned to the table, he stood for a moment, stirring in cream, then sat down.

"Rejoice," I said. "This place will soon be a distant memory."

"It's bullshit," said Woody.

"*Now* you swear?" I asked.

Woody looked down. "If I look back on anything, I can't help but see everything staring right back at me, especially the hard times."

"Maybe that's why we never hear from anyone again."

"That's why I left you the *Endurance*," said Woody. He'd willed to me his ship in a bottle. "You're the only one who cares enough to remember."

"Thank you."

We finished lunch in silence, then went outside and descended the steps.

"Stay safe, my friend," I said.

"At all times. And you."

We hugged like brothers being torn apart for good. Woody proceeded down the driveway and disappeared into a low, dense fog. This was all Woody's choice.

Woody would be separating from the service upon his return stateside. There would be no forwarding address or means to reach him. He wouldn't tell anyone where he was going. Then again, even he didn't know where he was going—not exactly, anyway. I did know that Woody would travel by car and that he would drive until he found a city, or a town, or a village that felt like "home." What home would feel like, Woody didn't know. But there was no way, he was certain, that it would hold any reminder of his past.

I took a moment to stand near the Bunker entrance, but far enough away to gain no advantage from the rush of exiting heat.

How does anyone know what they're made for, let alone what anyone else is made for? *One day I'll get out. One day I'll go home. What is home? It's the battlefield. It's the battlefield. The Bunker isn't the battlefield, it's only a battlefield. Just like Russia is the battlefield for Ivan, and East Germany is only a battlefield for Ivan.* My map depicted a whole lot of *a*'s. Going home, my return would be to *the* battlefield from *a* battlefield.

I returned to the office.

"Stand right there," said JED.

"For what?" I asked. "You plan on sucking my dick?"

JED sat down at his desk as I entered.

"My diet," he said. "Keep an eye out." He pulled out a flask and poured a double shot.

"What are you doing, dude?" I asked.

"I told you. My diet."

"*Liquor?*" I asked him.

"Not just *any* liquor. Whiskey. *Has* to be whiskey."

"*That's* your lunch?"

"No, it's my diet. Actually it's half my diet. Plus two MoonPies."

"What?"

"Yeah. The MoonPies are my carbs, and the whiskey burns up the calories."

"*That's* your diet?"

"And it works," JED said. "I'm down seven pounds since nine days ago. Three more and I make my weight check by Friday."

"You realize that whiskey is high calorie?"

"All I know is alcohol burns, and I'm losing weight. It's got to be burning the calories."

"You're going to make out just fine in here, JED."

At the end of the week, on Friday, the office went to minimum manning for the holidays. Over the break, each inmate would pull one duty shift.

"Chisolm," said Chief. "Phone."

I picked up the phone.

"Chisolm here."

"It's Timmons. Your Bootstrap orders are ready for pickup."

The first of my six courses would begin in eleven days, on the third of January. I could not technically sign out of the Bunker before my orders were published.

"I'm rolling," I said.

"Hey," yelled Timmons. "Tell JED to get his ass down here. He's got to weigh in *today*."

"Can't you just pen it in?" I asked.

"Wish I could," said Timmons. "They want eyeballs on his fat ass."

"I'll let him know," I said. "See you in thirty." I hung up.

"JED, they want your ass down there for weigh-in."

I signed out under OFO and put on my coat.

"I'm out, you chicks and dicks," I said as I walked out of the office. "Don't get yourselves killed while I'm gone."

60

March 19th, 1989

Roy,

I am proud of you.

You might remember that your uncle Don served in Korea. He never had much to say about it, but I'm sure you've got plenty of stories to tell.

I understand that you're no doubt dealing with a lot of concerns. That's the military, if not life itself. You've come a long way. Your mother would be proud at how you've turned out.

I ended up adopting those two old horses. They'll live out their time at the rescue center. I go almost every day.

Just nine more months, Roy. You're going to be fine.

Say your prayers.

Dad

61

After four full months of Bootstrap, I returned to the Bunker on Monday, May 8. The mousers were up early and active. The sound of their success echoed between two support buildings. I carried a satchel with me as I pushed through the clanking turnstile.

I arrived at my office. The coat rack outside the door was gone. I looked inside the office, and the desks were gone too. The room was filled with boxes stacked floor to ceiling—the markings indicating that the contents would be shredded and burned.

"Can you tell me where the RSS office is?" I asked a passerby coming out of Intel. I didn't recognize him.

"Down one deck. Second door on the left."

"Got it. Thanks."

Whereas my office once occupied the space between the OPS floor and Intel, I knew from the directions given that the new location was in a lower-classification NATO space. A few other US national offices operated the same way, doing their work in a secure classified suite, while maintaining space in the NATO areas.

As I approached the new quarters, debate poured out the open door. I entered slowly and surveyed the layout. No one noticed me. It was a big square space three times the size of my former shop. A bright-white six-person desk stood in the middle of the room. Three people could sit on each side, with drawers to the right of each chair. A centered shelf ran the length of the desk at about eye height. No one was sitting there. Instead, cubicles had been assembled around the perimeter of the office, with a five-foot-high partition encasing each one. There was meanness to the way the room was set up—an "us versus them," or maybe more a "me versus you," configuration. Those present debated from within their encampments via shouts across the room.

"Sounds like you got a dildo up your ass, Mr. Spock," said JED.

"How do you know about dildos, JED?" asked a voice, presumably one Mr. Spock.

"You don't need to be an expert to know that sound."

"From personal experience, obviously," said Mr. Spock.

"Shut up," JED said.

I took two steps in.

"Honey, I'm home!" I shouted.

"Holy hell," said Chief, popping up from inside his perimeter.

"Reporting for duty, sir," I said.

"Son of a bitch," said JED, gophering up from his position.

"He lives," Chief added.

"All straight and neat and pretty," I said, continuing to survey the layout. "Where's home?"

Mr. Spock exited his domain, walked to the cubicle closest to the office entrance and slapped his hand on the outer partition. "Right here," he said.

"Airman Spock, I presume?" I asked, reaching for a handshake.

"Just Mr. Spock."

"*Mr.* Spock?" I asked, askance. "OK, I'll play your game."

Mr. Spock was an airman first class. He pulled a pointed Spock ear from each pocket and put them on.

"Trekkie," said Spock. "Anyway, here's your bunk."

"I see that," I said. "I mean, that you are 'Mr. Spock.'"

"Heard a lot about you," said Spock. "Good to meet you."

"I'm sure all good," I said. "Interesting to be back."

I slapped the partition to my cubicle. "At least it makes for a quick getaway."

"Or welcome detail, more like it," said JED.

"Do we get that many visitors?" I asked.

"Only if they can find us," said Spock.

"Where's Burnsie?" I asked.

"You mean where is he at the *moment* or where does he *sit*?" asked Chief.

"Well, both."

"Right now, I think he's at the Brook," said Spock. "But when he's here, or *if* he's here, he sits in that one."

Spock pointed to the far-corner cubicle.

"What are you doing in here?" I asked Chief.

"They got rid of DDS."

"No way. How come?"

"Not enough people to keep it running."

"Are you *kidding* me? It only ran on weekdays, and daytime at that. How many people can that take?"

"It had its moments."

"Sounds like someone got wind of you guys going home to Momma."

Except for its use as our war game computer system, DDS was sitting idle. Occasionally, Intel needed historical reports, but none were time sensitive like the ones in RSS. Despite this, Hancock soaked up the staff like a genius. His team arrived each morning, powered up the system, then shut it down at the end of the duty day. They were known as the "fuck 'em" or "Foxtrot Echo" crew. Foxtrot Echo often took midday breaks to go home and fuck Momma. And sometimes they fucked other mommas. But the DDS team made it back religiously for shutdown each day. This was per protocol and as directed by the authority of Hancock. He stuck to his agreements.

"Hey now," said Chief. "Shh shh shh."

"If they killed DDS, that means the bitch didn't put out," I said.

In the Bunker, one could never officially claim that something wasn't needed. If you wanted to kill it, you'd say it wasn't "funded properly" or that it wasn't "staffed well enough" to continue operations. One demanded ever more, until what you were fighting for was cut off entirely, swept aside and forgotten.

62

"Sergeant Chisolm, sir, meet Tech Sergeant Gilbert," said Chief.

I'd made sergeant just as I entered Bootstrap.

"He's as uptight as it gets," whispered Chief in my ear.

"Here we go again," I whispered back.

"Tech Sergeant Gilbert sits next to Burns back there," said Chief, pointing to Gilbert's cubicle.

Gilbert exited his cubicle to meet me halfway, and we shook hands.

"Sergeant Gilbert is a twofer," said Chief. "Southwark's and Hancock's positions, combined."

"I'm due to leave on TDY for a week," said Gilbert. "When I'm back I'll sit with you and go over the basics, Sergeant Chisolm."

"That sounds like a wonderful plan, sir," I said.

Gilbert gave me a condescending once-over, then returned to his cubicle.

"So is Watkins still in this game?" I asked, turning back to Chief.

"Up here last month. The usual. Staff meeting days only."

"OK, so with DDS gone, how did WintEx go?"

"They did a three-day tabletop exercise," said Chief. "Can you believe that?"

"Tabletop?" I asked. "That's kindergarten. Who's that going to keep in line?"

"Ivan's been quiet too."

"I thought it was weird that no one contacted me for anything. Not even DiAPERS."

"You've apparently done something right, Chisolm," said JED. "It's either working or Intel isn't doing shit back there."

"I've done it right, alright," I said. "Very strange."

"What did you do this whole time?" asked JED.

"School," I said. "Pretty much all I had time for. That, and one long weekend free for Presidents' Day. Went to Paris."

"How close are you now?" asked Chief.

"Five more courses. I'll have my bachelor's degree completed in the next two terms."

"Son of a bitch," JED said.

"I'll be damned," said Chief. "You're going to make it."

"Told you I would," I said. "So don't ask to be damned on my account."

"Then what?" asked JED.

"The Air Force asked me to extend another year or reenlist altogether," I said.

"No shit," said Chief. "Are you considering?"

"Declined!" I said.

"Out *and* edumacated," said Chief. "If that ain't the shit."

I retreated to my cubicle, where I took custody of a 1950s steel US government desk. In addition, I acquired a wheeled steel-and-faux-leather chair from the same era. The partitions were bare. The fluorescent lights throughout the office were bright with a blue hue and hummed like Frankenstein. Pale-yellow walls created an annoying level of brightness.

A month before returning to the Bunker, I'd come across a world map for sale in the exchange on the Brook. Though the map itself was new, the plastic cover it came in was caked with dirt. There was little interest in our world, at least from this perspective. I bought it. Now I took the map from my satchel and hung it at my desk.

"Why the map?" asked Chief, peering into my cubicle on his way out of the office.

"It's my plan," I said.

"Where's your calendar?"

While most inmates hung a short-timer calendar at the one-year point from their departure, I instead chose the map.

"No calendar. Just the map."

"And?"

"That is the question."

"You've avoided it like ten times already," said Chief. "What *is* your plan?"

One late-winter night, lying in bed with my night-light still on, I stared at my new world map folded inside its plastic cover. Going home to America, to buy in to the structure—this would be insanity, I reasoned. No longer could I contort myself to suffice to my last breath. I had every wish to torch all the tightly fenced-in freedoms accorded to and allotted by income earned.

You'd have to be a lunatic to believe that's how things were always and forever meant to be. This was no longer my America. This was not the freedom for which I fought. *If I get out of the Bunker only to go back, I'm really getting out and staying in.* Then it dawned on me. It would take time to execute my plan. But until I had it ironed out, I would share it with no one, not even Rachel.

"My plan is to figure out what's new in this joint," I said.

"You pretty much know what's new," said Chief.

"What exactly happened to Hancock?" I asked, deflecting.

"Finagled his way to Ramstein on account of his spouse down there."

"Good for him."

"With DDS quashed, he had some ammo to back him up on getting out of here."

"That ain't the only reason he needed to leave," said JED.

"Then why?"

"You going to tell him, or should I?" Chief asked, looking over at JED. He didn't wait for JED to reply. "Well, he was chief of Foxtrot Echo, after all."

"He's weird," JED said.

"Hancock?" I asked. "Don't break my ears."

"Hancock had been on Ginger for months," JED said.

"Holy hell," I said. "Him *too*?"

"Go figure," Chief said. "You get all the chances in the world to get out of this bitch, and the motherfucker chooses to stay in here for some bitch."

"I guess that explains why he usually stayed all day while his team was OFO," I said.

"You think that's nuts?" asked JED.

"I'm pretty sure I know nuts," I said. "And I told you not to break my ears."

"Apparently, Hancock wasn't into *fucking* Ginger."

"Wait a minute," I started, "he's into Ginger, but *not* into Ginger?"

"Oh, no. He's into her alright," Chief said.

"Yeah," said JED. "He loves licking her pussy, but only after she's been fucked first."

"Holy mother of pearl necklaces," I said. "You *can't* be serious."

"If I'm lyin' I'm dyin'," Chief said. "Or JED's dyin'. But I doubt he's lyin'. He's usually got good intel."

"If anyone would, I suppose it'd be you, wouldn't it, JED?"
I asked.

"If that ain't the shit," said Chief.

"I disregarded my own advice," I said.

"What's that?" asked JED.

"Not to ask questions."

Toward the end of the day, I left for the OPS floor. I had an important stop to make.

"My old friend," I greeted Wagner upon seeing him. He had just arrived for the swing shift.

"Ah, Mr. Chisolm. I wish it were under better terms."

"You gotta be thrilled."

"Words cannot convey, Mr. Chisolm."

I knew this was Wagner's last shift in the Bunker.

"You're going to miss this place."

"I miss it already," he said.

"On your way to Japan, as I recall?"

Wagner had received orders late the prior year for Yokota Air Base, just outside of Tokyo.

"Yes, and soon," said Wagner. "Due in by June 12."

"Do you think we solved everything?" I asked.

"If not, then it isn't known."

"You'll be able to visit Nagasaki."

"I've got family there, somewhere. I put in for everything in Asia but hoped for Japan."

"This isn't chance, you know?"

"I know it isn't," said Wagner.

"Do you think one of your top nine had anything to do with it?"

"Maybe one in particular."

"Which one?" I asked.

"'You can do what others say can't be done,'" said Wagner, with a look of immense satisfaction.

"If ever there was a keeper, that's it," I said.

"I believed it," said Wagner. "After I opened that one, I got my job back. Then I got my orders. And not just *any* orders."

"Any word of advice, old-timer?" I asked.

Wagner paused and scratched his temple.

"Once you're in, they've got you by the balls."

"Why does it always come back to our balls?"

"Be cautious, is all I'm saying."

"Probably one of our best deductions," I said.

"I'm leaving you with this fortune," said Wagner.

"You can't," I said. "That would jinx you. You have to keep it."

"It can't jinx me. It already served me. Besides, I'm not throwing it away. I'm giving it to you."

I wouldn't take the fortune from Wagner. Instead I reached out with an open palm for him to place the fortune in my hand. Seizing someone else's good fortune cannot be a good thing.

"I accept, sir."

I placed my new fortune with the two others in my wallet: "Yes" and "Adventure awaits."

"Hey, wait," I said. "What's your final tally?"

"One forty-seven," said Wagner.

"I believe that is a record."

"It is one sorry state of affairs that such a record is even up for grabs."

"You will be sorely missed, Mr. Wagner."

"This was a place and time, Mr. Chisolm."

"You must write, sir."

"As I shall."

63

"We were there, babe, 6209," I said to Rachel.

That had been our room number at the hotel in Paris over Presidents' Day weekend. I was reminiscing about that brief getaway on this mid-May Saturday morning. We were having coffee inside a café on the village square in the center of Sankt Veldhoven, Rachel's hometown.

"I get *gänsehaut* when I think about it."

"Genzee?"

"Goose skin. I get goose skin when I think about it."

"Oh," I said. "Goose bumps."

Rachel smiled at me. I looked into her eyes, tracing their shape and colors.

"Yes," said Rachel. "I get goose bumps."

"Where are you taking me today?" I asked.

"Let's finish our coffee. I want to show you instead."

"Want to know something?"

"Yes, babe," said Rachel.

"I can't imagine not being with you."

Ever since I once mentioned that I like it, Rachel always kept her hair the same way—bangs down to her eyebrows and cut straight across, shoulder length everywhere else. Spring had arrived, though it was still chilly in the mornings. Despite this, Rachel wore one of her plaid thigh-length skirts, along with stockings, Mary Jane pumps, and a fitted red shirt.

"Because of my mind, right?" asked Rachel.

"That too."

We laughed.

"Indian for lunch?" I asked.

"I'd love to."

We frequented a local Indian restaurant. That was our favorite food.

"Ready, babe?"

"Of course, my love."

Rachel took me on a journey in her lime-green Citroën 2CV, about half a mile over switchback roads, lanes, and side streets. Cobblestones agitated the tiny car. The town predated any thought of designing straight-through boulevards. From the café in the city center, we were probably only a quarter mile away as the crow flies.

"This is it," said Rachel.

She slowed down and drove the right-side wheels up onto a sidewalk. We stopped along a row of townhouses—one yellow, then gray, then drab green, then gray again. Across the street on this one-and-a-half-lane road stood similar townhomes. All of them were three floors high. You entered all of them directly from the sidewalk. Because of the narrow lane, exiting a house would require caution.

"What am I looking at?" I asked.

Rachel pointed to a sand-beige townhome directly across from us. The early-morning sun was shining on that side of the street.

"You see the stone above the door?"

"Looks like 1837."

"My great-great-grandpa put that stone there."

"Wow," I said, evaluating the facade. Each home shared a wall with two others, except for the homes at the end of the block.

"Everyone in my family up to my mom lived there."

"That long and you're the first one who *didn't* live there?"

"My sister and I were born here in Sankt Veldhoven, but not in this house."

"Is anyone still there? I mean, from your family."

"No, but my family goes all the way back in this town."

"I don't know what to say."

"I wanted you to see this."

"It's interesting. I'm not sure what to say."

Rachel held the steering wheel with her left hand and placed her right hand on my leg, then looked at me.

"We don't leave for just anything," she said.

Her warm, gentle touch conveyed a lifetime of love.

"I understand," I replied, with painstaking calm.

Such conversations had become ever more impassioned the closer I came to my end of tour.

"I love you, Roy."

Our magnetic attraction never relented.

"I love you too. More than you know."

Rachel bit her lower lip. Her eyes welled up.

"You know why I showed you this house?" she asked.

I said nothing but turned a bit more to face her head-on.

"I would give up everything to be with you, anywhere you go, Roy."

I took a deep breath. "Which makes me all the more careful about promising anything." I held her hand on my leg.

She glanced again at the house, then looked at me. "I know that, Roy."

I kissed Rachel's tears, then her lips. She closed her eyes, then took a long, slow deep breath.

64

It'd be safe to say that Dad was a frugal man. His father bailed on the family when he was young, and he often reminded my older brother, Buzz, and me that he had to work while still going to school, to support his mother and two younger brothers. Because of that, Dad always kept a tight rein on the family's cash flow. At five years old, I rolled up watering hoses for two cents. At eight, I cut grass for twenty-five cents. I did not receive an allowance, but I knew I'd be compensated for my hard work.

The family would on rare occasions go out for breakfast, but only on Saturday. This was a prized treat. We could choose anything on the menu, so long as it was under some specified limit. After Dad moved the family to Chicago to follow his career, I wished that for once we could go out for breakfast on a school day. The biting-cold winters dictated to Mom that we have a warm meal before school. Buzz and I gorged on oatmeal, but not by choice. Mom had a science to the whole procedure.

The best part of the day was waking up. Once the oatmeal was simmering, Mom would make the first pass at getting

Buzz and me out of bed. Only we'd stay in the sack until Dad turned on the heater. He'd shut the damn thing off at night. By virtue of Buzz's seniority, I was required to jump out of bed first. I'd take my position over the one floor vent in our room, getting frigid air at first, then warm air. Buzz would wait until the air got hot. At that point, he'd jump out of bed, hammer me, and take over my position. I'd hold my ground as long as I could. That usually lasted until Mom's second round.

In the meantime, Mom would set the table, fill the bowls, and go out in the winter chill to start the car. Our "environmental" concerns revolved around making our vehicle environment properly warm in the winter. Sometimes the car would run for several minutes before we piled in.

When we were finally underway, Mom would tune in to Paul Harvey. She loved his daily report. The school commute was long enough to get much of the spiel. I didn't know what he looked like, but Mr. Harvey sounded like family. Mom always gave a damn about the family. Dad too. He just worked his ass off, so we hardly ever saw him.

"It's your father's way of caring for the family," Mom always reminded us.

I wanted to turn out just like Dad—the man who knew everything and could solve anything. Buzz and I looked forward to summer vacations for many reasons, not the least of which was going to work with Dad. Each summer, we held a one-week internship arranging supplies for the ladies who worked night shift in the photo finishing plant Dad managed.

"That's the John Hancock," Buzz said.

"That's Sears and Standard Oil," I said.

Though we'd long been able to identify the tallest buildings in the Chicago skyline, we still ran through their names every time we saw them. I wanted a corner office in one of those towers and didn't care what job I'd have to do to get it. They'd really have you buying it to get one of those.

I harbored no illusions about what my father went through to keep the family afloat. Those long hours when Dad was not around, odd hours. They framed my mind. There were a few times Dad talked about giving a guy a pink slip. I'd wonder what those pink slips looked like or, worse, what the hell the guy was going to do with that piece of information. Live out of a goddamn box, as I heard it. And that's what I saw. The box people were all over downtown Chicago on the occasions I went to work with Dad.

"Our ancestors feared the wilderness," Miss Ohen told us. "They feared what they couldn't see, but they also feared what they *could* see—everything around them that wanted to kill them."

Yes, that. All of that and more. We never escaped that. Not our ancestors, none of us. Hell, not even Dad, with his strength and grit, could escape it, what with being forced—I mean *choosing*—to pack up the family to follow a career to have a salary in order to survive every day and every night. It is *still* written in our DNA, this fear. We survive to this day in fear.

It was the first week of May. I had just returned to the office from picking up books for my next class.

"Come have a seat, Sergeant Chisolm."

Gilbert stood at the entrance to his cubicle.

"I'm good," I said.

"We're mutineers," said Spock from that direction.

I poked my head around to see Spock sitting in Gilbert's cubicle.

"Like on the *Bounty*?" I asked.

"He's serious," said Spock. "He says we're mutinying."

"Mutinying?" I asked. "You're kidding, right?"

I looked in at Spock, who shifted in his seat. JED and Chief remained hidden in their cubicles, signaling their presence for duty by a single cough each.

"Spock says you questioned my leadership," said Gilbert, returning to his seat. "Come on in here, Sergeant Chisolm."

I looked at Spock. He stared pensively at me.

"That's mutiny," said Gilbert. His permanent smirk disguised whether he was serious.

"You guys are kidding, right?" I asked.

"I don't think so," Spock said.

"The UCMJ is clear. I can have you busted for mutiny." Gilbert picked up a copy of the UCMJ from his desk.

"So you *are* serious?" I asked.

"Spock said that you are critical of my leadership style."

Spock kept quiet, but his worried eyes pleaded with me to come up with something to disarm Gilbert.

"Now I get it," I said. "It's your pencil dick."

"You son of a bitch. I'll have you for insubordination now too."

"So you *do* have a pencil dick."

The three others hiding in their cubicles tried to hold back their howling.

"God*damn* you," said Gilbert. "Stay put, Chisolm. I'll be back in one minute."

He rushed out of the office.

"What are you *doing* talking to that asshole about what I say, you dick?" I asked Spock.

"It's no big deal."

"It's obviously a big deal," I said. "What did you say to him, anyhow?"

"The guy's one pancake short of a full stack," said Chief, now standing in his cubicle.

"I told him about the stuff you say from your classes," Spock said.

"*That's* the problem," I said. "You threatened him with logic."

"Where's your head, man?" Chief asked Spock.

Gilbert returned.

"Frazione will be calling you, Chisolm."

I took the phone call when it came in.

"Sergeant Chisolm, what the hell is going on up there?" Frazione asked.

"All I know, sir, is that I came in the office after picking up books for my next semester, and I'm told there is a mutiny afoot."

"Sergeant Gilbert says that you were insubordinate."

"Unsure about that, sir."

"Well, what is he talking about, then?"

"Someone might have used the words *pencil* and *dick* in the same sentence, but I don't know anything about being insubordinate, sir."

"*That* is insubordinate, Sergeant Chisolm," Gilbert shouted in the background.

"What's he saying?" asked Frazione.

"In all honesty, sir, Sergeant Gilbert did state that Airman Spock and I were starting a mutiny."

"Quit the charade, Chisolm," shouted Gilbert.

"With all due respect, sir, who on earth would think that I would start a mutiny?" I asked Frazione.

"I'm not sure what he's talking about," said Frazione. "But you knocked Schmink's project out of the park. Intel loves it."

"I'm glad to hear that, sir."

"Please put Gilbert back on the line."

"It's for you, Sergeant Gilbert," I said, holding the phone out for him.

Gilbert yanked the phone from my hand. There was a bit of silence.

"I'm going by the UCMJ, sir," Gilbert said.

Silence.

"He doesn't know when to keep his mouth shut," Gilbert continued.

Silence.

"That qualifies for it," said Gilbert.

A long pause ensued.

"Fine, sir," said Gilbert. "Goodbye."

Gilbert said nothing.

"Well, what did he *say*?" I asked.

"Shut up, Chisolm," said Gilbert. "Get out of here, Spock."

Gilbert remained seated and silent at his desk the rest of the day.

The facts had been circulating for some time about a New Year's Eve gathering at Chief's place in the Q. The inmates present had gone overboard in drink. Conversations ensued. Who had the bigger this, that, or the other thing. Of course, the inmates could get downright insane, alcohol or not. At some point, Gilbert claimed to have the biggest dick. Debates raged. Anyone could claim anything. Gilbert, regrettably, half passed out, wanted to prove what should have been left to doubt.

Fear never left us. It was only displaced along the way because we learned how to draw lines. We drew lines and learned how to follow those lines. Anything and anyone who could follow our lines wouldn't need to be killed. If anything doesn't follow our lines, we kill it. We just need the lines so we know what to kill. I didn't know anything about lines back then, but my sixth sense told me the truth. And sometimes all you can do is follow your sixth sense.

However they gain power, those with authority over others know their capacity. They have followed the lines to their logical conclusion. This is our nature. This *is* nature. This is our condition. They know full well that when they crack the whip, the rest will scurry to their respective corners, heads down, in angst, in fear that another shoe may fall, hopefully not on them. I'd hated the drill since day one. But I always found a retreat. It was no different during those sunny Cold War days in West Germany, when my retreat meant midday sabbaticals from the Bunker.

Just before the inmates broke for lunch, I'd scoot out. That way I avoided anyone asking me where the hell I was going. Besides, I never knew how long I'd be gone. I never kept an eye on the clock. Since the cafeteria building stood adjacent to the Bunker entrance, I had to extricate myself a few minutes early. Once in my car, I'd roll out of the parking lot and down the long road through the pines, driving off in silence to the edge of my hill. I parked on the same grassy turnout every time. This spot afforded me a view south and west of the surrounding valleys. I'd pass my noon sabbatical watching them roll out in front of me. I'd always stay as long as I could. Sometimes for an hour, sometimes longer if the requirements of retreat dictated those terms.

Being five miles out from the Bunker granted a million miles of freedom. As long as I could practicably stay, I stayed. No one knew. I never told anyone. I knew how to keep secrets. This was my entitlement. There was no guilt. This was the Cold War. I did everything I could to warm up. In the event of a clear day, I was liable to be found there on that hill. Passing clouds were OK, but overcast days, no matter how warm, no way. Under circumstances otherwise beyond my control, I maintained this position.

Birds in flight, soaring for hours, circled in the updraft as air ascended from the valleys and hillsides. Patches of forest remained on the hilltops, while the hillsides had been organized into farmland. In the valley depths stood villages. The clearing provided spectacular views into the distance but offered increasingly scarce opportunities to see the birds—a true shame, since they would migrate annually away from there, then return to less and less domain. Not my concern, right? Whose concern was it, then? Who has any right to say what is right regarding any decision over anyone or anything else? That was a goddamn tragedy, that the view came at the expense of the birds.

I would drift back to the days of riding in the back seat of the Chevelle. If not that, if not home, then I'd recount the day I arrived in country, the moment I stood at the gate to the Bunker, the commitment I made to go beyond this place.

At around the same time each day of duty on my hill, an old woman would pass my car. There happened to be a cemetery up the road from where I'd park, and she always went there. She never wore anything other than black. Even her boots were black, and of the combat boot variety. She lived the role model from my imagination, and it was no stretch at all from the stereotype of German grandmothers portrayed in old films.

Once she got to the cemetery, I could make out that she was cleaning a select few headstones. Following that, she'd lay flowers on them and stand for a while in front of each one. I was never close enough to hear her say anything, but she would gesture at each gravesite, maybe talking with the dead about how she'd soon be with them.

Whether I spent minutes or hours on this hill, it didn't matter. When I left, my conscience would be clear and my bearing trued.

The inmates couldn't always understand what they wanted, but some were forever standing at the ready to grab their handle and get the others back in line. Left to their own devices, the inmates gridlocked in crisscross lines over who the hell had control over their lives.

"Are you serious?" JED asked. "*Now?*"

JED had just gotten a Thursday-morning call from the orderly room and been told to report to the Brook for a random weigh-in. The random weigh-in gave the Air Force a continuing opportunity to ensure that members met the standards of appearance, fitness, and reality. This, apparently, was JED's fourth random weigh-in within five months.

"You were told to get going," Gilbert said.

"I've got Intel lined up to take a look in half an hour," said JED.

"Intel says it's their highest priority," said Chief. "All the way from the top."

Chief's singular responsibility now was being our point of contact for the Intel teams on software testing and deployment days.

"Summary Counts, PR 89-018," JED confirmed.

"*Hey*," said Chief. "We've been preparing this all week."

"JED, why haven't you left yet?" asked Gilbert.

Gilbert would not stand for the mission getting in the way of an order.

"We promised the major delivery *today*," said Chief. "This is feeding upstream reporting."

"No questions," said Gilbert. "Now get down there, JED."

JED grabbed his car keys and got up to leave.

"Fine," he said, looking at Gilbert. "You handle it."

"We've had production on hold all morning," Chief tried to explain. "The databases will be too far out of sync by the time JED can make it back."

"*Too* bad," said Gilbert.

JED headed for the door.

"Wait a minute," Chief said, pleading with Gilbert. "It'll be another two weeks before we can restart the process. Who's going to tell the major back there?"

"You are," said Gilbert. "You're their point of contact."

"How about making a call and saying JED will be in tomorrow? One day isn't going to make a difference."

"One more time, and this is for both of you," Gilbert said, gritting his teeth. "Get going. Your program will wait."

"You don't understand what the hell's going on around here, do you?" asked JED.

"Now *that's* a goddamn mission statement," I added.

JED exited the office. Gilbert smiled. I didn't need a clock. The seconds ticked by in my head. There would be no reasoning with the unreasonable. I followed JED out two minutes later, around the hallway, down the stairs, through the tunnel, past the turnstile, and free of my incarceration.

65

The clear, sunny day proved my Bunker exit was a good decision. I spent the afternoon hearing arguments in the court of my mind. I deliberated "us"—Life, Liberty, and the Pursuit. The big ones. I was killing myself trying to reconcile the difference between what I wanted out of life and what others would make of it. Falling into this abyss, unable to grasp any tether to climb back out to what was home, could be only one thing— my penance for some sin of which I yet did not know, but for which I was going to make good.

But *why*? Always *why*? And then it came to me, this game. Everyone works god-awful hard to make something of it. But they, *them*, those bastards never give up. To *them*, the rest must conform within a specific and channeled way—and we end up buying it at any cost. Then there is no other tolerable way on God's green earth. Inmates got what they could from living, but how much living could they do with only the slop thrown down in front of them? Others, them, *they* cut our incisors. After the incisors are cut, we are channeled within the lines. We have no choice.

If the inmates made it to twenty, to life, they could have

BUNKER MENTALITY   303

it. I surveyed the banged-up remains of lifers who'd been contorted into form. JED didn't want it. He just couldn't label what was going on. What he saw, he didn't like. No one likes it up front. But when that's the only thing up for sale, what are you going to do? JED was taking a little longer than usual to choke it down.

This was a show of force. The inmates, they were the numbers. These numbers could be statistically used to scare off the Russians. We had sixteen trillion troops on the continent to back up our big dick nuclear warheads. If the Russians didn't kill us, our compliance by the numbers would. One must show up. One must fill a hole.

I had received a postcard from Wagner the day prior.

C

I made it.
We said we'd find our way home. I'm home.
I am right at this moment standing on ground zero.
I swear I can hear my grandfather calling me.
Stay safe, my friend.
W

On the front was a nuclear mushroom cloud sketched over a city. A stamp in English on the back read "Nagasaki."

I had the right commandment at confirmation, but the wrong question. Killing is all that *is* done. I could see it on my map. I could hear it in the second hand of every clock. I could read it in every contrail. We can't have this "freedom" nonsense. Why else do we have all these lines and all this time and just where the hell do you think you're going, anyhow? Who the *fuck* do you think *you* are, Johnny?

Once you can't take it upon yourself to use your own intellect, without distraction, by default you lose it to whatever circus is in town. And then they've bought it. You can't go back to the good old anything. This was the inmates' dilemma: We've got here and now. These, *now*, are the days that will be what we make of them. And if you don't take control, you will be medicated according to need, or otherwise trimmed to a narrow tolerance—following proper procedure, of course.

The Bunker itself held sway over the inmates, no doubt. But at a much more rudimentary level, the inmates came out of the larger context. The inmates weren't *born* with the mentality. They *bought* into it. And the earlier the better, for all concerned. They hungered for the real, for the genuine. They were starving. They were gullible to any semblance of what they had never known, but what they believed was authentic. I thought I had no tether to grasp and pull myself out. I was already out. They were the ones with no tether. The inmates succumbed to the superfluous distractions offered, to the meaningless and ever-changing pursuits set in front of them. We all have our incisors cut early. We all have the same indoc since day one. We all are ramped up quickly to play, to orchestrate our own demise.

Over and over and over again, like ever-stronger doses of chemotherapy, I drank of pure reason in undiluted form. The only distraction I had was the confines of my mind. This was my tonic. I dredged my mind's containment to determine if there was such a thing as *real* freedom that could be experienced outside the white picket fence. I wanted to kill the idea of living life within the lines of a prescribed and narrowly defined way. I am an American, rest assured, *you*, in America. But I will not be condemned for holding tight to what you let me discover. You gave me no choice.

Dad, I say my prayers every day. Not the least of which is that I'll find myself beyond the freedom proffered—bound on one side by the distraction of being buried alive, and on the other side constrained for fear of falling in. And if you do not fall in, you're out—and I mean out of your fucking mind.

To you back home who have the luxury of not knowing of this place, to you back home who have the comfort to choose a "what now, where to, and why not," you can be certain that I haven't wasted a single moment. There is no time I haven't spent trying to find a way out. Because of your generosity to place me at the fore of this war, I've had the time. And if I may, I'd like to take this opportunity to thank you for your benevolence.

It is this perpetual motion, the relentless pursuit, unattainable in a relative way, that creates this phenomenon. I saw enough of it. Once you're *in*, there simply is no other way, no way at all to reconcile the difference between what you want out of life and what others would make of it. The weight of the structure ensures your compliance. Ambition is trimmed to a narrow tolerance. Pursue, Johnny, pursue, but you better damn well do it in an acceptable way. The mind is incipiently tapped and distracted to pursue something ill-defined and constantly moving. And people buy it. Always. That's what gets me. People dutifully conduct the chase and cling to their tenuous positions, hunkered down in this horrendous bunker mentality.

66

Humidity was baked into the air on this late-August morning. Except for me and two others, everyone was seated. The three of us stood at the front of the stage, facing the squadron in the base theater on the Brook. At the scheduled time, the Shirt yelled the call to attention. He and the commander then marched to the stage from the back of the room.

The Shirt read:

> Citation to Accompany the Award of the Air
> Force Commendation Medal
>   To Roy Chisolm
>   Sergeant Roy Chisolm distinguished
> himself by meritorious service as
> Intelligence Operations Programmer,
> Intelligence Systems Support Branch,
> 427th Communications Squadron, United
> States Air Forces in Europe, Borlingau
> Tactical Integration Center, West
> Germany, for his contribution toward the
> Treaty on Conventional Armed Forces

in Europe. Sergeant Chisolm designed
a series of reports, used by American
negotiators in their discussions between
NATO and WARSAW PACT alliances.
Sergeant Chisolm's technical expertise
and diligence to work through chal-
lenges made the reporting system a
success. His efforts and resourcefulness
played a key role in the Intelligence
Operations Center winning the United
States Air Forces in Europe Intelligence
Center of the Year Award. The distinctive
accomplishments of Sergeant Chisolm
reflect credit upon himself and the
United States Air Force.

"The Intel commander put you up for this, Sergeant
Chisolm," my commander said as he pinned the medal to my
chest. "You nailed it, son."

"Proud to serve, sir."

"I know you are, Roy."

I rendered a salute, then remained at attention. The Shirt
read congratulatory remarks for two others standing to my left
for volunteer work they had done organizing a summer picnic.

I stared over everyone's head to a red pinpoint light at the
back of the theater. If only ten Hail Marys could solve this
penance. I was shoehorned into the silence of my brain debat-
ing nothing and everything.

I recalled one Chicago winter when I came across kids
who'd been destroyed on account of drugs. That year Mom
worked a part-time job as a shuttle driver to help pay for Buzz
and me to attend parochial school. She drove around town
picking up children with special needs and delivering them to
a rehabilitation center. The trek to my school coincided with

part of her route, so Mom saved time by picking up her "passengers" along the way.

I saw two of them each morning—one whose mother had overdosed on heroin, and the other a kid whose LSD trip had gone awry as he ended up running into and being hit by traffic on a busy road. Neither could speak coherently; they slobbered incessantly and had erratic and sometimes violent twitches or body movements. All I know is that it freaked the shit out of me about ever taking drugs. I think Mom did this on purpose.

One of the kids came from the poor side of town, the other from the right side of town. Though economics might have been an instigator as to what someone bought, it played no role in their outcome. They were the same at that point—captured in a complete loss of freedom from someone buying it.

Following commander's call, I returned to the dorm, hung up my full-dress coat, and headed to the Bunker.

"Did you get in for your eval yet?" I asked JED.

A week earlier, the inmates played a game of keep-away with JED's MoonPies. The game ended when JED recaptured three of his MoonPies and pounded them into paste. JED won, which means he lost. JED was referred to a psych eval.

"I don't need an eval."

"You need it, my friend," I said. "*You* might not think you need it, but *they* think you need it."

The inmates were now aware of JED's propensity to snap and lash out violently. Gnashing his teeth became his show of will. Pounding MoonPies was just one execution of that will.

JED fidgeted.

"Let's go to the OPS floor," I said.

We arrived and sat down at the operator desk.

"Do you think you gave them an excuse to do it?" I asked.

JED's gnashing began. He remained silent.

"I'm not like them," I said. "You're not like them. They don't want you *not* to be like them. They're trying to turn you into them."

JED would be taking over my projects upon my departure. I showed him how to handle data imports for my software and write custom templates for one-time reports. But if he couldn't get lost in writing programs, or drinking whiskey and eating MoonPies, he acted a lot like the kids in Mom's shuttle—mumbling under his breath or otherwise making no sense unless asked point-blank to repeat a comment. Unfortunately for JED, because of his willful execution of force, he unwittingly volunteered for the Bunker special education program.

"They want you medicated," I said, "because they think it will get you with the program."

"Fuck this place," JED mumbled.

"There you go again," I said. "You keep saying that, but they're really fucking *you*."

JED looked through me.

"Hello?" I asked, waving my hand in his face. "Do you hear what I'm saying?"

"You got something wrong?" asked JED.

"*Me* have something wrong?" I asked. "Wake up."

"A psych eval," said JED, still staring. "They want me to get a psych eval."

"Yeah, we determined that."

"I know they're going to put me on something."

"Everyone is on something," I said. "So, accept their pills, just don't take them. But settle down."

"They can't do this."

"Do what?" I asked. "This is their program. You signed up."

"Do you ever feel the walls are closing in?" asked JED.

"Not really," I said with twitched eyebrows.

"I sweat from it, especially in the tunnel."

"Then you're normal," I said.

"I want out of here. I need to transfer out. *Something.*"

"To where?" I asked. "And more importantly, why?"

"I don't know. *Anywhere.* How the hell have *you* survived?"

"Because I know the *why.*"

"Then why?"

"My why only applies to me," I said. "Short answer? I made a promise."

"The long answer?" asked JED.

"Violence, aggression. They're in our DNA. It is only a question of *why* we fight. That, and a little bit of *when.*"

"What?" asked JED.

"Why and when. As for when, today is just as good a day as any. But it doesn't have to be today. It could be tomorrow or a hundred years from now. But if not today, the day will come. It always does."

JED squinted.

"As for why, it's actually pretty simple."

"What are you *talking* about?" Jed asked, cocking his head back and throwing up his hands.

"Focus, goddamn it," I said. "I'm imparting million-dollar wisdom here."

"OK, OK. I'm listening."

"Someone somewhere always *needs* something. It always boils down to what someone *needs.*"

"Am I crazy or are you crazy?" asked JED.

"Think about it," I said. "When someone needs what you've got and they can't get it any other way but from you, and you won't give it to them, you're inches from violence. This is our world."

"How do you think up this shit?"

"I've had enough time in here to earn a Nobel Prize in the logic."

"Maybe put it another way?"

"There is this thing we call the American Dream. Ivan surely has some kind of Russian Dream. If there isn't enough of the *stuff* needed for all our dreams to come true, we get into nightmare territory, which is where we are now. At the moment, we just call it the Cold War."

"That doesn't even relate to me."

"Wrong," I said. "This relates to everyone, at every level, at all times."

JED stared at me.

"They need your compliance," I said. "You don't want to give them your compliance, but they *need* your compliance. You scare them. You're not like them. Medicating you is just their way to get you to play ball."

JED scratched his chin.

"I see what you're saying," he said.

"They want you to get in *line*."

"But *why*?" JED shouted.

"*Now* you're asking the right question. Why? All it takes is some asshole encroaching on someone else—in our case, the Russians trying to move in on us. In your case, them wanting to move in on *you*."

"This is how you've made it?"

"You don't need a textbook or teacher to tell you. Listen to yourself. Your need is to survive this place, and you yourself get violent if anyone gets in the way of how you try to survive it."

"That's insane."

"You'll learn," I said. "You just need to know *why* you fight. Then you won't go crazy from wondering what you are doing here, or anywhere."

"I don't get it."

"We're going in circles," I said.

"Just more bullshit."

"They *need* you to be like them. They *fight* for you to be like them. You're out of line, and they only know to follow lines. I ask you, *Why* do you fight? If your answer is true to yourself, you will find peace. You'll kill yourself otherwise."

JED calmed, offered no reply, then got up and walked away.

67

In the Bunker, religion had always been as much a given as the right to self-defense by any means. This was the military, after all. How could one be in the armed forces and not believe in the right to bear arms? How could one possibly die in armed conflict and not believe in God and an afterlife?

"Why are you even in the military?" Spock asked.

"I got a right to be here," said JED. "Just like you."

When it came to God, only the name might be different— the One, the Father, the Almighty. Just so long as an inmate didn't inform anyone else that they might believe in Xerxes the Car-Waxing Monkey, they were golden.

Spock and JED debated from the safety and comfort of their respective cubicles.

"Can you believe this guy?" asked Spock.

"Can you *believe* this guy?" parroted JED.

"How can you be an atheist on active duty?" Spock prodded.

"There is no God," said JED.

Chief was throwing darts. Gilbert was OFO to Ramstein.

"Prove it," said Spock.

"You're the one with a God," said JED. "*You* prove it."

JED lodged his defense now because Spock had tried to proselytize him.

"Spock, you're a shit stirrer," I said, standing up within my cubicle.

"Yeah, well what do you know, Chisolm?" asked Chief.

"I know there is a God," I said.

"How?" JED asked.

"Faith and science are not at odds," I said.

"They're not even related," said JED.

"They're the exact same thing," I said.

"You're talking out your ass," said Spock.

"How?" JED asked again, standing inside his cubicle, looking at me.

"Science is observation," I said. "Faith is belief. If anything, they complement each other."

"That's still not proof," said Spock, exiting his cubicle and stretching his arms.

"I'm not the one demanding proof," I said.

"More bullshit," added Spock.

"Pure logic," I said, "which you of all people should understand, Mr. Spock."

The fluorescent lights hummed.

"*Science* can't tell me why I'm here, and neither can any belief in some *god*," I said. "No one anywhere has ever been able to answer the why. Why did it all begin, or does it even have a beginning? The best anyone can do is say *this* is what *is* because I see it, or because I believe it."

"There ain't no God," insisted JED.

"That's a double negative," I said. "God exists, says the atheist. Proven!"

"I have proof there is no God," said JED, hushed, resolute.

"And your theory is?" asked Chief.

"I had a sister," said JED, pausing. "Or, I have a sister. I never know which one to say."

Chief stopped his game. Spock stopped fidgeting. I stood with my arms crossed, listening.

"I was fourteen. It was summertime, a cloudy Saturday. My twin sister was picked up early in the afternoon by her friend's parents on their way home from somewhere. Becky spent the afternoon at her friend's house. Rain came and went all day. It was pouring late in the day. My mom called that evening to find out if Becky needed a ride home. Becky had left her friend's house that afternoon to run home during a break in the rain. We spent months trying to find her."

"Sorry to hear that," said Chief.

"Mom slowly went crazy. Dad's I-can-fix-anything strength left him like sand drained from an hourglass. Every evening, he sat in the garage, looking out and waiting for Becky to ride up on her bike. She loved that bike. 'She'll be home,' Dad kept saying. Each night after sunset, Dad closed the garage door, came in, and sat in silence in his chair, with the lamp on next to him, staring. Strange thing: all that time, Becky's bike was in the garage. It's still there. She's never been found."

I heard a chair creak.

"Becky and I were close. Sometimes I still talk to her. I tell her to come home. I tell her it's OK. But it's not OK. So don't ever tell me again about your God."

I left for my hill.

68

As I observed aircraft trace their routes above me, I recalled a moment eight months earlier, when I had just been handed my orders for Bootstrap.

"My guy at Ramstein says he was on it," said Timmons.

"He" was Ed, and Ed was assigned to Ramstein, where both of us worked on a project that spanned both locations. Ed left for the US on leave December 21, 1988, out of Frankfurt. Connecting on a stopover in London, Ed boarded Pan Am's *Clipper Maid of the Seas*, known as Flight 103, which was blown up over Lockerbie, Scotland.

Since then, every time I see a contrail, I am reminded.

My hill afforded me full and frank recognition that corroboration between what I know and what I once knew failed. Thankfully so.

I returned to the office after listening to the echo of half a dozen flights.

"They bent me over," said Chief, infringing upon my peace.

"How's that?" asked Spock.

"They extended me to my ETS."

"I thought you applied for an early out?" I asked.

Chief had waited three months for word of his curtailment, only to receive thank-you-for-your-service, so-we're-extending-you-in-the-Bunker orders.

"Ouch," I said.

"They've now got me leaving ten months *after* I'm supposed to."

"You didn't even get to pull your pants down and enjoy it," said Burns. "I hear we may have a RIF coming. Budget crunch of some sort."

Burns had come by the office to stir up commotion about a possible Reduction In Force.

"Then how did we get JED?" I asked. "And Spock?"

"Still leaves more than half a dozen positions unfilled," said Burns.

"If that isn't the damnedest thing," I said.

"I don't think they can do it legally," Chief tried to rationalize. "I'm going to personnel."

"Good luck with that," said Gilbert. "You're screwed."

"They're not letting you go because we need people here," said Burns.

"You're going to plead your case to the same people who extended you?" I asked. "Brilliant."

"The military doesn't care," Burns said. "They own your ass."

"That's the most intelligent thing I've ever heard you say, Burnsie," I said. "It's always *them*."

What our ApPLe hadn't completely ruined, a deepening federal budget crunch did—a harsh wave of vacancies. The budget crunch was interpreted differently by each inmate, but it scared most of them. If an inmate was close to twenty, they were worried. If an inmate was halfway to twenty, they were frightened. If an inmate wanted out but had too much time left on their enlistment, they were fucked.

I liked Burnsie. You knew where you stood with anyone

retired on active duty. Help them get to twenty, or at least don't impinge on them getting there, and you could live large. Burns had nothing to prove. His prior experience in programming matched many at his rank—none.

The Air Force had little choice but to cross-train more senior ranks into the career field. Junior enlisted programmers like me often earned their chops and then took all their experience and fled the military for high-paying civilian jobs. This left few to move up through the ranks. There was also a bonus pay incentive for anyone wanting to cross-train from another career field.

After all, what could one hope to do after a military career in explosive ordnance disposal? Cross-training gave many senior-ranking inmates experience in the programming field, if only on paper.

The next morning, I walked in on time and went to my desk.

"It's too quiet," I said. "Someone say something."

No one replied.

"Who's in here?" I asked.

"Me," said Chief.

Gilbert walked in ten minutes late. But who was counting? I focused on coursework for an evening class.

JED walked in thirty minutes late.

"Tighten it up, JED," said Gilbert.

Someone was counting.

"I had a flat," JED claimed.

Gilbert met JED in the middle of the office. "You can be replaced," he said.

Gilbert had intended the comment to make us all duck and cover. His D&C maneuver had no impact.

"Replace me then," said JED.

We all knew that an inmate *could* be replaced, but if they were, it would not be any time soon.

"Plan accordingly," said Gilbert. "If you'd left *early* enough, you'd have been here on time."

JED gnashed. He squeezed his fists.

Gilbert continued. "Get your act together."

"Picking at scabs," I said.

"Stay out of it, Chisolm," said Gilbert.

"I am hearing you, which means you are bringing me into this," I said.

"I'm late on account of a flat," said JED. "You're making this a huge deal."

"If I let *this* slip, and I let *that* slip, *then* what happens? By next month, you end up like Chisolm over there."

"That's what I mean," I said. "You want me in on this? Now I'll be in on this."

"I'm not bringing you in on anything, Chisolm," said Gilbert. "I'm not going to lighten up."

The public flogging made JED snap up stiff as a board.

"I'm not late for anything," he said.

"Oh boy," said Chief, now looking over the top of his cubicle.

"Get over here," said Gilbert.

JED headed for the exit. Hell, the hairs on the back of *my* neck stood up.

"Fuck this place," JED said, pulling our massive steel door behind him with a full swing and a giant thud.

Aggression had no place in the military. Unrestrained, JED created a real problem. Threatening behavior like this was entirely at odds with our mission—a willingness to destroy everything, but carefully targeted only toward the narrow slice of populations numbering in the hundreds of millions around the world who, collectively, had the misfortune of not being us. It would be crazy otherwise, and therein lay JED's error of judgment. The choice was really his. In an odd way, I suppose there could have been some measure of victory for JED to have chosen violence. But with all this attention he didn't need, JED would be placed on even stronger and mandatory "keep the voices inside only" pills.

In fifth grade, I had a friend who came from a real Catholic family—an eight-kids-big family. With so many children, how much attention could any one of them get? But the Goat got attention, at least in school.

"Quack quack quaaaack," the Goat loved to blurt out in class.

Sister Jenice, AKA the Duck, had her back to the class. This young nun was our English teacher that year. Her waddling gait when she walked full stride down a hallway did not help her cause.

"Alright," the Duck began, slapping her desk. "*Who* did that?"

The Duck knew who did it, but instilling personal responsibility was a part of our education. The responsible party would need to speak up.

No one broke the code of silence. The Duck pressed on with the lecture.

"Quack quack qua—"

The Goat had a bias toward goats, but no matter the animal chosen, the attack launched the minute the Duck faced the chalkboard. If you could name an animal, the Goat did his dead-level best to mimic it.

"Mr. Unitas! Stop that right now."

The Duck addressed us students with the respect afforded a "mister" or "miss," but her soft voice couldn't command the authority required to stop the Goat. Making matters worse, because the Goat now had the room's undivided attention, there was no stopping him. I felt sorry for the Duck, but the class had expectations. The Duck's lesson followed lunch recess. Unfortunately, by the end of our thirty-minute lunch break, we were pinballs.

The Goat continued until there was one of two outcomes—the Duck buckled and ran out of the room crying to get Big Momma, or the Duck buckled and ran out of the room *not* crying to get Big Momma. Big Momma was Sister Agnes, the school heavyweight—in terms of both physical size and age. Big Momma packed walloping, gale-force-wind lungs and an unbreakable yardstick used for smacking desks. There would be no negotiating with Big Momma. But with seven siblings, what else could the Goat do?

"Mr. Unitas," with respect, Big Momma began, "what are you going to do with your life?"

Sweat rolled off Big Momma's brow and beaded on her dark mustache. She stood in front of the Goat's desk, yardstick in hand. The words sounded like a question, but Big Momma didn't want an answer. She walked to the front of the room.

"Do you know what happens to delinquents?"

She threw this bone out for the entire class to scarf up.

"They'll grow up," Big Momma pressed on, as if reading a crime novel. "They'll become criminals and a menace to society. They'll go to jail. They'll get bread and water and that's *all*."

Big Momma made "delinquents" sound like axe murderers. She ended her sermon with a whack to the Duck's desk. When the flat edge of the yardstick hit parallel to the desk, the shock made our ears ring. Everyone jumped when Big Momma got it just right. She was good at it, like greater than fifty-fifty good at it.

"Now, *why* do you do this?" Big Momma asked rhetorically, giving us more food for thought.

She studied our faces.

"Your parents work very hard for you to be here. Don't let me hear again that you've disrupted class, Mr. Unitas."

Big Momma panned the room, looked into the eyes of each of us, then walked out. We were quiet the rest of the day. In fact, the Goat might maintain silence for a week or two before going rogue again. As we moved deeper into the school year, the Goat honed his timing to the Duck's breaking point. He adjusted. He learned when to cut it off just right. But until he perfected it, Big Momma showed up, yardstick in hand.

Gilbert was our Goat, all grown up. Both could hurl senseless attacks to break the insecure. Like the Goat, Gilbert kept vigil over the opportunity to practice his animal instinct. The only difference in Gilbert's case was that there was no one around the Bunker to keep him caged in. That, and no one really gave a fuck.

69

"Thirty pound-feet of torque," said Dad.

Deep in one of those Chicago winters, Dad was giving Buzz and me a lesson in auto repair. We spent two days in our carport, covered in oil and grease, replacing a transmission during the ass-biting cold. Dad looked down through the engine compartment at Buzz lying on his back.

"Alright, alright," said Buzz.

"Be *careful*," said Dad.

Dad always said to be careful. No matter what you did, he always said it.

"Ah *shit*," Buzz said.

I heard a snap.

"What happened?" asked Dad.

"The bolt broke, *damn it*."

"Ah *shit*."

The strange thing about this was that the bolt was thin and only a half-inch long. And that Dad didn't yell at Buzz for cursing. Four of these bolts were used to hold the driveshaft to the transmission u-joint. Buzz over torqued and broke one of them. Who would have thought that such a small and unassuming part was critical to moving such an enormous weight? Buzz crawled out from under the car and disappeared. I didn't. Dad and I spent the rest of the afternoon finding parts to tap out the broken bolt and replace it.

I wouldn't be torqued down in any manner. By Halloween, my degree requirements were complete. My escape plan was almost in place. Following in the footsteps of those ahead of me, of those contorted into silence to do as they were told— that world had become foreign to me. They saw no way out. I saw no way back to embrace what was, but instead to work in earnest at understanding *why* it is. I couldn't stand if not standing on my hill. I couldn't see but for seeing west. I couldn't move, if not of my own will.

No, not me. Not to the manicured lawns, the perfect straightaways, the careening boulevards. No more locked in, no more lines, no more death by the numbers. I sought no tether, no hold on me, no sway over me. I would not return to the confines. Instead, I contacted the Black Label Cargo firm out of New Orleans. Black Label offered a position on one of their ships. I could remain at sea, using my computer skills on board, sailing to ports around the world. There would be no landlocked return. Neither stranglehold of country nor physical geography would ever again subvert me. I had pursued this road of no roads since summer.

I leaned back in my chair to study my map.

"Hey, Burnsie," I said. "Any chance of you getting out before your time's up?"

This was, of course, rhetorical to a lifer, but the silence in the room at the moment was intolerable. For old time's sake, I had to come up with something to spark debate.

"I think I'm going to stick it out."

"You know what they do to anything that sticks out, right?" I asked.

"Yeah, yeah," said Burns.

"They're going to keep you down, brother," I said.

"I'm way over halfway," said Burns. "It'd be stupid to get out."

"What if they do a RIF?" I asked.

"I'm not planning on that."

"What could they offer you as a buyout?"

"Wouldn't do it."

"For one hundred million?"

"OK, for that," said Burns.

"For one million?"

"Maybe."

"For one hundred thousand?"

"Stupid at that point."

"You'd have cash money and you'd be *free* from this place, or any place," I said. "They'd be buying *your* way out. How twisted is that?"

Burns paused for a moment.

"Never going to happen. No one would just *give* me that kind of money."

"But if they did, you could be free," I said. "And why not? You've cursed it before."

"I wouldn't do it because no one's got that much," Burns said, agitating in his seat.

"They've got that much," I said. "It's only a question of what they're willing to buy with it."

"What does that even mean?"

"Just casting conundrums," I said.

"Uh-huh."

"OK. One more," I said.

"My head is exploding."

"Just one more."

"Fine."

"Would you ever get out just to get out? No reward. No regrets. Just because you discovered that you can't stand the weight. To be *free*? Unowned-by-any-motherfucking-thing *free*?"

"You're out of your goddamn mind, Chisolm."

"Always," I said. "That, I concede."

"Chisolm, have you ever fit in?" asked Chief. *"Anywhere?"*

"Where do you think you're going to end up?" asked Gilbert.

"I know what it means to fit in, but you'd have to see it to believe it," I said. "As far as where I'll end up, right where I want to be."

"Put up with a little BS, you get a guaranteed paycheck, life's easy," said Spock. "Pretty sweet deal, if you ask me."

"Easy?" I asked. "Yes, so long as you buy it."

"Getting out is shortsighted, Chisolm," said Burns. "You're the one giving up everything."

"No, not quite accurate," I said. "I'm giving up *something* for *everything*. And I've got a plan to do it."

Silence.

"I'm giving up the certainty of pressed, starched minds, shirts, shorts, shops, manicured lawns, and a dick-sucking perfect princess who won't take it up the ass two days after the honeymoon."

"Psychotic," said Burns.

"I just want unvarnished memories of weed-infested landscapes and no roads in sight. I want nothing but the chance, and the choice for everything."

"Out of your mind, Chisolm," said Chief.

"Yes, and the other things," I said. "I am out of it."

The inmates had their moments of accuracy, unintentional as they may have been.

"I want the chance at a wrinkled life, wrinkled like old hands," I concluded to those present. I put my right palm to my heart, then walked out of the office.

I must have been no more than four years old in my earliest memory. Dad took Buzz and me to my great-grandmother Mimi's house. We had gone to fight back her yard and get it in order. The question of "order" confused me. The unusual perfection of weed stalks and wildly uneven grass patches made for ideal running paths. Mimi's chaotic garage added to my exploration and discovery. Of course, leaving this all to itself would never do.

"The sun will always keep you warm and happy," Mimi said, embracing my face with her aged hands.

Mimi always wore a black linen dress, even on the hottest of Southern California days, on account of my great-grandfather having passed away years earlier.

"Yes ma'am."

"I have something for you, Roy."

Mimi reached into her purse and retrieved a folded white handkerchief. She carefully unfolded it and held up a two-inch-long carved wooden cross. The cross was attached to a necklace strung with small wooden beads.

"What is it?" I asked.

Mimi put the cross and necklace in my right hand. She folded my left hand over it, then clasped her hands around mine and looked into my eyes.

"This belonged to your great-grandfather."

Just then Dad entered the house. He stopped inside the doorway.

"I want you to have this, Roy," said Mimi.

"Thank you, ma'am," I said in a hushed voice, mesmerized. I knew this had to be from God.

"You're welcome, Roy." Mimi leaned into me. "Can you remember something very important?"

"Yes ma'am," I said, eyes wide open.

"*Never* break a promise," Mimi imparted to me, with a firmer hold of my hands.

A strong sense of knowing overcame me, yet I hadn't any questions needing answers.

"No ma'am," I confirmed. "Never."

Dad looked on, still unmoved from his position, as Mimi put the cross around my neck and tucked it under my shirt. It hung down to my belly. But in the years ahead, the cross found its proper position—directly over my heart.

I have kept vigil of that moment ever since.

Shortly after my family moved to Chicago, Mimi passed away. I still feel her words as if they were spoken to me two minutes ago.

I returned to my hill on several occasions from mid to late summer and even going into fall, always around the same time and only if it was sunny and clear. On one Indian summer day, I drove up beside the graveyard, parked next to the low brick boundary and wrought iron fence, got out of my car, and looked in. I knew no one there, but I didn't feel out of place.

I entered and inspected the row of gravestones that the grandmother used to clean. Whereas once these were religiously maintained, grass had grown up around them, and the headstones were covered with dirt. Any flowers placed there were now long gone. As I turned to leave, I noticed a new gravestone. It stood at the end of the row where the grandmother once cleaned the others. I hadn't seen it before because this new headstone was flush with the ground.

Gertrude Maria Brandt, Geboren 14.04.1912, Gestorben 02.06.1989. This had to be the grandmother. She was born the day *Titanic* hit an iceberg, and she survived World War I and World War II. I hadn't seen her since late spring. I recalled Gertrude's commitment and faith, just as I recalled Mimi's words. I said a prayer for them both.

I turned to leave but was stopped in my tracks. The intense calm of knowing returned—as if I had just taken a most difficult exam. There would be no need to wait for the graded result. I knew every answer perfectly, and my questions were many.

The Indian summer soon ended, and with that came the long gray skies of fall.

I never again returned to my hill.

70

Friday, November 10, 1989, began much like every other day in the Bunker. I'd been working in earnest to complete preparations for my sailing. The process was lengthy and included a physical exam along with documentation of my degree and programming background. After completing a specialty training course, I would be running a ship computer system. My secondary role would include navigation training. This day turned out to be a beginning for me, and an ending.

The inmates exited the Bunker early in the morning. We crammed into the mess hall to see history unfolding. Along with other inmates from our NATO partner nations, we watched in stunned silence as a West German sledgehammered a hole through the Berlin Wall on live TV. With less than seven weeks left for me on active duty, the Cold War ended.

Fear is *their* crutch. They say drugs are a crutch—truer words were never spoken—but that is only half right. They're a business too. Just like everything else consumed—religion, television, candied apples from the five-and-dime—everything is a crutch and a business at the same time. And you buy it. That *is* our way of life.

71

November 13th, 1989

Roy,

Happy Thanksgiving!

Congratulations on completing your college degree. What a milestone!

The news has a lot of coverage about the Berlin Wall. I can't imagine the history you live in over there.

You are the man I raised you to be.

I'll be waiting for you.

Love,

Dad

72

On Thanksgiving Day, stragglers joined me in the chow hall. A few chose to eat alone, as I did. The gyration of the dishwasher conveyor belt distracted from the stillness in the dining room. This was a good day. I liked these days. Not for the weather, but for the time afforded me in finding answers, and for the occasional revelation.

I read a letter that I had received from Black Label the day before. I would report for duty on the third day of the New Year. At their New Orleans home port office, I would undergo training and certification. Once that was complete, I would set sail on the *Seltan Seas*. No roads, only course and bearing.

Outside, low gray clouds held the temperature well below freezing. The branches on one tree were long since barren. I knew this tree from my first week on station. Damned if it didn't matter what the world launched its way. I gave thanks for many reasons, not least of which was following orders to the Bunker, without reservation.

After my meal, I drove off the Brook to a turnout alongside the access road and waited for Rachel. She always spent Thursdays at lunch with her mom and grandmother. I respected this, so I timed our arrival accordingly. A few minutes later, Rachel showed up. We got out and stood between our cars.

"I need to get going," I said.

"Why are you in uniform?" asked Rachel. "It's a holiday." Her lip trembled.

"It's official travel. I have to be in uniform, holiday or not."

Rachel tried to pull away, but I held her and pulled her into a bear hug. She leaned back, grasping my jacket collar with both hands.

"Roy . . ."

"Don't read into this," I said, holding her tight. I put my mouth to Rachel's ear and whispered. "I'll be back in two days."

Her eyes welled up. She let go of my collar.

"I love you," I said, nodding to her with a slow blink.

I turned to open Rachel's door. She got in and rolled down the window. I leaned in to kiss her as she looked away.

I kissed her ear and whispered, "I love you," then returned to my car.

I rolled down my window and held up the palm of my hand. She stared and nodded as I slowly pulled away.

73

"These guys never give up," I said.

"Who's that?" asked Chief.

"The RAF," I said. "They killed the head of Deutsche Bank this morning."

One week to the day after Thanksgiving, I had just read the flash from the AP wire.

"What assholes," said Chief.

"Why do you think they did it?" I asked.

"They're animals."

"We're looking in a mirror," I said.

One of my pastimes on the Brook had been an occasional visit to a one-room library. Instead of buying what was sold in the exchange, I chose to find what no one saw. I visited this secluded place on the second floor of a rarely visited wing of the main building. I spent time looking for works that might not have been touched in years, maybe even since their original placement on the shelf. I conducted my forensics, calculating the time since last touch by the amount of dust built up on the book's spine and top edge. Riffling through the stacks one day,

I came across a real find by Gwendolyn Brooks. I tucked the images from *In the Mecca* into my sense of freedom.

I loved *In the Mecca*. The impoverished left to live in decay. Snot-nosed black kids running rampant, ready to scare whitey if he'd ever return to the neighborhood. At least the children could dream about having a white Christmas. The children of the Mecca converted the circumstance, alright. They lived, albeit in a condemned building prostituted as a legitimate shelter.

The indigent didn't register in my existence when I was a kid. They had no choice. I had no choice. They were on the outside of the confines, somewhere else where they couldn't quite take hold of the pursuit. I loved hearing that the whole deal was up for grabs. By whom, for whom, from whom? The Father, the Son, and the Holy Ghost. Brooks's work bullied me. I owed no one anything. My decisions weren't a zero-sum outcome. It bothered me that the children couldn't find a way out of the Mecca.

It served to harden my resolve that my pursuit would not be winnowed down to merely accepting these facts—what did you expect me to do? Would you have found it more appealing were I to carry the encumbrances to which I had been assigned since birth? Fuck you. Fuck you if even for a fraction of a momentary lapse in your memory you feel that is *my* burden. Let me rephrase that: Fuck you all to hell.

"I miss Wagner," I said.

"That's a flashback," said Chief. "Whatever happened to him?"

"He went home," I said.

"Where's that?"

"Ground zero."

"Smart-ass."

"I'm serious," I said. "Nagasaki."

"No shit?" asked Chief.

"No shit," I said. "Got orders to Yokota. Family was from Nagasaki."

"You've yet to say where you're going," said Chief.

"I have rejected all offers of compromise," I said.

The room fell silent.

I owe some untold ransom for the calm of my hill. Even in a thousand years, I could never repay the fair price for the peace of standing in rows during prayer before school. And I couldn't try to calculate any sum worthy of the warmth from Mimi's hands. For this and much more, I am forever indebted.

74

December 16th, 1989

Dad,

I've buttoned up just about everything over here.

I want you to know something that has weighed on me for a long time.

When I left home that day in '84, it was because I didn't know what to say. All I knew was that I had to figure out life on my own terms.

I wouldn't have been able to do this without you. I am proud that you are my father.

I am so sorry I wasn't there for Mom. I used to think we had all the time in the world. I won't make that mistake again.

I'd very much like to see your horses.

I've said my prayers.

See you soon.

Roy

75

My annual performance review was my final official action. Frazione chose to personally meet with me. I rated the highest possible marks for job knowledge. I rated the highest possible marks for military bearing. I rated a firm substandard for adherence to AFR 35-10.

With four days left in country, I marched my final walk out of the Bunker.

"Chisolm!" JED shouted. "Wait up."

I stopped and turned. JED caught up with me halfway down the driveway.

"There you are," I said.

"I've been looking all over for you. When are you gone?"

"Gone?" I asked, surprised. "I *am* gone."

In JED's defense, I had never hung a short-timer calendar.

"I mean last-duty-day gone. I didn't want to miss you leaving."

At that moment, I heard a jet overhead and looked up, and in the contrail being painted, I knew I was gone long before that day.

"Right now, JED. I'm turning in my tickets at the gate."

"I found the rock. I found the note."

Over Thanksgiving weekend, I'd driven to Frankfurt, where I took the overnight military duty train to Berlin. Full dress uniform was required to ride the train, since it traversed East Germany. I didn't take an overnight bag, as I wouldn't need much time. While there, I wrote a postcard to Wagner.

> W,
>> *I stand at Checkpoint Charlie.*
>> *The Wall has fallen. This war is over.*
>> *I have found my way out.*
>> *Eternal peace to you.*
>> C

Twelve hours later, I caught the overnight train back to Frankfurt.

The "rock" was a part of the Berlin Wall I had chipped off. I was determined to hold a piece of what once stood between us and the terror of Cold War enemy annihilation. I left country with no clock. I left country with no crystal. Instead, I took a piece of the Wall and split it in three. I kept one piece of the Wall for myself, and this—along with the *Endurance*—was all that I took with me as tangible record of my part in this war.

The second piece I gave to my father. I would not set sail before seeing him. On my stop home after leaving country, Dad and I spent two days talking and laughing and crying about home, and the life we once lived as a family, when life had nothing to do with death. The details of this Cold War, of the Bunker—these would wait for another day when I again would find my way home. I didn't know how to share my stories. Not then, anyhow. Though really, I wasn't sure if ever I could.

The final piece was for JED. To accompany his piece of the Wall, I wrote a note: "427th Communications Squadron,

Borlingau Tactical Integration Center—whoever finds this, to the last day of this war, I never gave up."

I placed both the rock and the note in a small box held shut with a rubber band. I wrote the words "Cold Warrior" on the box and left it in JED's desk drawer on top of a book that I knew he'd been reading.

"What makes you think it's from me?" I asked.

"Who else would do shit like that?"

"Do you understand it?"

"How *should* I understand it?"

"It is a continuation of a thread begun long before you and me."

"How do you mean?"

"We all fight our battles. We all fight our wars. Just be certain that *why* you are fighting is for an outcome you can live with."

JED stared at me, unblinking. His eyes showed the calm confidence I had at the cemetery. I turned to walk away, made it ten feet, then looked back. JED stared. I held up the palm of my hand. JED replied with his hand up, palm open to me. No words were spoken. We dropped our hands in unison. I turned and continued to the gate.

You asked me to go. I went. You asked me to forgo what we once shared. I did. But just so you know—and you must know—I too ran. For freedom. From lockstep, structure fucking mentality. These were glory days. I could see them vividly. Certifiable only when during the present, there is never a desire to be somewhere before, in some time already past tense.

I played just as integral a role as anyone else. I was your boy sent overseas to fight this Cold War, to fight for freedom. A hero's welcome? I don't need one. I only wanted to let you know how things went on my end. I fought valiantly. The reinforcements just never showed.

I handed my tickets to Gold Tooth. He buzzed open the

gate as I gripped the handle one last time. I exited the compound and closed the gate behind me, struck at once by the chill of memory from three years prior. I turned, facing west, and recalled my first day at that gate. Overtaken by the classics, I fell into the sound of "Someday We'll Be Together," and I knew right then that I lived in the best moment.

With my feet planted firmly in the December cold, I remained long enough to remember the few words Hlavacka left with me in place of a goodbye. Upon my departure, he said, I would be history. This presage frequented my thoughts up to that very last day. When I left—after I was long gone—I knew that to all whom I didn't know, and to those whom I never met, I was history.

I spent my final night in country with Rachel. In her bed, we lay facing each other. She looked in my eyes. I combed her hair with my fingers.

"Remember our plan?" I asked.

Rachel smiled through the duress of our last night together.

"You finish training on February 11. You sail on February 19."

"Yes," I confirmed. "I'll be writing you in a few days."

"Want to know something, Roy?"

"I do, beautiful woman."

"I've loved you since I met you."

We spooned, looking up at her ceiling mirror.

"Want to know something, Rachel?" I whispered.

"Always, Roy."

"We're under the same stars. When I look at them, I know you see what I see."

"I will look for you, for us."

"Never forget our stars," I said. "I'll be looking there, and I'll be thinking of this moment."

"I will never forget."

I pulled Rachel tighter against me in silence, so all she

could feel and sense was my strength of conviction. The next morning, she drove me to Rhein-Main. Before leaving, I tucked a small box under Rachel's pillow. In it, I left my best fortune—"Yes."

We skipped breakfast. For the first time ever, we had no appetite.

The week before I sailed, I returned to Europe, where Rachel and I orchestrated a rendezvous in Paris. I reserved the same hotel and room, 6209. We spent that week charting a course together in life. This was also part of our plan.

I promised Rachel.

ABOUT THE AUTHOR

Copernicus Paul was assigned to Strategic Air Command and later to the US Air Forces in Europe during the Cold War. A Southern California native, he holds a healthy measure of contempt toward those who deny true liberty and freedom to anyone, especially through means of fear or force. Copernicus is a cancer survivor and lives in gratitude for every day on this earth.